WANDERING SOULS

ANGELA VAN LIEMPT

First paperback edition August 2022

Cover design by Natasha MacKenzie,
Miss Nat Mack Studio @missnatmack
https://www.missnatmack.com/

ISBN 978-1-7782544-0-6 (Paperback)
ISBN 978-1-7782544-1-3 (E-book)

Published by Dawn Publishing
www.dawn-publishing.com
contact@dawn-publishing.com.

For my sister, Kelly.
Forever a part of me.

The boundaries which divide Life from Death are at best shadowy and vague. Who shall say where the one ends, and where the other begins?

Edgar Allan Poe

One

Time doesn't heal all wounds—at least not according to Drew Harlow. Getting out of bed every day to face the world was struggle enough. Healing? That was for other people. *Normal* people. All she needed was to get through one more year of high school. Graduate. Move on.

Shuffling through the sand, she seated herself at the edge of a waterlogged tree trunk. She came to this same spot at Jupiter Cove every day. Sitting alone on the empty beach allowed her solace to think without interruption. Without everyone asking her if she was okay. Here, she could stop living on autopilot and breathe—really breathe—keeping time with the steady pulse of the waves as they washed against the shore, dragging small rocks and pebbles back into the deep.

The late October evening left her chilled and shivering. The wind rolled up and over the rocky cliffs leaving her long hair a mess of tangles in its wake. She zipped her sweater and wrapped her arms around her bent knees for warmth.

Somehow, she'd made it through the summer without Shane. He'd been gone nine months now. Nine months and she still had no answers. Shane was gone. Dead. How could she move on when she *knew* he couldn't be gone?

Shane wouldn't leave her. She knew it in her bones just as assuredly as she knew her own name. If his car had crashed into the Coda River, someone would have found him. But his body had never been found. He'd disappeared with nothing left behind other than his car sinking through the icy water.

Heartache gripped her every day. It was like an ice block that refused to melt. Her eyes watered and she dabbed them dry before tears could fall.

A crisp wind sent another shiver across her skin. It was late, and she was cold, but she dreaded going home. Gran would still be up, ready to ask her all sorts of well-meaning questions offering up one platitude or another that didn't help her at all. She got it; Gran meant well, but there were times…

Drew stood and wiped sand from her jeans before turning for the weathered, wooden steps to the top of the cliffs. She plucked her shoes from the sand and held them as she put one foot in front of the other up the narrow, crooked stairway. No traffic busied the coastal road tonight. It rarely did on Sunday nights. Not in Atlas Cliffs.

But there were other things that moved in the dark.

She scurried across the road to her house. Moths dived toward the streetlamps—like little suicide bombers without a cause. Crickets chirped, but not as fast as they had just weeks ago. Maybe they knew their days of singing were coming to an end.

As she neared the porch steps, she heard a faint voice, barely a whisper, uneven and hoarse. Someone, or rather *something* lurked in those shadows.

"Please, go away!"

They usually left when she asked. Usually.

Drew's breaths quickened, misting in front of her as the air chilled around her. She closed her eyes, waiting, hoping, but the voice rustled again, closer, like dry leaves scraping across the pavement. She hated that she couldn't make out the words. She never knew what they said. But she wasn't going to stick around to find out. They always whispered the same, unintelligible nothings at her. Maybe they did it to torture her? Or maybe they couldn't help it. Either way, they'd been a part of her life for as long as she could remember.

She sprinted up to the yellow door and dove inside, throwing the deadbolt. She leaned against the wall. Could a door keep away whatever prowled outside?

Drew waited, listening. Whatever lurked out there seemed content to remain in the cold night and standing around in the vestibule wouldn't change anything.

A glow of scattered night lights lit the parlor in warm light. The slow drip of the kitchen faucet hitting the metal sink was her only greeting. No ghosts—*and no Gran either.* She must have gone to bed early. Just as well. Maybe a life of being alone was Drew's destiny. Her mother had taken off to chase her dreams and follow some guy around the world, only to leave Drew behind with a shattered father. He'd made his living at sea working on fishing boats, but even he'd left her—he sure as hell couldn't drag a five-year-old with him. So, he'd brought her here to live with Gran.

He used to come home every couple of months with gifts in tow to make up for missed birthdays, and money to help Gran, but those visits had become fewer, the times between them growing more distant until Drew couldn't remember the last time she'd seen him. And if he did come home, he'd never earn back the title of *Dad* in her eyes. That ship had sailed. Literally.

She took her bone-weary body up the creaking stairs. She'd been up way too early for work and spent the rest of the day on the water. Surfing alone kept her sanity intact.

A stained-glass lamp glowed atop a pedestal table in the hallway, giving Drew soft light to navigate by. Gentle snoring escaped Gran's closed door, and not wanting to wake her, she crept to the end of the hall and into her bedroom, turning on the light. An easel loomed in the corner, complete with unfinished artwork. She ran her fingers over the textured canvas. She hadn't painted in months. Painting used to calm her, but nothing did anymore. Not since Shane.

Rummaging through a pile of wrinkled clothes, Drew found a t-shirt to wear to bed. She shoved the rest onto the floor to deal with later. Changing quickly, she flicked the light off before crawling into bed, burying herself under the duvet.

Tomorrow was Monday. Another week of school. Another week of work at the Casting Spoon, a local restaurant on the boardwalk. Another week of biding her time before she could leave this place. Another week without any news about Shane. Soon, it would be a year since his accident.

Something had to be done. If she couldn't find Shane, perhaps she could at least find out what had happened. Not what was in the police reports, but what had *really* happened. Anything to have some peace. Peace for her. Peace for Shane.

***

Drew fell into a fitful sleep, knowing what was coming: the recurring nightmare that came every night. Tonight, was no different. She always hoped for a beautiful dream where she could see Shane again, one where she'd want to stay forever. But that dream never came. Only this one. It was the same every night, and it terrified her. Knowing it was a dream didn't help. She could never wake from it of her own will.

Just like the night before, and the night before that, Drew found herself walking along a forest path. Dampness penetrated her body to the bone, freezing her feet with each step. Salt air whirled around her, whipping at her thin pajama bottoms. Below her, rocks and pine needles stabbed her toes. Above her, a full moon illuminated thick fog that rolled through the trees. Spiders seemed to hang from every low-hanging branch, balancing on thick webs. A particularly large one with furry legs weaved its silk around a grasshopper, who struggled in its death throes.

Drew rubbed her bare arms, now pricked with goosebumps. She pinched the skin on her arm, hard, but all it did was leave her bruised and hurting. Why couldn't she shake herself out of this? She continued, unable to stop.

She jumped, startled as something screeched overhead. It was just an owl. The bird glared at her with yellow eyes, not of this world.

The trail narrowed ahead and closed in on her. She forced branch after branch aside only to have them swing back in her face. Ahead of her, tangled bushes rustled, a low growl rumbling from within. She quickened her pace to a run, only to catch her foot on an exposed root, tripping her. She crumpled to the ground, winding herself.

Struggling for breath, she used an overhanging branch to pull herself up.

That was when everything changed. That is when it always changed—warping, morphing.

The trees melted around her like too much candle wax, the terrain turning rugged, rocky, and wet. Stone slabs rose around her, entombing her in some sort of underground tunnel. She couldn't breathe. It didn't matter that she knew this wasn't real—it *felt* real. The wet stone beneath her feet was hard and slick; the damp air was cold and penetrating.

Her hands clawed over the walls and ceiling, mud caking in her nails. Something crawled over her arm, and she slapped it. She was going to die. Dream or no dream, if she didn't get out, she'd suffocate.

A strange force, like she was a puppet on strings, compelled her forward, step after step. She couldn't stop. She didn't want to stop. This was either the way out—or pushing her farther into darkness. A peculiar light brighter than any bulb sparked in the darkness ahead of her, illuminating the exit to the cave, and growing brighter.

But this light was meant to torment her. She knew that. Just as she knew she would never reach the exit.

She couldn't, because a stark figure stood before her, blocking her way.

The image sharpened, like a camera finding its focus. She saw him, not two meters before her, a man, bone-thin and deathly white. He wore a long, ragged coat, which he slung over his skeletal shoulders, and a hat. He turned to her with vacant eyes, completely devoid of color.

She didn't know who he was, only that he came every night.

Wake up!

The words yelled in her head, but the dream kept rolling on, relentless. It had to end. It always ended. And she'd wake up. Her body trembled and her knees buckled. She hit the ground. Hard. A sudden burning pain cut through her thigh. She ran her hand over her leg, and the thin material of her pajamas came back warm and wet. Blood. Blood coated her hands. And all the while the man gazed upon her and did nothing.

He hovered over her. His cadaverous, wrinkled skin moved as his jaw contracted. Wild, silver hair hung to his chin.

But then something happened. Something that wasn't supposed to happen—that *never* happened.

Lifting the sleeve of his ragged coat, he revealed a bony arm and wrist, which he turned toward her. A round, shiny object dangled from a chain hanging over his corpse-like finger. He used that finger to point to a mound of moss-covered dirt in front of a towering barren tree. His thin, pursed lips moved again, but no words came out. Drew's soundless scream ripped from her like a helpless victim in a silent film.

***

Bolting upright, she gasped for air. Sweat gathered on her forehead and her hair stuck to her cheeks. She lifted the blankets to feel her leg. No blood.

Breathe, Drew. Breathe!

Another dream. She wasn't freezing in the wilderness. She was at home, in her bed. The digital clock glowed 7:14. She grabbed an elastic hair tie from the bedside table and secured her damp hair off her clammy neck.

What in the hell did it all mean? Night after night, it was the same. The forest. The cold. *That man!* But this time was different. This time, he'd pointed at something. The dream—the dream that was always the same—had changed.

Her eyes burned from a lack of good sleep. Her head ached and she flopped back on the bed, letting them close again, only to have the alarm blaring at her. With her face still planted in the pillow, she hit the off button so hard it almost broke. This constantly troubled sleep was kicking her ass. Gran had pills to help her sleep. Maybe she should try one. If she didn't decipher the dream, and fast, this was going to kill her. Maybe if she could figure it all out the nightmares would stop, and she'd be able to sleep—peacefully!

Peeling herself out of bed, she headed for a quick shower, not bothering to wash her hair. She just needed to get through the day intact. Finish the day. Finish the year and move away from Atlas Cliffs. Maybe if she left, she'd be free from this curse, the dreams, and all the encounters with…*them*. She didn't even know what they were. What was she supposed to call them? Ghosts? Shadows? Wandering souls? Her haunted hometown seeped into every inch of her skin like a sunburn. Yes, she had to get away. Get *far* away. Maybe she would attend college in a big city where no one knew her.

Would the shadows follow?

Time wasn't on her side. Wrapped in a towel, she dashed to her bedroom and sat on the pink-cushioned chair. Staring at the reflection in the dresser mirror, she leaned closer. A sun-kissed glow clung to her cheeks and shoulders. Bright copper hair dangled out of the elastic all over her head. She yanked it out, flinching as it pulled a few strands along with it. She flipped her head upside down and ran her fingers through to ease the mess of tangles, the curls loosening into gentle waves. A cascade of freckles spread across her forehead and nose. Gran called them *bricini*. Little stars. Maybe they were cute when she was little, but not anymore.

Dark circles beneath her eyes popped against her pale skin. She grabbed a tube of concealer and blended it to cover what she could. Mascara and lip gloss helped too, but it was all a façade, a lie that covered up everything going on inside her. If anyone actually saw what she did—the sad, troubled face staring back at her in the mirror, how would they react?

Not well.

It never went well. The only person she could talk to was Shane. But he'd been taken from her.

She dressed in stretchy jeans and a plain t-shirt but caught a glimpse in the full-length mirror behind her door and grimaced at her disheveled appearance. A distraction from her tired face would be better. Yanking the shirt off, she chose a loose, V-neck tunic with an abstract print instead. It would have to do. Grabbing her backpack, she ventured down the stairs to the kitchen.

Gran sat at the bench seat by the kitchen window and looked up with smiling eyes. Her ashen hair draped over her shoulders in unruly strands, but it matched her hippie soul. Drew grabbed a blueberry muffin from a plate on the counter and sat across from her at the table. She pulled a piece of the soft muffin and popped it in her mouth, not ready for the tart berries as they hit her taste buds.

"Good morning. Want me to make you something? That muffin isn't much for breakfast."

Drew smiled. Even after all these years away, Gran still hung on to her Irish accent. "No. I have to go, or I'll be late."

"Aye. Always running." Gran turned the page of the newspaper and put on reading glasses.

Drew pushed her chair back and got up. "I'll be home late. I work tonight."

"Have you heard from your father?"

Her insides clenched. Just the mention of her father was enough to set her off. "No. Gabe doesn't contact me anymore." Gran should have known that. Gabe hadn't called her since her birthday last January. One week before the accident.

"The boat will be out longer than they thought. He'll call when he can."

"Whatever. Let me know if I can bring anything home." Drew bent down and hugged Gran who patted her arm.

"I'm working until dinner. I don't need a thing, dear." Gran looked up over her glasses. Lines deepened across her forehead. "He loves you, ya know."

She doubted that. Gabe didn't know what love was. How could someone claim to love you and turn their back on you time and time again?

"That's debatable. Anyway, aren't you supposed to be stepping down and letting Nellie run the shop? I don't think this is what retirement is supposed to be, Gran."

"I'm keeping my nose out of it. I'm a silent partner now, and we have a deal. She agreed to keep me on part-time. The woman has good business sense, I'd say." Gran winked and fanned the paper out in front of her on the table. "Be safe, dear."

"I will. Say hi to Nel for me."

Drew threw her bag over her shoulder and waved behind her as she walked from the kitchen to the foyer. Shoving her feet into a pair of Converse, she bounded out of the front door with her car keys dangling from her fingers, and down the porch steps.

Their aging Cape Cod house stood across the road from the cliffs and the crashing waves below. Years of salty air had whipped the warm-hued cedar shingles to a faded gray. The sun danced across the water and cut through the sea breeze warming her face, unusual for the end of October, a false calm before the storm. For coastal New England, it meant storms and snow. Just like the night Shane had disappeared. God, she missed him.

A familiar nagging feeling that something was off came over her again, like when dark clouds move in on a clear day and everyone *knows* a storm is coming. She should skip school and go out on the water. What could she learn in school feeling like this? But she'd missed too much already. If she wanted to graduate, she had to break the cycle.

She tossed her bag into the back seat of the old Volkswagen. Rust started to eat away at the blue paint, and she was paying to have something fixed every other month. She wished she could afford a new car, but the busy season had wound down with the end of summer, and that meant fewer hours. She'd made enough to pay her bills, and she refused to burden Gran by asking for money.

Sliding into the front seat, she started up the engine. Adam's Ale Road wound its way along the cliffs taking her deeper into town. The rock face protected the land from the ocean—most of the time. Rolling the windows down, she inhaled the salty air. Gulls swooped over the cliffs contemplating their next meal. Leaves on the trees turned their new shades of red, yellow, and orange. It was a gorgeous late-fall day. Postcard perfect. If her insides matched the world around her, she'd be fine, but she was far from that.

The face of the old man from her dream kept creeping back into her mind, but the images were distorted, and foggy. His features, which were always so clear to her in her dream, were so frustratingly vague in the light of day, like a name she couldn't quite remember. She couldn't shake the feeling that he'd appear without warning like he was somehow watching her. It was impossible, of course. He only—and always—existed in her dreams.

She rubbed tight muscles in the back of her neck. Her car swerved as she rounded the turn into town a little too fast and she slowed down. Had Shane gotten distracted and lost control of his car like this? The roads had been slippery that night and he crashed.

At least they said he did. But they'd never found him. She couldn't wrap her mind around it; there was something she was missing.

Side streets branched off the road as it wound through town along the water. Seagulls owned the sky. They cried in warning fighting for food scraps. A sinking feeling came over her. Not the same constant unease that hung over her like a storm cloud. This was different and she couldn't put her finger on it.

But dammit if she wasn't going to.

Two

Drew pulled up to the stone pillars and curled iron gates marking the entrance to Marble Gate Estates. The non-functional gates may as well have a sign that said, 'Atlas Cliffs Elite'. The imposing manor where Piper lived exuded luxury. Drew drove along the circular driveway and stopped at the elegant entryway beneath the steep roof.

Drew didn't have a sibling, but if she could choose her own, Piper would be that person. They'd met the first day of middle school and clicked. Their backgrounds couldn't have been more different, Piper from a wealthy family and Drew...well. But none of that mattered; they were as solid as friends could be.

Highlights of bright fuchsia decorated Piper's bob, which spun as she bounded toward the car and hopped in. "Hey!" Her face dropped when she looked at Drew. "Are you okay?"

Piper had been trying so hard to help her move on and heal but Drew feared losing her friendship if she continued to dump problems on her every time they hung out.

"Yeah, sure," she said, somehow managing to

sound breezy. "Didn't sleep much, is all."

"Dreams again, huh? Still the same creepy old dude?" Piper asked.

She nodded, keeping her eyes on the road.

"I'm worried about you, Drew. Maybe you should talk to someone. Like a professional. Someone who deals with these things—"

"No one deals with these *things*. And if they do, they don't call them *shadows* or *souls*. They call them hallucinations and schizophrenia, and then they give you pills or lock you up. Or both!" She pushed the hair from her face. "Piper, I don't know a single professional who could help me."

"I can't imagine seeing what you see, but that's not what I meant," Piper said. "Grief can mess you up, and after the shit you went through last year? Maybe that's why you're having nightmares, or—"

"The nightmares aren't from grief. I know grief. There's something else going on." Her hands ached and she loosened her death grip on the steering wheel.

Piper's face lit up. "Is it the *ghost people*?" Piper whispered the last part.

Drew had always been open with her about what she saw, the people, the wandering souls—whatever they were. But she hadn't talked about it since…well since Shane. "You really do believe me, don't you?"

Gran was Drew's family, and she didn't know where she'd be without her. But Piper was the only one who knew her secret, and if Piper thought she was crazy and gave up on her, she'd be more lost than she already was.

"What? Of course, I do. You're my best friend. I trust you with my life."

"Trusting me and believing me are two different things."

Piper put a hand to her heart. "I, Piper Arlott, solemnly swear that I have always believed everything you've told me." She dropped her hand. "Seriously, Drew. I'm here for you. You know I am."

She caught herself smiling. "I know."

Drew followed the winding road to Atlas Cliffs High School. The L-shaped building lay nestled right next to the downtown area. Idling buses rumbled into motion, lurching away from the drop-off lane. She turned into the student parking lot, jamming on the brakes as a slew of kids rushed in front of the car, before pulling into an empty space.

She switched off the car, but neither of them moved.

Piper faced her. "Tell me about the dream? What happens?"

A pit formed in her stomach just thinking about the old man. Nothing about the nightmare was normal— even for her! She shook her head, not knowing where to start. "It's like I know I'm dreaming and can't wake up. It feels more intense each time. I'm walking on a dirt path. I can hear the river. Coda River. Where— where Shane died. The old man—and we're not talking about a gentle elderly guy, I mean, he's like something out of a horror movie! He's standing there, pointing and mouthing words."

"Words? What words?"

"That's just it! I don't know. I hear him, but I can't *hear* him."

"So…it's like another language?"

"No! Yes! I don't know. It's changing, Piper. The dream is changing." She held her hands up. "Last night I had blood on my hands. I think I was injured."

Piper tilted her head to the side and scrunched her face. "He hurt you? Like, for real?"

Drew shook her head. It was like the line between real life and her dream world had crossed over, except she didn't know where or when. She knew ghosts existed, and if the man *was* a ghost, then what did it want with her? "Something is going to happen, Piper. I can feel it."

"Oh, I don't think it's like a bad omen or anything. It's probably just a dream, Drew. I mean, it's one messed up nightmare. But don't you think that's all it is? A dream. You've said so yourself, the ghosts never hurt you. They're just *around*."

She wanted to believe Piper, but wished she understood; unless she experienced life the way Drew did, how could she ever get it? How could anyone? "Sure, maybe. Let's just go. We're going to be late."

Drew opened her door and climbed out, grabbing her bag from the back. More car doors slammed, with kids shouting and laughing as they barreled toward the front entrance steps.

They walked side-by-side in silence following the crowd through the rusted double doors.

"I have to stop at my locker. I'll see you in first period."

Piper grasped her arm. "You sure you're okay?"

"Yeah. I'll see you in a few." Drew forced a smile.

Piper waved as she got lost in a sea of people down the hall.

Drew glanced at the west wing lockers, her gaze narrowing in on one locker in particular. It had belonged to Shane, their lockers separated by a row in between like bookends. It was hard to believe so much time had passed. Harder to believe he was gone. Standing there with everyone rushing around her, it was just like that day she'd met him. The snow had melted, spring was in the air, and the end of grade ten was in her sights. She'd been running late for class and stopped to get a book when they met face-to-face.

His brow furrowed in deep thought as he shoved books inside his locker. Everything about him was dark, from his black jacket to his jeans bunched over boots. Everything except his eyes. They were the lightest shade of blue she'd ever seen. They were so bright. Mesmerizing. He ran his hand through the hair that fell over his ears. The self-assured way he stood struck her the most. Tall and lean. Mysterious.

He caught her staring at him. "Hey. I'm Shane…and you are?"

He'd noticed her—with her pale, freckle-faced, unruly mop of red curls—yet *he'd* spoken to *her*. Heat shot to her face. She could feel herself turning sunburned red. "Drew," she said, at last.

She gathered herself together, shaking off embarrassment. She was not *that* girl, the one who gets rattled by some guy, regardless of how cute and charming, or how distracting his blue eyes were when he looked at her.

When he looked at her, she found herself pulled in by his mixed chaos of light and dark—like a magnet. All thoughts of classes, teachers, or missed assignments vanished from her mind. All she saw was him. Her stomach fluttered; she couldn't think. She couldn't speak in sentences, which must have been obvious as she'd stood there tongue-tied.

"Okay, Drew. Nice to meet you. I'll see you around."

Someone bumped into her with a thud—and just like that she was back in the present.

Shane was gone.

"Hey. Where'd you drift off to?"

"Huh?" Drew spun around. A small-framed girl she'd never seen before stood in front of her staring at her with intense, amber eyes. The girl twisted her hair around her finger and released it letting it bounce to her chin. She did this repeatedly. Her small mouth curled in a smile. "Must be a good daydream."

"I'm sorry, do I know you?"

"Maybe. I'm Enid."

She wore a white sweater with tiny red hearts all over it and light-washed jeans. "Are you new here?"

"You could say that." Enid winked at her.

The warning bell rang above their heads. Drew checked her phone for the time and looked at Enid just as she pushed the same strand of hair behind her ear. A tiny scar trailed across her smooth cheek. Enid fluffed her hair back over her face covering it.

The second bell clanged. She didn't have time to get to know any more about this girl. "I'm late. I have to go."

"I'll talk to you later then," Enid said.

Drew waved and sprinted into the classroom. Large windows lessened the claustrophobic vibe. The walls were bare except for a smart board and a few motivational posters with words of encouragement.

Keep going.

Don't give up.

Believe in yourself.

Bullshit.

She plopped down at the empty desk behind Piper.

"Guess what I heard," Piper said as she turned around, clapping her hands in delight.

"Mmm. There's a gas leak and we all get to go home?"

"Funny girl. No. This weekend—"

"Miss Harlow, Miss Arlott. Do you have something to share with the class?" The teacher glared at them.

Piper turned to face the front and answered for them as she popped a bubble of chewing gum. "Nope. All good here."

Piper always had one adventure or another up her sleeve. Drew referred to this as the 'Piper Effect'. If it weren't for her, Drew wouldn't have been able to leave her house the past year. Even attending school was damn near impossible for her. Piper made it better. Or at least bearable.

Piper glanced back at her with a warm smile as the

teacher introduced her lesson of the day, *Poetry and the Spoken Word*. Drew's eyes felt heavy as she tried to pay attention. The minutes dragged on.

Finally, the bell rang. And like Pavlov's dogs, everyone stood. The chatter in the room increased and chairs scraped against the floor as students beelined for the door. She waited until they cleared out before leaving the room to avoid the frenzy.

Piper walked beside her plucking lint off the pocket of her denim jacket with black polished fingernails. "So, like I was saying. There's going to be a party Friday night at Haven. I work Thursday and I'll be off, so Cole and I are going. I really want you to go too. And before you say no. Just hear me out—"

"I can't. You know that. I'm not going back to Neptune Point. It's where the accident happened. The lighthouse that everyone calls Aurora, and that abandoned house…it all gives me the creeps."

"I get it, I do. But it's just that. A boarded-up house."

"It's not just the house. It's…it's all of it."

"We'd just park by the clearing—Haven. People are always hanging out there. It's not so scary. You wouldn't even have to see the lighthouse, or anywhere around there."

Thinking of it made Drew feel sick to her stomach. "You'll have Cole by your side, you don't need me there."

"Of course I need you there! It'll be like the old days. The two of us hanging out again."

"The two of us?" Drew bumped Piper's shoulder

with her own. "You've spent the entire summer wrapped up in Cole. I'd be a third wheel. How are things going with you guys anyway? He seems nice. I like him for you."

Piper smiled. "Things are good. I really like him. He's crazy smart. Not like the type of guys I usually go for which sucks because I do like pissing off my parents." Piper stepped in front of her placing both hands on her shoulders. "But enough about me. Come out with us Friday. Get back to the world of the living. We'll leave if it's too much. I'll have your back."

"You guys go. I'll catch up on homework, so I don't fail."

"You won't *fail*. At least consider it. I think this could be good for you. See some people. Have *fun*. You can't stay in this head space. It's not healthy."

"I *do* see people. I don't need to see more. Trust me."

"That's not the people I mean," Piper said, sighing. "What if this one time you put a little trust in me? Try it my way?"

"Your way? I like mine better."

Piper's answer for all things sad was to shove the feelings under a rug and do something exciting to forget them. Putting on a fake smile and parading around a campfire at Neptune Point was the last thing Drew wanted to do. People would stare with pity wondering what she was doing there. She picked up her pace toward the next class with Piper at her heels.

"I'm sorry, but your way of living like a hermit hasn't been working. You only leave the house for work and school!" Piper's voice softened. "Drew. It's been almost a year. Would you stop walking so fast?"

Drew slowed. "I'll think about it."

"Good!"

Drew looked at her phone. "I'm going to be late for class."

Before she could escape the conversation, Claudia Sloan sashayed up to them like a peacock spreading its feathers. In true Claudia fashion, she owned the space surrounding them. Like Piper, Claudia lived in Marble Gates and came from a wealthy family. But *unlike* Piper, Claudia had a snotty, holier-than-thou attitude.

Claudia cleared her throat. "Hello, ladies. Am I interrupting? Did I hear weekend plans underway? I have to say I'd be surprised to see you at Neptune Point, Drew. It's been a while. Are you sure you're up for it?"

Piper balled her hands into fists at her side. "To answer your question, yes, you are interrupting. Don't you have to be somewhere to be?"

Claudia eyed Piper. "I was just saying hello. Nice hair by the way."

Drew rolled her eyes and grabbed Piper by the arm before she started punching. It wouldn't be the first time. She met Claudia's eyes dead on. "We're leaving."

Claudia beamed a flawless smile. "I thought of all people, you would like to hear what I have to say."

Piper crossed her arms. "Nothing you have to say would interest—"

"I wasn't talking to you."

Drew's body tensed. "What could *you* possibly have to say to *me*?"

Claudia put her hands on her hips. "Oh, I don't know. A little something came up that I just happened to be present to hear."

"What are you talking about?" Drew asked.

"Someone found a bag."

"A bag? What does a bag have to do—"

"Looks like it might have belonged to your boyfriend."

Drew held her breath. Sweat gathered on the back of her neck, and she reached her hand up to rub it. This was impossible. If it was true, why hadn't anyone reached out to her?

"How could Shane's bag just turn up after months?" Piper asked.

Claudia held her hands up. "I'm just the messenger. You're welcome by the way."

"You're lying," Piper glanced toward Drew and back to Claudia. "His case is closed. He's gone. What's wrong with you?"

Speechless, Drew leaned against the wall. Could it be true?

Claudia smoothed her hair and stared at Drew. "I'm a lot of things, but a liar isn't one of them. Maybe it's nothing. A man turned a duffel bag into the police. I heard my dad talking about it on the phone so it was a one-sided conversation, but from what I could tell, they questioned Paxton Bishop." She tapped her chin. "Isn't that Shane's father? Anyway, that's all I know."

Drew's jaw tightened. Shane's father was a local paramedic. She'd only met him a handful of times. Shane and his father struggled with Shane's mom leaving. It was something they'd had in common.

"What did Shane's dad say?" Drew asked. "What's in the bag that points to Shane?"

"No idea about his dad. I told you, I'm just the messenger. But I guess there were some clothes— shirts, socks, a rolled-up rain poncho…" Claudia twisted lipstick-coated, red lips to the side and put a finger up in the air. "Oh, and an antique pocket watch with some engraving inside." Claudia picked at her fingernail.

"The watch?" Drew practically choked on the words.

"Sounds like something you're familiar with. Anyway, it's probably nothing, but that is what I found out. Like I said, thought you'd be interested." Claudia scowled at Piper. "I actually do have somewhere else to be. If I find out anything else, Drew, I'll let you know." And after detonating her grenade, Claudia strolled away with her heeled boots clicking on the scuffed tiled floor.

"She's making it up," Piper said. "Don't trust her. When has she ever tried to help you with anything?"

She hadn't. That didn't mean it wasn't true. Claudia had plenty of time and opportunity to torment her, so why start now?

A red exit sign at the end of the hall beckoned to her. A part of her wanted to charge for the door and get away from school, and this conversation. But what could she do with all the pieces to a puzzle she had no idea how to solve? Her feet remained planted in place.

"I don't think she's making it up," Drew said.

"Shane always carried that watch. His mom gave it to him before she left. How could Claudia know about that?"

"I don't know." Piper looked as shocked as Drew felt.

"He'd been trying to figure out where it came from."

Piper paced back and forth. "Alright. Let's just say these *are* his things. What does it change? I'm so sorry to say this, Drew, but Shane is gone. This doesn't bring him back. Maybe you shouldn't be digging for something that isn't there."

"I know he's gone!" Drew wiped under her eyes. She knew Piper didn't mean to hurt her, but why did everyone insist on reminding her that Shane was gone? She, of all people, didn't need a constant reminder. "I've lived it every day for months! Every single day I go over our last conversation in my head, trying to think of a word. A clue. Anything that might lead to answers. What if they missed something? What if I've missed something?" She took a deep breath. "Maybe it means I'll get to hold something that he once held, and that will just have to be enough."

That feeling hit her again. The profound tugging of a missed clue. A still shot of the dream popped into her mind. The round shiny thing dangling from the old man's finger. Round. Gold. *The watch.*

"Piper, I have to go."

"Go where?"

"I need to see that bag," Drew said.

"Well. I'm coming with you." Piper stood with her

arms folded. Drew mirrored her.

"You can come on one condition," she said. "I don't want to hear any more on why I shouldn't be doing this."

"You have my word." Piper pretended to lock her lips throwing away an invisible key.

"Alright, then. Let's go."

Drew bolted for the double doors with Piper at her side.

Three

Drew sat with Piper in her car at the police department. The brick building was tucked on a side street downtown. A couple of uniformed officers exited a police car and headed inside. A woman with a no-nonsense buzz cut stood looking at her phone in one hand and gracefully holding a cigarette in the other. She wore dark blue pants and a matching shirt tucked in neatly. No badges were visible, only a lanyard with tags dangled from her neck, but she wore a belt with a gun in a holster at her side.

"So, how should I do this exactly? Just walk in and say 'Hi. Rumor on the street is you have the bag of my dead boyfriend'?" Drew cringed at her own words.

"That could work," Piper said and shrugged. "Come on. We'll go together."

Piper got out of the car and after hesitating, Drew followed. What if they turned her away? Maybe it wasn't Shane's bag at all…but the pocket watch. How else could Claudia know about that?

The woman flicked ashes from her cigarette and watched as they walked toward the white framed door. Drew pulled it open and stepped inside. Plexiglass protected a long counter. A man behind the desk spoke on the phone in a deep voice that didn't match his face. He looked up and held up a finger. *One minute.* A minute to figure out what she'd say.

The call wrapped up and he stood and placed his palms on the counter facing Drew.

"Can I help you?" His voice sounded slightly muffled through the divider.

What do I say to him? "I'm Drew Harlow."

Silence followed. Piper nudged her and she continued. "Um. Yes. A bag was found and turned in here. It belonged to someone I know—*knew,* I mean."

The man sighed. He didn't look very old. Not much older than some of the guys in her school.

"Can you be more specific?" he asked.

Something inside her switched from nervous to anger. This man didn't know what she was talking about, nor did he seem to care.

"Shane Bishop. The boy who…disappeared last January. The bag belonged to him. I need to see it, please."

"Are you family?"

"Yes. Well, sort of."

He sighed again, this time with a groan. "Are you, or aren't you?"

"I am…Well, I was, his girlfriend. Look. I knew him better than anyone. If that bag belonged to him, I'll know."

Hidden from his view by the counter, she fidgeted with her jacket zipper. Focusing on the small piece of metal kept her calm.

He scanned her face and peered over at Piper who stood silent for the first time ever. Drew almost forgot she was behind her.

The woman from outside walked in carrying an aroma of cigarette smoke; the smell reminded Drew of her father. He'd come home after working at sea for a few brief days and sit on the front porch of Gran's house smoking while she played in the yard. She'd been so happy to have him back. But that was a long time ago when she was just a kid and oblivious to what life had in store. She snapped back to the present. The woman held her card up to a panel and opened a door when it beeped. Using her foot to keep it ajar, she turned to Drew.

"What brings you in today?"

The deep-voiced officer spoke before Drew could respond. "She claims to be the girlfriend of the boy who went missing last January. The bridge by the lighthouse—"

"I know the case." The woman held Drew's gaze. She pushed the door open wider. "Come in."

Drew turned around giving Piper a wide-eyed glance and a nod to follow her. She walked into the room with Piper at her heels to find a space that appeared larger than it looked from the outside. Cubicles and offices filled the room, papers were tacked to walls, phones rang, and a low hum of chatter between officers and regular clothed staff filled the room. How busy could it be in Atlas Cliffs anyway?

The woman gestured to a smaller room at the back and closed the door behind them. She waited for Drew and Piper to take a seat at a round table in the center of the room before sitting across from them. She folded her hands and eyed Drew with striking features. Gold hoops hung from her ears.

"I'm Detective Valerie Porter. You're Drew Harlow, right?"

Drew didn't think the other officer mentioned her name. How did this woman know who she was? She sat speechless for what must have been too long because Piper kicked her chair leg and spoke for her.

"This is Drew and I'm her friend Piper."

Drew bit her lip. "I'm sorry. How do you know my name?"

"Like I said, I know this case. I know you were the last person on record known to have spoken to Shane Bishop."

"Yes, ma'am," Drew said.

The detective placed a black notebook on the table and folded her hands over it. "That accident happened some time ago. Why are you here now?"

"I heard someone found a bag that might've belonged to Shane. I really need to see it."

"What exactly did you hear?" The detective's calm demeanor gave nothing away.

Drew glanced at Piper who shrugged. She breathed deep, trying to gather her thoughts before speaking. "Claudia—a girl at school—she told me a pocket watch was inside the bag. Can I look through it? Please."

Detective Porter leaned forward and pulled a pen out of her pocket. She opened the notebook to a blank page. "Was Claudia a friend of Shane's?"

"Claudia? God no. She knew him, but it's a small town."

The detective started writing but Drew couldn't make out her scribbles from across the table. "What's her last name?"

"Sloan. Claudia Sloan," Drew said.

Detective Porter paused and raised her head. "Dominic Sloan's daughter? Of Sloan Enterprises?" She appeared surprised.

"Yeah. Claudia said her father was talking to someone, and she overheard."

Drew didn't understand; she was under the impression that Claudia's father was involved in the investigation somehow. Claudia loved to remind everyone that her father practically ran Atlas Cliffs like royalty or something.

"Shane used to carry that pocket watch everywhere. It's old and had an engraving on it. Is it true? Was it in the bag? Can I please see it?"

Detective Porter scrutinized her. She closed the notebook, picking it up as she stood. "I'll be right back." She left the room for a brief moment, returning with a brown duffel bag that she placed on the table in front of Drew. "This is the bag. It was found on a cargo vessel by a deckhand a couple of weeks ago. There was no evidence found on the bag, or the items inside, pointing to Shane Bishop, or any wrongdoing. Maybe this will put your mind at ease."

Drew ran her hands over the rough canvas and turned the bag over but didn't recognize it. The name Ezra was written in black Sharpie in small print at the bottom.

As if she could read Drew's mind, Detective Porter pointed to the black ink. "Any idea who Ezra is?"

Drew shook her head. "I've never heard that name before." She started to unzip the bag but stopped. "Can I look inside?"

"Be my guest," Detective Porter said.

Piper leaned over and tried to look inside as Drew stood and opened the bag, pushing her chair back to give herself space.

She reached inside and pulled out a pair of blue jeans, a long sleeve shirt, and a thick flannel jacket. They appeared too big to be Shane's, and they didn't look like anything he'd ever worn before. In a knee-jerk reaction, she held the jacket up to her nose and inhaled, desperate to prove it could be his. There was no sign of Shane. These could have belonged to anyone. What was she thinking coming here?

Drew dropped to the chair, yanking the bag with her, and frantically searched through the pockets. "Where is it? The watch. Didn't you find a pocket watch?"

"I'm sorry, Drew. This is it. There was no watch."

"It's gone?" Drew whispered. The image of the old man gripping the watch in his bony hand flashed in her head. She looked at Piper who sat quietly beside her and turned her attention back to the detective.

Defeat hit Drew in the stomach. She flipped the bag over and stared at the name written in black marker. Maybe the bag belonged to someone named Ezra, and this had nothing to do with Shane. But Claudia knew about the watch! She'd overheard her father saying the bag might belong to Shane!

"All I have done—all I do is think about Shane and what happened that night. He *disappeared*. They never found a body. Nothing but his car in the river. What does that even mean? Don't you need a body to prove that someone is dead?" Drew almost threw up saying the last part.

"Detective Porter," Piper said. "Please understand. Drew's my best friend, and this past year has been really hard for her. She came here hoping for answers." Piper turned to Drew. "Claudia must've been lying about the watch."

Drew pinched her fingers under the table trying not to burst into tears. Claudia was nasty, but she couldn't be lying about this. Something wasn't right.

Detective Porter leaned against the wall, stoic. Observing. Her face softened and she retrieved a card from the breast pocket of her blue shirt and handed it to Drew. "If you need to talk, I have some great resources I can put you in touch with. Call me and I can help you set something up."

Drew turned the card over and over in her fingers feeling brushed off again. No one had told her anything back then, and here she sat in this tiny room, feeling no further ahead now.

Biting her lip, Drew shoved her chair back. She stood tall as if facing a bear in the wild. Nothing going to get solved here. "Thank you for your time today, Detective Porter." She nodded to Piper. "Piper, let's go."

Piper gave a little salute and jumped up to walk beside Drew.

Detective Porter opened the door and directed them into the hall toward the lobby. They left the building and got in the car. Drew pulled out of the parking lot, leaving the station.

"Do you want to go back to school?" she asked.

"Hell no. Home please," Piper said.

Drew knew this town with its labyrinth of streets well. They were etched into her mind like a wood carving. Piper flipped through the radio channels before settling on a rewind station playing Duran Duran's *Ordinary World*. Drew had always loved that song, but since losing Shane it hurt to listen to.

"How are you?" Piper said.

Drew sighed. "I'm frustrated. Claudia overheard something and I'm going to find out what it was. There's no way she could've known about Shane's watch."

Piper turned down the music and shifted to look at Drew. "Maybe. Or maybe she'd seen him with it before. I don't know. Just be careful with her. She can't be trusted."

Drew pulled the car along the side of the road and put it in park. She faced Piper. "I feel like a piece of myself is dead inside and I don't know how to fix it. People tell me to move on with some sort of 'new normal', which, don't get me started on what that looks like in my life because *normal* doesn't exist for me." She sat back facing the front again. "What if somehow, Shane walked away that night?"

"Oh, Drew. Don't do that to yourself. If that watch does exist somewhere, it doesn't mean anything. Shane died that night. There's no way he could've walked away. You must know that." Piper looked at her with an expression so pained that Drew nearly crumpled into a fit of crying.

Adjusting her seatbelt, she signaled and pulled back into traffic with tears in her eyes. Piper was right. Shane couldn't have survived. Because if, by some miracle he had, he would've contacted her.

"I get it if you don't want to go to Haven Friday night," Piper said, "so why don't you sleep over at my house instead? We'll watch movies and eat junk food, like the old days."

"Yeah, maybe. We haven't done that in a long time, have we?"

"We sure haven't. I think we're past due."

The light turned red at the last intersection before the fancy community where Piper lived. A group of people crossed the street in front of them leaving behind a clear view of a man leaning against a brick building. A mess of white hair hung from under a hat.

There is no way it could be him!

The sun reflected off something shiny in his hand. He held it up with his thumb and index finger as though showing it to her.

Shane's watch!

Horns blared. Piper frantically tapped her arm. "Drew! It's green!"

She hit the gas, squealing the tires, and peered in the rear-view mirror to find he'd disappeared.

Piper turned around in her seat. "Did I miss something? What were you staring at?"

There was no way he could be the same man from her dream. He wasn't real. Every muscle in her body tensed.

"I um…I thought I saw someone I knew."

She slowed to a stop in front of Piper's house. Piper grabbed her book bag from the backseat and looked at Drew. "Do you want to come in? Talk? You know my parents are both workaholics and never home, we'd have the house to ourselves."

"Thanks, but not this time."

"Alright. We'll make a plan for this weekend instead." Piper got out of the car and gave a peace sign as she walked up the cobblestone walkway; her pink Doc Martens stood out against the gray rock.

Drew backed out of the driveway, but instead of veering away from the privileged neighborhood, she turned left. Her Volkswagen crawled along until she found Claudia's house. Like Piper's, the sprawling estate was large enough to get lost in, although she'd never been inside. People living this way couldn't have any problems.

She hung back watching as a man exited the residence. He carried an authoritative air in his sharp-looking tailored suit.

Dominic Sloan. She recognized him from the news that Gran insisted on watching every evening at dinnertime. She wanted to speak to him and find out what he knew about Shane, specifically who had he talked to the night that Claudia overheard him.

In a split decision, she turned into the driveway as he opened the door to a dark sedan. He stopped and stared at her as she exited the car.

"Mr. Sloan? I'm a friend of your daughter's. Do you have a minute?"

"Is something wrong? Is Claudia okay?"

"Yes, she's fine. What do you know about Shane Bishop?"

The keys he was holding slipped from his fingers and hit the pavement. He bent down to pick them up before standing and smoothing out his suit jacket.

"Shane Bishop. I'm not familiar with the name."

She bit her lower lip. "Remember the accident at Neptune Point? His car was found in the Coda River."

He looked thoughtful but didn't take his eyes off her. "Right. Of course. I remember hearing about it. Why are you here exactly?"

He knew the story. But most people in town would've heard about it.

"Claudia heard you talking to someone about a bag that could've been—"

"My daughter heard no such thing." He exhaled and lifted his wrist to check his watch. "I'm late for a meeting. What's your name? I'll let her know you stopped by."

"I don't mean to keep you, but this is important. If you have any information about that bag or Shane, I'd appreciate it. Even the smallest detail would help."

"I'm sorry, Miss?"

She thought of making something up, but he'd tell Claudia about the encounter, and she would know it was her. "Harlow. Drew Harlow."

"Miss Harlow. Claudia can be a bit of a storyteller at times. She means no harm, but clearly has hit a nerve."

"I don't believe she was telling a story because she knew about a pocket watch that belonged to him. Were you speaking with police? I was just there—"

"I really must go. I'll let my daughter know you were here." He opened the back door of the dark sedan and threw his briefcase on the seat.

She stepped forward. "Wait! Please."

He slammed the car door shut and turned back to her. "I'm going to give you a piece of advice. Stay out of matters that don't concern you. Do you understand?"

"This does concern me. If you have information that could help his family understand what happened, wouldn't you want to do everything in your power to help? Especially someone like you who is well connected in this town." Her words came out braver than she felt.

His face reddened as he stepped toward her, swinging his finger in her face. "That boy is dead. Case closed. If you know what's good for you, you'll—"

"I'll what? Let it go? What do you know about him!" She folded her arms across her chest gripping her keys tight.

"I don't know anything about him! This is ridiculous. Get off my property or I'll have you charged with trespassing!"

He moved closer, his hand raised and balled into a fist. He towered over her, and she stumbled backward against the hood of her car. She put her hands up ready to push him away or defend herself if he struck her. She couldn't imagine he would hit her!

He froze and looked around. Dropping his hand, he spun around and strode to his car. He climbed in and closed the door, hiding behind the tinted window. The engine came to life and revved before backing out of the driveway.

What in the hell was that all about?

Dominic Sloan wasn't the warm gentleman portrayed on the news at all. Like his daughter, he hid behind an image of what he wanted the world to see. He was hiding something.

Drew glanced at the house. It appeared dark inside. Cameras were angled at varying entry points; she felt like she was being watched. She got in her car, closed the door, and drove away leaving Marble Gate Estates in the rear-view mirror. For now.

Four

Drew slept in past her alarm. A knock sounded at her bedroom door. Nightmares of the old man kept her up most of the night and she had a splitting headache.

"Aren't you late for school?" Gran asked.

"I'm not feeling well. I'm staying home today."

The door opened a crack. "Do you need anything? I was going to work but can stay home."

"No, it's okay. I'll be fine. Go to work. It's just a migraine."

"Alright then." The door closed and opened again a second later. "Don't miss time this year. You don't want anything standing in the way of graduating."

"I know. I won't. Bye, Gran."

This time the door shut with a click. She pulled the blanket over her head. The thoughts wouldn't stop coming. She couldn't understand the correlation between a random stranger's bag and Shane's watch showing up nine months later. How could it be possible? Everyone assumed he'd died in the river, but she'd always questioned it. If he was dead, why couldn't she see him like the other souls? And what did Dominic Sloan have to do with any of it? He knew something. A person didn't become enraged like that for no reason.

***

Once she was sure Gran had left, she got up and went to the bathroom for some ibuprofen to relieve her aching head. She went downstairs to the kitchen for toast and juice. Her headache subsided, but the thoughts did not. She shuffled back upstairs, heading for bed again.

At the top of the staircase, she froze. Her arms and the back of her neck tingled, and not in a good way. Panic tightened her chest. She wasn't alone.

She heard the humming first. It came from Gran's room, slow and melodic. It echoed through static as if someone turned on a radio searching for a clear channel. She looked around but couldn't find the source of the sound. She inched closer and reached out to close Gran's door. Her shirt sleeve rustled as something brushed against it. She stepped back, but not before she felt the faint pressure of fingers wrapping around her wrist.

Never had a ghost touched her.

Who—or what—was in the bedroom?

A woman's voice continued murmuring the song.

"Go away! Please go away. You're not welcome here." She'd try asking politely, it had always worked before. But the grip on her wrist tightened. This one wasn't leaving like the others. *Something* wanted her to pay attention. The grip on her wrist tightened, holding her, vice-like.

"You're hurting me."

This time the hold on her arm released. Drew pressed her body close to the doorframe and gripped the edge. A blurred figure sailed across the room, hovering over the trap door on Gran's floor. The door led to a space under the stairs below, but it had remained closed for years. If the ghost wasn't floating over it, she could open it and crawl inside.

The figure appeared more clearly now, more focused. The woman wore a long nightdress that twirled around her as she turned in a slow pivot, coming to face Drew. The ghostly woman stared at her before shifting a gaze downward in erratic movements as if searching for something. Blood trickled down her arms and soaked into the dress, staining it crimson.

Drew struggled to breathe. She couldn't conjure up enough saliva to swallow. Her knees buckled beneath her, and she slid down the wall to the floor. The woman gaped at her with vacant eyes before vanishing.

Drew covered her face and fell apart, crying hard. Not once had a soul looked at her like that. Never covered in blood. So bright and red. *The Crimson Lady.* Who was she? Had she been murdered? If so, why come here?

What she'd give to be like everyone else and have a normal existence. How lucky would she be if her biggest worry consisted of what to wear in the morning, or if the cute boy from the party liked her. Instead, she'd been labeled as the girlfriend of that poor kid who died, and everyone looked at her with pitying eyes.

Shane had opened a gate for her. He understood her, or if he didn't, he accepted anyway. He'd been her first love. Her first *lover*. And in a blink, he'd been ripped from her life.

Nothing good lasts. She would have to accept that sooner or later.

She settled on the window seat in her bedroom and stared out the open window. She fought the urge to pull the curtains closed and crawl back into bed. The last time she'd done that, it had taken a month to rejoin the world. She couldn't do that again. Not when new information about Shane demanded her attention. She needed something to help refocus her energy.

Surfing was the only thing that ever allowed her to experience a glimpse of something other than the daily anxiety and depression plaguing her. She could go out on the water and recharge her damaged battery. She grabbed her wetsuit from the hook behind her door, changed, and left her bedroom. Hurrying down the stairs and outside, she let the door slam behind her.

She crossed the road with her surfboard under her arm to Jupiter Cove. The rugged cliffs and steep rocks never appealed to tourists. They stayed away from this part of town, which suited her fine. Kicking off her sandals she walked barefoot along the dirt path. For a moment it reminded her of her dream and the old man… She looked behind her, but no one was there.

She hurried down a steep stairway made of stones. Markings of age-old inflections were etched into the rocks like a mystical language she'd never understand. Waves drenched the beach below pushing closer with every surge. She perched her board nose-first in the sand and heaved a sigh. The ocean tugged at her. Who needed school when this existed outside her front door?

The lady in the blood-covered dress was a world away out here. All the tension inside her melted away, if only for a little bit. A couple of locals bobbed in the water and nodded at her before paddling away. These were the last weeks of the season before winter seized them all.

Winter. January would mark a year since he vanished. She needed to find out what really happened to Shane that night. It was strange that he was at Neptune Point during a storm in the first place. Was he running from something?

The older locals told tales of a Greek God banished to this town after siding with the Titans in a war against the Olympians. His sole purpose from that day forward was to hold up the heavens forever, keeping the sky from falling and crushing the townsfolk. His name— Atlas. This was how Atlas Cliffs came to be. Or so the story goes.

Shane always thought it fascinating. He'd been convinced the town held dark secrets... Maybe that's why he was at Neptune Point. Maybe that's why something happened to him.

Her hometown didn't enchant her, not as it had him. Maybe she saw too much; no one else could see the dead wandering around them.

She grabbed her board and moved through the water past the whitewash. Launching herself forward, she paddled beyond the shore break where she sat upright with legs dangling. The swell rose and peeled toward shore, and she licked her lips tasting salt from the sea mist. Gulls flew overhead, but she didn't hear their cries. All her thoughts stopped. There was only her body, the board, and the ocean.

She maneuvered her longboard through the water. Heaving with all her strength, she moved one foot forward and let her hands release, rising to balance on both feet. This was the moment a partnership with the ocean took over. A connection with nature. She held strong on her board, moving with the wave as free as the air surrounding her.

The first few waves were flawless. A larger swell rolled in with more force, and she turned too fast losing her balance. Holding her breath, she jumped off the board covering her head and plunged ass-first into the water. The pull of the undertow dragged her deeper. Her hair floated above her in the churn of whitewater.

Was this how it had felt for Shane? Had he plunged into the river unable to break the surface only to be carried out by the current? The sun seemed farther away with every second. What would happen to her if she let herself float where the water took her? If she drowned, would she come back to wander? Who would be able to see her?

An alarming need for air pushed her into survival mode. She reached for the leash attached to her ankle and pulled, kicking her feet, and clawed her way up. Light reached her again. Her lungs burned in desperation. Hands wrapped around her arms and hauled her up. Saltwater went up her nose and down her throat and she broke the surface in a fit of coughing.

"Are you okay?"

She wiped her eyes to see. Nico DeSarro sat poised on his board as he held a hand on hers, not letting it go. She gripped his in return like a tether to life. She nodded, unable to speak. Wet hair clung to her face and down her back. She slowly moved to a sitting position, gulping in precious air, and shivering with cold. Or panic. Maybe both.

"I saw you go under. Rule number one, Drew. Never surf alone. Remember?" A charismatic introvert, Nico's gentle eyes framed with long lashes observed her with care. His wet hair stuck up all over the place appearing glossy black in the sun.

She coughed the last of the water out of her smoldering lungs. "Where is your surfing buddy? I don't see anyone with you either."

"I'm looking at her. At least, she used to be that person. I haven't seen you out here in forever and suddenly you ditch school and don't message me?" With a playful smile, he placed a hand against his heart. "I'm hurt."

Nico. Seeing him was a throwback to simple times before she'd ever met Shane. He embodied home.

A concerned look crossed his face. "Seriously. Are you alright? You went down hard."

"I'm good. I think." She wiped hair from her face and looked herself over. "No cuts or blood."

"Come on. I'll paddle in with you."

He maneuvered alongside her as she used every bit of strength to make her way to shore. He peeked over a few times, and she gave him her best Everything-Is-Great smile. She couldn't remember when she saw him last. For as long as she'd lived in Atlas Cliffs, Nico lived down the road. His dad ran a reputable auto repair shop located on their property. Growing up, they spent their time on the water teaching each other how to surf.

He had been the boy who helped her build sandcastles on the beach when they were kids, making sure the tide couldn't reach them. The one who fixed up an old bicycle and taught her to ride when other kids had their parents around to teach them. He bought her flowers for her tenth birthday because they didn't bloom in January.

Now, they hung out in different social circles and rarely crossed paths. The water became their meeting place; they would make huge bonfires on the beach and talk for hours. But when she met Shane, his pull was stronger than the boy next door's.

Seeing Nico today triggered buried feelings of warmth and security. The realization hit her hard. She didn't know the ability to feel alive—really alive—was still within her.

She carried her board up the beach with Nico at her heels. She unzipped and peeled the wetsuit down to her waist revealing only her black sports bra. She didn't feel exposed, not next to Nico. He didn't stare at her, and she knew he wouldn't make a rude comment. Her wet skin quivered from the cold air, and she rubbed her arms to tame the goosebumps.

"Here." Nico handed her a towel and she wrapped it around her shoulders.

"Thanks."

He freed his chest from the clinging material exposing a lean build and broad shoulders. She'd never noticed him quite like this before and the last thing that came to mind was 'boy-next-door'. They weren't the same kids anymore. She wondered, for the first time, what it would be like to kiss him. Pulling the towel tighter around her, she looked away. This was *Nico*. Why was she thinking about making out with him? And why did she feel so nervous?

"Do you need anything? Water?" He dug around in a backpack leaning against a piece of deadwood. "Here. You're shivering. Put this on." He handed her a gray sweater.

"No. I'm good." Her breath caught the way it did in the cold air of winter. He'd changed since the last time she'd seen him. Older looking, maybe.

The muscles in his arm flexed as he held it outright. "It won't win you a fashion contest, but it'll keep you warm. Take it."

She dropped the towel and pulled the sweater over her head. Warm fleece smelling of sandalwood mixed with sunscreen caressed her cold skin and wrapped her in nostalgia. It was big enough on her that the sleeves hung past her hands and the bottom hem fell somewhere near the lower half of her wetsuit.

"Your dad's shop has merch?" She pulled the hood on her head and smiled. "I think you're wrong about the fashion thing. It's not so bad."

"I'll tell him you said so. He'll order a dozen more for the storefront."

"I assume you're still working for him?" She pointed to the DeSarro and Sons' decal on the front.

"Yeah. I guess it's my fate, right? I'm helping him restore an old Mustang. It doesn't feel like work. It's more fun than anything. Plus, I get to keep the car."

"Have you driven it?"

He laughed. "It's almost roadworthy. By the end of the week. Why? Are you interested in a rip along the coast?"

His silent confidence showed in the easygoing way he stood. At complete ease with the world and in his own skin. Drew wondered what that felt like. Looking away, she eyed the rock steps. She picked up her board and didn't respond. Did she want to go for a ride with Nico? It was a loaded question. Piper told her to have "fun". Going for a drive up the coast with him sounded exciting. And terrifying. But her heart remained with Shane, and she couldn't let him go until she figured out what had happened to him.

Nico pulled a hoodie over his head and threw the towels in his bag before tossing it over his shoulder. "Promise me something. Next time you go out on the water, just ask. I'll go with you. Better than going alone. It would be like old times."

When life wasn't so damn complicated. Nothing about Nico was "old times" anymore. "I'm not sure if I'll be out again for a while. Especially after today."

"I get it. But consider it an open invitation in case you change your mind." He gestured for her to climb first, and she sauntered up the uneven terrain as he followed.

At the top, she turned to face him. Ocean wind blew seagrass to its side and wet strands whipped her face. "Thanks, Nico. I don't know what happened out there."

"You wiped out and it scared the hell out of me, is what happened. I saw you catch a few good ones and started to swim over. Next thing I knew, you went under." He put his board in the back of his truck and leaned against it. "I didn't have time to think. Just dove and grabbed you."

She thought of the seconds sinking under the surface and her throat hurt. Shane's face popped in her head. The familiar ache returned. "I guess it just wasn't my day."

"I know you've had a rough year—" He averted his eyes. "Word travels… But if you ever want to hang out or talk…I'm not far, Drew. We could just hang out like we used to—"

"Maybe. I'll keep it in mind. I've been busy with work and school. I haven't had much time for anything else."

"Says the girl who ditched for the day."

"Says the guy who also ditched for the day and is with said girl." She laughed and ran her fingers through tangled strands of wet hair. Heat flushed her cheeks, and she dropped her flip-flops to the ground looking down as she stuck her feet in. "I should go."

She pulled her arms out of the sweater and he stopped her. "Hang on to it. You can return it next time."

The unspoken promise hung in the air. Nico

wanted to see her again, but he was an acquaintance and nothing more. He never could be. The baggage she carried clipped her wings and she kept her secrets close.

"Bye, Nico." She turned her back to him and walked toward home across the road.

The truck's engine roared to life behind her. "Drew?"

She stopped and shifted to face him. He sat with his head out the window, once again resembling the boy she'd known forever. "Yeah?"

"My number hasn't changed. Keep in touch." He waved and sped down the road.

She walked up the driveway. An ominous presence replaced her home's usual protective feeling. Paint on the porch peeled, displaying natural wood underneath that creaked with each careful step. Gran was still at work. Nothing appeared out of place. Curtains billowed inside the upstairs window. It was just the wind; she'd left it open.

Would the Crimson Lady be inside again? She walked inside and ventured upstairs. The space where the ghost swirled earlier now stood empty. No humming came from the room, only silence.

She unwrapped the wetsuit from her legs and hung it inside out. Chilled to the bone, she darted to the bathroom and turned on the shower tap until steam billowed. Hot water scalded her cold skin for a few seconds until she adjusted. She scrubbed the salt from her skin and lathered her hair with shampoo. The scent reminded her of her mother. They'd all lived in an apartment in Bar Harbor. Her favorite pastime was playing with the expanse of make-up and perfumes covering her mother's dresser. She loved to spray the contents in the purple glass bottle all over herself, leaving behind the scent of waterlilies and musky vanilla clinging to her skin. She never heard from her mom anymore, except for a postcard or letter on occasion. Sometimes if the stars lined up and the moon was blue, she'd get a phone call for Christmas or her birthday. Considering her birthday was in January, sometimes that meant one call to cover both. It was rare these days. How could a mother leave her child? Maybe Drew was unlovable. She pushed the thought from her mind. *One issue at a time.*

She rinsed, turned off the tap, and stepped out, dripping on the bathmat. Using a towel to wipe steam from the mirror, she moved closer patting her face dry. Who was this girl? A constant sense of free falling left a pit in her stomach. The warm feeling from being around Nico again dissipated.

A notification chime rang. Wrapped in a towel with a mess of wet hair, she ran to her room and hopped on the bed to grab her phone from the side table. It had been hours since she'd checked it.

She had missed messages from Piper wanting to know if she was okay and if she'd be back at school tomorrow. Just as Drew was about to respond, her phone rang.

"Hello?" she answered.

"Hey!" Piper exclaimed. "Are you alright? I've been texting for hours."

"I needed the day." Drew used the towel to absorb

water from her dripping hair.

"Did you talk to Claudia's father?" Piper said.

Claudia must be furious if she was talking about it already.

"I did yesterday after I dropped you off. He was standing in the driveway, and I thought I'd ask some questions. It didn't go over so well. He knows something, Piper, and I'm going to find out what he's hiding."

"I'm telling you, Drew, that family isn't one to mess with. I doubt Claudia's father knows anything. Like I said, I think Claudia is making stuff up. I don't know. The thought of you chasing after a dead end scares me. I don't want you to get your hopes up and crash all over again. I just want you to be okay again. Happy."

Happiness. The concept teased her but was beyond her reach. For some reason, Nico came to mind. The comfortable feeling of being around him today begged to come back. She shoved the thought away. It had been a moment of nostalgia, nothing more.

"Piper, I can't let go of the watch. Not until I find out how she knows about it."

Piper exhaled heavily. "I just worry about you. The longer all this drags out…I don't see how the end will be any different. Watch or no watch. Maybe Shane just dropped it somewhere, or someone found it at Neptune Point."

"Maybe. But why would it prompt a conversation with Claudia's father and who was he talking to? It doesn't make sense."

"It's weird. I'll give you that. Look. Tell me what I can do to help, and you know I'll be there."

"I know. Just don't think I'm crazy."

"Never. Promise." Piper paused and then asked, "Are you going to work?"

"In about twenty minutes, why?"

"Can you swing by and pick me up? I need a drive to the Book Nook. My shift's at five. I could ask my mom but we're not getting along at the moment."

Piper and her mom didn't get along most moments. Drew wished she knew what that felt like; to have a mom around to get along or not with.

"Sure. I'll be there soon."

Sitting on the edge of her bed, she dried her hair and spun it up in a messy bun. After dressing in a work uniform consisting of black pants and a white button-down shirt with *Casting Spoon* embroidered on the left side, she glanced in the mirror. Her weary eyes needed brightening, but she was out of time to let it bother her. She rushed down the stairs and reached for her jacket as a hand touched hers. She flinched, pulled it back, and spun around. A puff of mist dissipated up the stairwell into nothingness. The only sound was her shallow breaths as she stood in the entryway alone. Someone or something desperately wanted her attention, and she had no idea why. She opened the door, snatching her jacket off the hook, and darted for her car.

Five

Drew arrived at school to pick up Piper. Mobs of students gathered outside, boarding busses and cars. She stood beside her car and shielded her eyes from the sun that wasn't warm enough to combat the chill in the air. She could almost smell winter coming as November crept closer.

Piper barreled toward her pulling her into a hug. "Claudia is such a bitch! Demanding that I tell her where you were all day! I can't stand her. Strutting around like she's queen of the world."

"Queen of the underworld perhaps." Drew caught herself laughing for the first time in days.

"What exactly did you say to her father? I've never seen her so mad! I wish I'd known you were going there. I would have joined you."

"Like I told you, all I did was drive by and he happened to be outside. I only asked him who he was talking to about the bag and if he knew anything about Shane's accident. I didn't expect him to get so nasty."

"Nasty? How so?" Piper asked.

"He yelled at me. Told me to stay out of matters that don't concern me. He was a real asshole to be honest. I don't know, it was weird. You don't act like that unless you're trying to hide something."

"Well, you set Claudia off that's for sure. I've never seen that girl so rattled. She's been telling people you trespassed on her private property and her dad almost had to call the police. It's about time someone knocked her off her high horse."

"I wasn't trying to knock anybody off anything. I only want the truth and I'm not backing down until I find out what that is." Drew zipped her jacket up as the wind picked up. "Enough about Claudia; I don't care what she thinks. Her father is another story. One that I intend to follow up on by the way."

"What are you going to do? Should you report it to the police? Wouldn't that be the icing on the cake for her highness!" Piper said.

"Please. Report Dominic Sloan for being mean to me? Think about it. Me, Drew Harlow from the edge of town. I was in his driveway, *trespassing* as he put it. I wouldn't have a leg to stand on. I'm letting it go—for now."

"Are you sure? It sounds odd. Doesn't he fund a children's hospital? A man of his social status should be making good impressions on our youth not attacking them. Especially a seventeen-year-old girl for God's sake!"

"He didn't exactly attack me unless pointing a finger in my face counts. He was angry about something."

"Alright. But stay away from that house from now on. I don't trust any of them, least of all Claudia." When she said Claudia's name, Piper made a face like she ate something sour. "What did you do all day anyway?"

Drew hesitated. Warmth flushed her cheeks, and she hoped it wasn't noticeable. As soon as she mentioned Nico, Piper would ask a ton of embarrassing questions.

"I was out on the water," she said.

"Surfing? Wow. And you didn't freeze to death? Were you alone?" Piper leaned against the car.

"Yes. No. Sort of." She kicked at some dead leaves along the curb, avoiding eye contact.

"Oh, damn. Spill it, girl!" Piper exclaimed.

"I *went* alone."

"What aren't you saying?" Piper gave her a playful look. She had a gift of making you feel comfortable enough to tell your deepest secrets.

"Nico was there. Just at the end though."

Piper clapped her hands. "Bingo! I knew it. I didn't see him in class today. He's gotten hot! Don't you think? What's up with him? I said hi to him last weekend at the Book Nook but didn't have time to talk. Didn't you used to be friends?"

Bingo indeed. Questions flew.

"He's alright. It was nice to see him again, it'd been a while." He was more than alright, but she wouldn't dare say that. Seeing Nico awakened feelings inside of her that she thought had been submerged with Shane. But the nice feelings were stricken with guilt. She had to hold her focus on Shane until the events around his death weren't so blurred.

To distract Piper from more questions, Drew

looked at her phone and opened the driver's side door. "We have to go."

"What? No details?" Piper pressed as she hopped in the passenger seat.

"There's really nothing to tell. It was good to see him. But that's it."

"I'm not letting this one go," Piper said.

Drew drove downtown and parked on a side street beside the Book Nook. The local bookstore appeared like one of the corporate chains, but smaller with a vintage charm. Drew couldn't tear her eyes from the place connected to the bookstore, a trendy café called Maze. It had always been one of her favorite places. She hadn't been inside for months, not since Shane's death. Just looking at it made her sad, so she avoided it.

A painting hung on the wall inside. Her artwork. She'd painted a picture of a girl perched on a swing suspended from trees. One of the ropes had snapped, but the shadow of a woman held it up, keeping the girl safe. She'd let Shane convince her to enter it in a contest and it had won second place. As far as she knew, it was still hanging on the wall.

Piper unbuckled her seatbelt. "Thanks for the drive."

"You're welcome. Have a good shift tonight."

"You too." Piper turned in her seat, facing her. "Are you sure you're alright?"

"I've got this. I'm going to be okay, I promise." She hoped she sounded convincing to Piper because it sure didn't to her.

"You deserve to be happy. Shane wouldn't want

you to live in misery for the rest of your life. He was in a terrible accident; the roads were icy as hell. Stop punishing yourself, Drew. There isn't any big mystery to figure out."

But there was. What was he doing at Neptune Point so late? The police showed up at her house when the phone records showed her number was the last phone call he'd made. If only she'd answered her phone, maybe she wouldn't be having this conversation today. To her, the whole situation *was* one big mystery. If only she'd been able to reach Shane before he left that night.

Sirens screamed and lights flashed as emergency vehicles coursed from down the street and parked at the duplex across the road.

Piper peered out the windshield. "Shit. What's that all about?"

A police car parked behind an ambulance and paramedics rushed into the building. A sinking feeling came over her. She chewed on her bottom lip. Death happened here and how she knew that wasn't in the realm of her understanding.

Piper wouldn't be able to see it. None of them could. Not the paramedics or the police. But Drew saw it, just as she always did. Death. As if on cue, the ghost of an elderly man wearing a white undershirt and pants held up with suspenders wandered by. He stopped and stared at her with a toothless grin through the car window. His face appeared washed out, gray, and sparse hair revealed age spots that covered his head like constellations. She held her breath, feeling her heart thump in her chest, and watched him shuffle by from the rear-view window. The man looked skyward, turned to wink at her, and disappeared. Her hands gripped the steering wheel and her ears buzzed until she heard Piper.

"Drew? Did you hear me?"

"What?"

Piper opened the car door. "I'm going to see if I can find out what happened—"

She grabbed Piper's arm before she could get out. "A man died."

"How—how do you know that?"

She knew the way she always knew. It was like the dead knew she—and only she—could see them and made a point of strutting around in front of her. Except this was the first time she'd seen one wandering while Piper was with her. "I just saw him go."

Drew stared straight ahead, hands still on the wheel. Dark clouds rolled in and blocked out the sun. Raindrops hit the windshield and she turned on the wipers. Lights flashed in the driveway beside them as paramedics carried a sheet-covered stretcher from the house. A glimpse of a beige pant leg showed from underneath.

Piper leaned back in her seat and closed the door, the sound echoing in the silence. She spoke slowly like she was talking to a child. "I know you see things. You've told me about it before. I guess I always thought maybe—"

"It was in my head?"

"No. Not that. I don't know what I thought. I've never seen you…in action. What did he look like?"

"An older man with no teeth wearing a white shirt and suspenders. He looked really sick."

"So…like a person?"

"Not exactly. I can make out certain things. Facial features, hair. Clothes."

She let her hands drop from the wheel. A shiver crawled through her. A wave of tired rushed her as it often did after this happened.

"Is it scary?" Piper asked. "What you see?"

"It terrifies me. I wish it would go away, but if anything, it's happening more than before."

"I don't know what to say. It seems impossible…You saw that man after he died."

Drew swallowed through the tightness in her throat. "Not so impossible for me. I saw him. I see *them*."

"I'm doing it again, aren't I? Making you feel like I don't believe you." Piper stared at her with a somber look on her face. "I do believe you, Drew. Okay? What do you need? If there is anything I can do—"

"Just promise me you will never tell a soul. You must keep this to yourself."

"Of course! I promise," Piper said.

If this got out? One word came to mind. Devastation. Outcast. Ostracized. That was more than one word, but the floodgates opened.

She met Piper's eyes with desperation. "Not a soul, Piper. Can you imagine the amount of shit that would rain down on me? People would think I was a freak. No one would believe me."

Piper shifted her gaze through the windshield at the

flashing lights. "You have my word."

"Thank you." She caught the time on the dash. "I better drag myself to work, or I'll be late."

Piper leaned across the center console and gave her a squeeze. She closed her eyes and hugged her back not giving in to the breakdown that wanted to take over.

"Are you sure you'll be alright? Maybe you should call in sick—"

"I need the money. I know all this is new for you, but it's my everyday life. I'll be fine. Really."

She wanted to crawl into bed and sleep for so many hours it would be bedtime again, but she couldn't afford to lose her job.

Rain pounded the car in bullets as Piper stepped outside and closed the door. She pulled her hood up and ran for the Book Nook doors. Drew started to pull away when her phone rang. She slammed on the brakes and directed the car back to its spot before answering, but it was too late. She missed the call and checked the voicemail.

Nellie needed her to stop by the bakery. It was too important for a phone call.

Something about her father.

She eyed the time on the dash again. If she hurried, she could stop by the bakery and still make it to work on time, but it would be close. Nellie got all the latest town gossip from the locals who came by the bakery, but nothing she could tell Drew about her father would matter. The last time he'd strolled into town was Christmas. He'd stuck around for her New Year's birthday and left right before Shane's accident on

January 11th. The day would be forever burned in her mind.

Where was her so-called father when everything collapsed? Yet a part of her wanted to know what Nellie had to say.

Dammit.

Making a quick U-turn, she veered onto Spinner Boulevard lined with restaurants, cafés, and boutiques—a busy part of town on any given day. All the leaves had fallen from the trees marking the entrance to Portal Park. Gran took her to that park when she was little and a little boy carrying a stuffed duck followed her around the sandbox. Gran asked her who she'd been talking to. She always remembered knowing that no one else could see them. She'd been too young to understand it then, and she was no closer to grasping it now.

Talking to Piper had opened an old wound. When she'd first told her about the ghost people, she shrugged it off like maybe they were imaginary friends. At some point being different proved to be a pitfall. Nothing about it was beautiful or unique and she'd learned to never speak of it. She had to bury her secret, losing herself in the process as she tried to fit in.

She'd vowed to never breathe a word to anyone else. Not ever.

Everything changed when Shane came along. She found herself telling him details about her life that she never talked about, and nothing shocked him. Not even her admission that she could see the dead. She'd never felt so free. After he disappeared, she'd tumbled back to reality in a world of confinement.

She slowed her speed and tapped the steering wheel as hordes of people ran across the street with raincoats and umbrellas. Little kids in rubber boots jumped in puddles sloshing water everywhere. She longed for that childlike carelessness. She couldn't remember if it had ever existed in her world.

Finally, she arrived at the white, two-story building on the corner of the block with a seafoam green door and matching shutters. A sign with bold cursive letters hung above the door, reading: *The Tough Cookie*. Its eclectic charm stood out like a blue jay among crows. An assortment of weathered round tables with multicolored chairs sat empty.

A jingle of chimes above the door announced her arrival. That sweet fresh-baked cookie smell reminded her of after-school days with Gran decorating cupcakes. Maybe those were her puddle jumping, carefree days, but she had no way of knowing.

Nellie Quinn held a pan in one hand and tongs in the other as she placed pastries drizzled with chocolate into a display case. The black t-shirt she wore revealed an intricate design of tattoos covering her arms.

"Hey, hun. You got my message?"

"You wanted to talk to me about Gabe?"

"He's in town." Nellie put the pan on the turquoise counter and smoothed out her short pixie cut. "A friend of mine is friends with some guys that work in the dockyard. His ship came in late last night for repairs. It's supposed to leave in a few days."

"He's in town?" Typical Gabe. Some things never

changed. It would have been nice if he gave a shit about reaching out to her or Gran. She wasn't surprised though. "Nellie, couldn't you have just told me over the phone?"

"There's more." Nellie nudged her red-framed glasses as they slid down her nose. "Someone found a bag on a container ship. Rumor is that it might've belonged to Shane because of some old watch that was inside."

Drew sighed. And Claudia had thought if it weren't for her highness, she'd never been privileged enough to find out a damn thing.

"You knew," Nellie said.

Drew sat on a stool across the counter from Nellie. This totally could've been a phone call, but Nellie meant well. She always did. "A girl at school told me and I went to the police station yesterday to see for myself. The watch wasn't there though. Do you know who found it?"

"I wish I knew. Believe me, you'd be the first person I'd tell." Nellie leaned her elbows on the counter and propped her chin on her hand. "Maybe it's not his after all. I mean how could it be? Hell, I wasn't going to say anything because I don't want you running on some wild goose chase. At the same time, I didn't want you hearing this from town gossip. You've been through—"

"I know. Thank you for telling me, Nel. Is Gran still here, or did she leave already?"

Nellie stood upright and flung a tea towel over her shoulder. "You missed her by about half an hour. And before you say anything, the only thing I told her was that Gabe was in town. I had to tell her, Drew. She'd want to know, and if I don't tell her, someone else will."

Nellie was right about that. Gran would find out if her son was close by and didn't call. "I get it," she said.

"It's a small town and people talk," Nellie said, "If I find out anything else, I'll let you know, but don't let this take over your life. I'm pretty sure it's just hearsay. The last thing I want is for you to rehash that awful night all over again."

"I already do," Drew whispered under her breath looking toward the window.

Outside, a man ran by with a little girl under the eaves to avoid getting wet. Both were laughing. Faces beaming. Anger stirred inside her; her own father couldn't even pick up a phone and call her. "I've got to run, Nellie. I'm late for work. Thanks."

Drew pushed the door open to leave and turned to see Nellie wave at her with the look of a concerned parent spread across her face—Or what Drew envisioned that to be.

Six

Drew drove through downtown toward the boardwalk on her way to work. The rain had stopped, and the clouds parted allowing the sun a final show before nightfall. The Casting Spoon came into view. An anchor and a lobster trap decorated the front entrance, with blue and white striped umbrellas lining the wraparound patio. Yachts with colorful flags docked below as tourists escaped their everyday lives and ventured to the coast. What would it be like to take a journey away from here? She longed to be a tourist in a place where no one knew her.

She parked behind the building to avoid the flow of traffic, got out of her car, and made her way to the back door marked *Staff Only*. Shoving the heavy metal door open, she walked inside, nodding hellos to the kitchen staff. During busy times, the conversation never progressed past small talk, and she never stuck around after her shift to get to know anyone.

Tying a black apron around her waist, she shoved a pen and notepad in the pocket and braced herself for the steady rush of customers. The door to the private room had been propped open. As usual, the large table sat empty in the center. It was a waste of space; no one used that room.

Her head ached and her cheeks flushed. Piper was right. She should've called in sick but needed the money more if she was ever going to be able to leave town.

Her first couple of tables were seated on the patio. Patrons strolled up the steps from their boats wearing sweaters and jackets. The fall air by the water was cold, and she shivered. At least she'd be busy running back and forth to warm her up. These would be the final days of the season. Winter would see to that.

She hurried to take orders and deliver fancy-plated dishes. Savory aromas filled the dining room inside, and her stomach growled. She'd eaten here once with Piper's family a couple of years earlier, but not since. On her off days, it was the last place she wanted to be.

Staff scrambled around her leaving the kitchen door in a constant swing. A steady hum of chatter and bursts of laughter filled the room and meals ended with decadent desserts and liquor-filled coffees. Her cheeks hurt from smiling her dimpled 'I'm a happy local' smile. If it wasn't for great tips, she'd be hard pressed to smile at all.

The chaos in the room closed in on her. Conversations sounded louder than they were. Her headache from earlier returned with a wave of nausea. Sweat gathered at her forehead and beaded down her back like a spider, but she didn't feel warm. Taking a deep breath was impossible.

Stealing away to the bathroom, she locked herself

in a stall and crouched down trying not to throw up. If she ran out of the restaurant would anyone notice? Not until her tables complained about their absent waitress.

Get your shit together!

She pushed hair off her forehead and stood up straight. She wiped her sweaty hands on the apron and pushed the stall door open.

A girl stood at the sink and stared in the mirror at Drew.

"You work here?" the girl asked.

The little scar moved as the girl smiled. What was her name again? E…something…

"Enid," the girl said, grinning.

Is she a mind reader?

"Enid, right! And yes." Drew pointed to the Casting Spoon on her shirt. She straightened the crooked name tag in the process. "I do work here. I have to get back—"

"See you around?" Enid still didn't turn from the mirror. Instead, she stared through the reflection at Drew.

She wasn't sure if it was a question or an invitation.

"Ah, yeah, sure," Drew said before hustling out of the bathroom.

Encounter number two with the girl—Enid—and she didn't know how to take her. Used to being labeled as different herself, she got that, but this? There was something off about this girl.

Drew smoothed the wrinkles in her apron and busied herself clearing tables as people left. An elderly woman assisted a man with his cane. A family of five boasted with excitement as they stood putting their jackets on. A couple spread a map out in front of them as they discussed their boating route south; the woman wore bright pink lipstick and talked with her hands. Drew felt like she was a ghost herself, wandering around people who couldn't see her. She moved between tables with a tray and a dishcloth as though invisible. She counted down the minutes as her final hour neared the end.

Icy air wafted toward her from the back of the room. Thinking the doors to the patio must be open, she went to close them—only to find them closed and already locked. Turning back, she stopped and gasped. Sitting alone in a booth by the windows was a man. The old man. He was creeping from her dreams into reality!

Still facing the back of the booth, she stared at him and stepped closer. He tapped long fingers on the table.

Impossible.

The sound of a dish hitting the floor resonated from the kitchen. Startled, she looked around.

No one seemed to notice him sitting there. Only her.

A wave of dizziness hit, and she thought she'd faint. It couldn't be him. There was no way it could be the same man from her dream; that man wasn't real.

With a stomach in knots and a mouth so dry, she couldn't speak, Drew approached him. She had to see his face and prove this was not the man in her dream. She caught her reflection in the window—his did not appear despite the fact he was sitting in front of her.

His head arched toward her.

His colorless eyes lit up with an odd glow. Was he blind? Did he see her? Was this even real? Questions charged through her mind so fast, that nothing made sense.

She stepped back staring at his narrow, lifeless face. His chin protruded as his thin lips moved and he spoke. This time, unlike in her dream, she heard him.

"The house of Aurora." His voice cracked into a moan.

Aurora, the lighthouse at Neptune Point.

"What about that old house?" she asked, her voice barely a whisper.

He pointed his skeletal finger at her face.

"Go. She's there," he hissed.

She stepped back. "Who is there?"

He dropped his hand down and when he lifted it, the watch sat in his palm. He moved his mouth again.

"Help her." This time the words, along with the man, faded into a breath.

"You're not making sense!" Tears burned her eyes.

Alone with her shocked reflection in the window, she turned around to stunned faces gaping at her.

She shifted her weight from one foot to the other and rubbed the back of her neck.

One of the new waiters, she couldn't remember his name, leaned over with a nervous chuckle. "Um, who are you talking to?"

"No one. I…I was just talking to myself."

She spun around searching for the old man, but he was gone, and he'd taken the watch with him. She had no idea how he could have that watch, but she was sure it was the same one that had belonged to Shane! She was sure of it. Had it been real? He was one of them. One of the dead. And he had escaped her dream and walked right into real life.

The waiter rolled his eyes and walked away. The others averted their eyes and ignored her, continuing with closing the restaurant.

People were going to think she'd gone off the deep end. Maybe they weren't wrong. The ghosts no longer wandered around her. They were getting bold and making contact—speaking to her. The line between the living and the dead was no longer clear.

***

Drew stepped outside of the restaurant at the end of the longest shift she'd ever worked. One of the lights buzzed and flickered until it burned out. A wind gust blew dead leaves along the pavement, and chimney smoke through the air. No one else was around, but she could've sworn someone was watching her from the dark corner of the building.

Zipping her jacket up to her chin, she dashed to her car and plopped into the driver's seat. What in the fresh hell was happening? He had brought up the house of Aurora, the old lighthouse at Neptune Point. The keeper's house nearby had been abandoned and boarded up for years. He wanted Drew to help…and who did he mean by *her*? Biting down on her lip she flinched at the taste of blood. This was a goddamn curse. In the absolute worst way. She wanted it to stop.

She started the car and blasted the heat. As soon as the windshield cleared enough to see, she raced out of the parking lot along the coastal road toward home. Maybe if she sped fast enough, she could escape the old man. Doubtful. He was everywhere! Would he show up at her house next? School?

This time he'd spoken to her.

This is crazy.

She could keep on going all the way out to Neptune Point. *Aurora.* But without electricity and no flashlight, she'd be useless in the pitch black this time of night. Alone in the middle of nowhere. Cold, terrified. Not a good combination.

Gravel crunched under the tires as she cut the turn too sharp up the driveway to her house. She turned off the car, grabbed her bag, and got out as hair spilled out of her ponytail. Brushing it off her face she looked across the road. The streetlight lit up the path to the beach below. Hours ago, she had stood there with Nico. Thinking of him made her stomach flutter. It had to be nostalgia, like how a certain smell or a song can spark a special moment in time. Nico was an old friend who lived down the street. Nothing more.

A rustling sounded in the bushes beside the house. She jumped back and banged her leg on a planter.

"Ouch! Shit!" She rubbed her leg as a rabbit darted across the driveway into the darkness. Great. Paranoia had set in. She hobbled up the porch steps and into the house.

"Something chasin' ya?"

"Fuck." Drew covered her mouth with a hand to

74

cover the slip.

"Potty mouth." Gran never missed a beat.

"Sorry. I wasn't expecting you to still be up."

"Couldn't sleep." Gran rocked in her glider watching television. She picked up her pottery mug of wine from the side table and took a long sip before turning her attention to Drew. "Brutal night? You look like you've seen a ghost."

"Brutal night about sums it up." If Gran only knew. She wasn't about to start spilling secrets, though. Not tonight. Not ever.

"Tourists still around wreaking havoc, are they?" Gran asked. "Leaf peepers we call them this time of year. It's good for business though. Don't worry, it'll be over soon enough when the snow falls."

Tourists were the least of Drew's problems.

She kicked her shoes off and hung up her jacket. Flames danced in the fireplace, the logs popping and crackling. Shivering, she leaned down close to the fire and held out her freezing hands.

Gran faced the television. "I got caught up in an old movie. Come sit with me."

She should go to bed and try to sleep, but who was she kidding? Between the nightmares and the Crimson Lady creeping around upstairs, if she could fall asleep, it wouldn't be restful.

Gran looked so lonely. A hint of the young woman she used to be snuck through the creases framing her eyes and mouth. She'd smoothed her wild hair into a long braid that hung over her shoulder. Gran once commented that a person only got lines on their face if they were blessed to laugh, cry, and live. At this rate, Drew's face would be wrinkled like a bulldog, and it wouldn't be from all the laughing.

Giving in to Gran's request, she sat on the overstuffed couch and pulled a blanket over herself.

"The bakery was busy today." Gran's eyes were glued to the television. "God, I love that place. Hardest thing I'll ever do is sell it."

Drew wasn't going to bring up Gabe. She'd leave that up to Gran. "You won't have to sell it, not for a while. And you can trust Nellie. She's family. She won't let it fall apart. It's in good hands."

"Aye. It's a good partnership. I couldn't manage it all anymore." She lifted the blanket revealing an ice pack over her knee. "My body and wallet had other plans."

A log in the fireplace snapped startling Drew. She'd been on edge ever since she saw the old man in the restaurant. She imagined he was in the house somewhere, waiting for her to go to sleep.

Gran continued talking, "I'm going to keep working until I'm dead. It keeps me young, and the money will help with a few repairs before winter."

Drew scanned the room. The house was older but had held up well as far as she could tell. If only there was armor to keep the wandering souls away. "I can help fix stuff and if you need money, I've got some saved," she said.

Gran turned to face her and for a split second, Drew saw her father in those eyes. The ache in her chest returned. Had she been so difficult to raise that he'd made himself scarce?

"Absolutely not!" said Gran. "I know he's in town. Maybe he'll stop by. And you'll need any savings you have for school next year."

Gran didn't voice an opinion on her life choices, except on the topic of school. She wanted her to have opportunities, but Drew would have to find her own way. She was undecided about school. All she wanted to do was leave Atlas Cliffs.

"I'm not sure what I'll do yet, Gran. Maybe I'll travel or something."

Gran raised her eyebrows. "Don't throw away your future. Your father told me he'd be back to stay a long time ago. We both know all too well how that went. I believe he'll come home to us, but for now, we've got to take care of each other. Save your money for school."

As sure as the Earth turned, Drew knew her father wouldn't be home anytime soon. Not in the way Gran hoped for. "I'm not a kid anymore. I know that Gabe swooping in to save the day will never happen. One thing he excels at is making promises he can't keep."

"He's done a fine job of hurting us both, hasn't he?" Gran said.

Drew pulled the blanket up to her chin and sunk deeper into the sofa. "That he has."

Gran got up from the chair letting the ice pack fall. She shuffled to the kitchen with a limp and returned with an envelope. She handed it to Drew. "This came in the mail for you. She left a message too. Just a phone number for you to call her. Said it's important she talks to you. I wrote it on the back of the envelope."

Drew turned it over. The return address read Bodega Bay, California, which meant nothing. It was the name that made her back stiffen upright. Joelle Marisol.

Mom. The word barely held meaning anymore.

Letters from her mother arrived a few times a year, and the return address never stayed the same.

She sat up and tipped the letter toward Gran, knowing full well she'd seen the name on the envelope too. "Check-in letter from Joelle," she said.

Gran sat back in her chair and pulled a blanket over her legs. "Aren't you going to open it? Not that it's my business." She couldn't hide her curiosity if she tried. It was all over her face.

Drew pushed the blanket aside. "I think I'd rather just go to bed." She got up to leave when a melody echoed from the television. It hit her like an electric shock. The Crimson Lady had hummed that song!

"Stay awake, don't close your eyes," a woman on the television sang to two yawning children. Drew shot a glance to the bottom of the stairs expecting a ghost woman covered in blood to appear. How could a sweet melody sound like something out of a horror film? She inched closer toward the entryway and looked up the staircase.

Gran blurted from the living room, "If your dad calls tomorrow, what do I tell him?"

"He won't call, Gran." She couldn't tear her eyes from the dark hall above the stairs.

"What if he does?" Gran persisted.

"Tell him…tell him whatever you want."

Unblinking, she stared upward holding the railing so tight her knuckles turned white. Was the woman up there?

Gran's defeated voice called from behind her, "Goodnight then."

"Goodnight," she whispered and started up one step at a time, continuing to the top of the stairs. She inspected the hallway, but no one was there. Darting to her room, she closed the door behind her, gasping, blood pumping in her ears.

Moonlight crept through the darkened room. She sat on the bed and held out the envelope. A phone number was scrawled on the back just like Gran said, but Drew had no intentions of calling it. Turning it over she ran a finger across the handwritten name and address. She wondered if her mother experienced any emotion when she wrote Drew's name. Sadness? Loss? She'd stopped reading them after Shane disappeared. It hurt too much. If she opened this one there would be no turning back. She'd rip through all of them and read about adventures her mom was having somewhere without her. Promises and *until we meet again* would be littered throughout.

This one would remain closed. She tossed it in a drawer with the others.

Exhausted, she changed out of her work clothes and crawled underneath the thick duvet. She was afraid to fall asleep and find the old man waiting for her in the nightmare that was seeping into real life.

She rubbed her eyes and picked up her phone. It buzzed as it lit up and Piper's messages filled the screen with romcoms they could watch on the weekend.

Drew typed a response and hit send before she could change her mind.

I've changed my mind. We're going to Haven Friday night.

She was going to that damn party at Neptune Point. It would bring up memories of Shane, but everything did.

Biting her lip, she scrolled through until she found his final message to her, the one he'd sent her the night of the accident. She couldn't stop herself from rereading it now and then in hopes that something different would jump out at her.

I found out something tonight. Something horrible happened. My mom was keeping something from me, and I don't know what to do. I think she's gone.

It was an ominous message and she'd never heard anything further on what could've happened to Shane's mom.

But there wouldn't be a tomorrow for Shane to tell her what he'd found out. She had gone to bed and slept while his car crashed. By the time she'd seen his message, it was too late. Those last words haunted her. She might never know what secret he had uncovered.

She'd give anything to have one more moment with him and hold his face in her hands. To look into his eyes again, those bright eyes, and feel his arms wrap around her. Her heart sat like a brick in her chest. She put her phone back on the bedside table and lay on her side as tears soaked her pillow.

She thought of the memorial service the

community insisted on holding for Shane in a local cemetery. Winter parkas were no match for the cold as everyone huddled in a candlelit vigil. Everything about it felt wrong. Shane had never been found, yet everyone assumed he'd died. His mother hadn't returned to town, not once. His father stood defeated among the small crowd as though he'd given up all hope. Drew couldn't stop crying. The whole thing was hell.

She flopped on her back and stared into the darkness at the ceiling. She thought of the watch and how it ended up in the hands of a dead man. The old ghost man's words played in her head.

Aurora. She's there. Help her.

She was the only person who could find out what happened to Shane. She wouldn't give up on him like everyone else.

Seven

It was Friday afternoon, and the bell rang to end the day. Drew dropped her books in her locker, slammed it shut, and spun the padlock. With her backpack hanging over her shoulders, she zipped her jacket and headed down the crowded hallway. People walked around her laughing and talking over each. Posters advertising clubs and events were plastered on the walls. A couple made out in a corner as though they'd never see each other again. It all added to the chaos in her head, making her breathless.

Somehow, she'd made it through the week. She'd failed another math test and had to stay in every day at lunch for extra help. Dreams haunted her every night. Most of it was like déjà vu, trudging down the same forest path, through the same underground tunnel trying to claw her way out, never making it. The old man was always there, waiting for her, echoing the same words:

Aurora. She's there. Help her.

But one thing *had* changed. The night after the restaurant incident, the Crimson Lady appeared in the dream—something she'd never done. She'd crept up from the ground wearing the same blood-stained nightdress she'd had on in the hallway, staring at her with pleading eyes. What the connection was, she had no idea.

"Drew!" a voice called from the packed hallway.

Drew rose on tiptoes to see over the crowd. Nico DeSarro moved with his casual stride, his face beaming as he caught up to her. He looked like he'd stepped out of a convertible with his wavy hair a beautiful, wind-blown mess. Maybe he'd gotten that Mustang on the road after all. It'd be cold for the top down in October, not that that would stop him.

Her stomach fluttered again, like the time on the beach. But this time her breathlessness was caused by the person in front of her rather than the chaos around her. Why did he affect her so much?

"Hey, Nico."

"It's good to see you. I've been thinking of you since the other day on the water."

"You—you have?" Heat flushed her cheeks as it so often did around someone she liked. Except she didn't *like* Nico—right?

"Well, yeah. I don't want that wipeout to keep you from surfing. I like hanging out with you." He smiled at her. "Are you going to Haven tonight?"

Haven. Piper had tried to talk her out of it—something about the stress of the week and how going back there might make everything worse—but she'd made up her mind. She'd be there.

"Actually, yeah, I'm going. What about you?"

He smiled again, and she couldn't help but smile back at him.

"I am. I can pick you up if you'd like. Consider it your opportunity to go for a ride before I put the Mustang away for the winter."

Well, that sounded very date-like. She could hear the thumping of her heartbeat in her ears. She couldn't go with him. Imagine the gossip if she showed up with Nico!

"I—I already promised Piper that I'd go with her and Cole."

His smile faded like he was disappointed. She wanted to say screw it all and go with him, but if she did, he might think she liked him—and that freaked her out. She was being ridiculous. He probably looked at her as a friend and nothing more.

"That's okay. I'll see you there?"

"Yeah. Sounds good." She didn't like how she reacted to him—heart racing, face blushing, distracted by his dimpled smile.

"Maybe we can go for a drive over the weekend sometime instead?"

"I don't know if I'll have time. I mean, maybe. I'm not sure."

He let out a breath. "I understand, Drew. I really do. You've had a shitty year. I guess I just miss our friendship. How about I message you? If you're free, great, if not, that's cool. No pressure at all."

"Okay." Her face was so hot. He only wanted to be *friends* after all. Where was her head?

"Awesome. I can walk with you."

"I'm good. I've got to stop by my locker." It was a lie, but she needed to break away from him and the attraction that threatened to pull her in. When Nico was around, she wasn't thinking about Shane. It would be fun to go on that ride with Nico, letting her hair blow in the wind along the coast. Didn't she deserve that after everything she'd been through?

Nico was the getaway car. The blue pill instead of the red one. He was the window when the door was locked. All she had to do was say yes and see what happened next. Friends? Maybe. But something inside of her knew he wanted more, and she did too. She could let go of everything else choosing to forget about Shane.

But there would be no peace. The choice didn't exist. Finding out what happened to Shane was the only way to freedom.

"You go ahead, Nico. I'll see you later."

Nico reached out a hand and touched her arm. That warm feeling came over her again. And as much as she wanted to, she couldn't turn it off.

"I'll see you tonight."

His hand dropped and he smiled before taking off toward the end of the corridor. If he only knew how much he'd gotten to her.

A couple of girls stared at her, whispering. Claudia's crew. Gossip swirled around them like wasps and when it came to Drew, doubly so.

Something isn't right with her, and

She's depressed, and

She hardly talks to anyone.

People could be assholes. Piper once gave someone a black eye for calling Drew a freak. Now the next rumor would be about her and Nico. She turned her nose up and walked away just as someone tapped her shoulder.

Enid popped up beside her out of nowhere. "How are you?"

"Do you make it a habit of sneaking up on people?" Drew asked. Enid laughed and a little scar over her cheek moved. Drew wondered how she'd gotten it.

"There's a party tonight at Haven. Do you know it?" Enid said.

She used the word, *Haven*. Only the local kids called the party spot at Neptune Point that.

"How do you know about Haven?"

Enid tilted her head to the side. "I've always had family here. I come back from time to time. I guess you could say, I'm familiar with Neptune Point. So, are you going? I'll be there."

Something about Enid triggered her to proceed with caution but she didn't know what. Enid didn't appear menacing. She wasn't rude. Quite the opposite. She had on the same white sweater covered in red hearts that she wore the first time Drew met her. She shook her head at herself. She was doing what she hated, judging someone without knowing them.

Drew softened. "My friend, Piper…do you know her?"

Enid smiled. "Can't say that I do."

"I'm going with her and her boyfriend." Drew leaned against a row of lockers. "Who's your family? I've lived here my whole life and I might know them."

Enid's smile dropped and the light hit her eyes

casting a golden hue. Dreamlike. "I doubt that you'd know them. Look. I'm just trying to make friends with you because, well, I have none. Am I going about it wrong?"

Drew laughed. "You're asking the wrong person. I'm no expert, but I think you're doing just fine."

"Good. So, go tonight. I'll see you there." Enid peered up at a clock on the wall. "I've got to run." She spun around disappearing into what was left of the crowd.

Drew trailed behind the stragglers toward the doors to freedom and bounded down the steps toward her car.

***

She arrived home to find a note from Gran letting her know she wouldn't be home for dinner. She made herself a grilled cheese and scrolled through her phone as she ate. There was a message from Piper, something about a night in watching movies should she want to back out of the party. She knew Piper well enough to realize that Piper was trying to give her an excuse not to go to Haven.

She messaged her back: *I'm going, Piper. I have to do this.*

It was set. Piper and Cole would be at her house around 6:30 to pick her up. Cole was driving because Piper was never allowed to drive her parent's fancy SUV.

She headed upstairs to take a shower and gear up for whatever the night would have in store. She wanted to be comfortable and warm but look good. She hadn't gone out in a long time; people might talk.

And Nico would be there.

Her head was all over the place.

Settling on a pair of dark-wash skinny jeans and a green sweater that matched her eyes, she dressed and looked in the mirror. The jeans fit her like a glove and made her feel pretty. She sat on the stool at her vanity and took her time to dry and straighten her hair.

Her pale lashes appeared nonexistent. She sorted through what little makeup she had for a liner pencil and mascara to line her eyes and coat her lashes. Sitting back, she gazed at herself in the mirror. For the first time in a long time, she looked put together. Confident. The mask hid everything going on inside. It was perfect.

The last time she'd gone to a party at Haven had been with Shane the previous summer. And here she sat preparing to go for the first time since he'd died.

Died.

She'd avoided using that word, preferring disappeared instead, but how could he be still alive somewhere?

A thumping subwoofer pounded out a rhythm, growing louder. She stood to peer out of the bedroom window and saw a white jeep pull into the driveway.

Grabbing a jacket from her closet, she darted down the stairs. She wrote a note back to Gran letting her know she'd be gone for the evening, and hurried outside, locking the door behind her.

Piper hopped out of the passenger seat pulling up

the waist of her skull-printed leggings. A pink crystal sparkled on her eyebrow. She hugged Drew, catching her off guard. "Are you sure you're good with this?"

"I am." She tried to sound confident.

Cole waved from the driver's seat. His glasses slid down his nose and he pushed the key-hole-shaped bridge back in place. Drew got in the back and Cole steered the jeep onto the road.

"Is that a beach over there?" Cole said.

"Yeah. Not many know about it, so don't spread the word." Drew was half-joking, but not really. That beach was her sanity, and it would be ruined if mobs of people started showing up.

"My mom hates the water," Cole said. "She never took me growing up. Now I want to go as much as I can."

Piper turned around to look at her. "Ready?"

"As ready as I'll ever be."

The road to Neptune Point offered unspoiled views of the ocean on the left. The tide edged close to shore at this time of day but with darkness approaching earlier now, she couldn't see much other than streaks of orange along rippled water.

Piper's laugh was infectious and pulled Cole in as she gossiped about people from school. Drew stared out the window, half-listening. She wished she could be as charismatic and free as Piper.

It wasn't long before they approached the Bifrost Bridge to Neptune Point. The road had been destroyed years before she was born, and the bridge was built in its place. It arched tall and wide enough to keep the water far below. Rounding the turn, the towering Aurora Lighthouse came into view at the outermost edge of the point. The automated light turned like a carnival ride above the rocky shoreline glistening under the moonlight. The boarded-up house was barely visible among the tall seagrass and dead bushes. For a moment she swore she saw a light between the cracks of an upper-floor window. She moved so close to the window her breath fogged the glass. If there had been a light, it was gone now.

What does the old man want with this place?

All she saw was a watchtower and a dilapidated house with no signs of life. She had no idea what she should be looking for.

They rounded the corner away from the lighthouse off the paved road. Cole drove to the open area of gravel and sand which was the makeshift parking lot. Vehicles were crammed wherever space allowed, and Cole pulled into a spot farthest away.

She was here. Back at Neptune Point for the first time in forever. It was like stepping into a time machine, except Shane was gone and she was alone. God, she missed him. She jumped out of the jeep and shut the door, scanning the wooded area ahead. An opening among the trees marked the forest pathway. It led to the clearing known by local kids as Haven.

Piper linked her arm around hers. "We can go back you know. If all of this is too much. Say the word and we'll take you home."

"No. I'm doing this. Let's go."

Music drifted through the trees as darkness settled

around them. Cliques of kids moved in waves toward the forest pathway holding flashlights and lanterns. The boys had a new swagger compared to the last time she'd been here. It carried a sense of invincibility. Their conversations filled the air with jokes and jabs at each other.

She walked alongside Piper who waved to people, never missing a beat. Piper beamed around Cole. He had a likable charm, and she could see why Piper stuck around. They were so good together, so easy, like what she'd had with Shane. They got each other in a way that was hard to match. That hollow ache hit her again from her chest to her throat.

Piper turned around to face her. "Is everything cool? You're still good with being back here?"

"Yup. So far so good." It wasn't true, but it didn't matter. Not at this moment.

The brilliant glow of a bonfire appeared as they walked deeper into the woods. Kids gathered around the flames holding their hands close as smoke billowed up into the night sky. The sound of the river echoed in the background. As she walked closer, she could hear banter among the crowd. A playful yell. Laughter. The skunk-like scent of weed wafted around her. She'd never smoked pot before. She was curious but she probably had enough visions as it was.

"I'm glad you came. It feels like old times," Piper said.

"You think? I don't know, Piper. So much has changed." Everything was different including her. Grief does that to a person. It wears you down like sandpaper and reshapes how you look at life.

People gravitated to Piper and tonight was no different. She'd always befriended everyone regardless of social group. As familiar faces strolled up to say hello, Piper's presence took the pressure off her to socialize. She wandered off, unnoticed.

She looked back at Piper who was flirting with Cole. Twirling strands of pink hair around her fingers, Piper leaned into him gazing into his face with doe eyes. Cole wrapped lanky arms around her and pulled her close.

Shane had been Drew's crash course into that world. Flirting. Kissing. Sex. It had all terrified her, but with him, all those fears disappeared. She'd fallen hard for him, and he'd loved her right back. Would she ever have that level of comfort with anyone again?

Nico.

There he was. Standing by the fire, sharing banter with a few kids from school. One of which was Claudia. His head turned her way and she ducked, bolting for a dried-out log along the edge of the forest. The sound of the water rushing behind her matched the fuzziness in her head.

Did he see me? Did she?

Claudia would be raging to give Drew a piece of her mind after the encounter she'd had with her father.

She looked around the crowd to the path leading back to the car. She could make a run for it, avoiding him altogether. It could be an opportunity to go back to the house by Aurora. That's what she was really here for.

But why is he with Claudia of all people?

No. Aurora. She had to keep her head straight. Keep focused.

Nico broke away from the herd and headed her way.

"Hey. I thought that was you."

"Hi. Yeah." She eyed the log behind her. "I wanted to get away from the crowd and sit somewhere." She didn't know what else to say.

"I get it." He shoved his hands in his jacket pockets. "Can I sit with you?"

Her stomach coiled into knots. "Sure."

She plopped down and he sat beside her, his leg touching hers. An electric current ran through her.

"I'm glad you made it," he said.

"I am too. I think. I wasn't sure I'd ever come back here again."

"It's been a while, hasn't it? Despite what you might think, I haven't been to many of these lately either. I remember when you used to come out here with Shane. It always surprised me because it's never been your thing. The social scene I mean." He looked down at his hands. "I'm sorry. I shouldn't have brought him up."

"It's okay. He was new to town, and it was a good way for him to meet people. But you're not wrong. I'm what one would consider a bit of an introvert."

"A bit?" Nico smiled at her.

"A lot."

"I am too but don't tell anyone."

"Could've fooled me." She nodded toward the

group by the fire. Claudia had her head tilted back in over-exaggerated laughter.

"I've known most of these people my whole life. Take me out of this place and put me in a big city? I'd fall flat on my face." Nico stared ahead and a muscle along his jawline twitched.

"Hardly! It's effortless for you. I wish it was like that for me."

"Don't sell yourself short, Drew. I love talking with you. It's so easy. Comfortable. That day on the water brought it all back. I'd forgotten how much I missed hanging out."

The combination of light from the fire and a full moon offered Drew a clear view of his broad shoulders under a dark shirt and jacket. Never one to make a bold move, she found herself wanting to reach out to him in some way. Shyness crept back in, and the moment passed, leaving her feeling like an idiot.

"I guess we sort of drifted apart, didn't we?"

"We did," Nico said and shrugged. "You were with Shane. After his accident, I wanted to check in so many times to see how you were doing but wasn't sure I should. You weren't in school for the longest time, and once you were back, I told myself you needed space or something."

"You weren't the only one not sure what to say. It's okay. I get it."

"I should've figured it out. When I saw you on the water, I couldn't believe it. It'd been so long. I'm sorry, I should've reached out before this." His intense, deep brown eyes looked at her. In that moment she caught a glimpse of the Nico she knew. The boy down the road. Only her feelings for him were different now. They were intense and it unnerved her.

But Shane was gone, and she had to find out what happened to him. That was all that mattered.

"Thank you. But it really is okay," Drew said. "It's still hard to believe he's gone. I miss him."

"I can't imagine what it's been like for you. Claudia told me about a bag or something. I don't believe much of what she says though, I refused to listen to her gossip. If you want to tell me about it, that's up to you."

The weight of a hundred bricks lifted off her. Claudia glanced over where they sat as though she had super-sonic hearing. Nico wasn't *with* Claudia. He didn't even seem to like her.

"Someone found a bag and rumors flew that it might be his stuff, but it's not. The police have it but can't confirm who it belongs to or where it came from. That's all I really know."

"Okay." He put his hand over hers. Heat rushed to her cheeks. It must've been the fire's warmth. She enjoyed Nico's company, but she didn't want to complicate her life any more than it already was. He oozed charisma pulling her in like a magnet. Her feelings were torn between wanting to shut down any possibility of friendship or God knows what, and desperation to feel alive and excited about life again.

Piper and Cole sauntered over. Nico released her hand, and she resisted the urge to grab his back again.

Nico stood. "I'm going to catch up with my

friends, but I'll come back in a bit. Cool?"

"Sure!" she said.

He waved and walked away.

Piper sat beside her. "See? He likes you."

"It's not like that. We're *friends*."

Piper bumped her shoulder into Drew's with a laugh. They had that kind of friendship. The sisterhood kind. Piper's way of helping her get through Shane's loss was different than others. She didn't do anything gently. It was more of a push with both hands on her ass out of a hole she'd fallen in.

A monstrous shriek trumpeted from somewhere above, and she jumped up. Music thumped in the background between the guttural cries. She looked up. A tree branch swayed from the weight of an enormous owl.

Piper and Cole were talking, oblivious to her panic.

Why was she the only one who could hear it? Her breath fogged in the air as the temperature dropped, plummeting into icy cold. Something was about to happen.

The owl dived toward her swooping by her face. Its feathers skimmed her cheek and she gasped, swatting in front of her.

A ball of light swirled between the trees. She stepped closer, leaving the blaze of the fire behind. A narrow path lit up in front of her in glowing light. It was like something out of her dream.

The owl flew closer to her landing on a branch not a foot from her face. It was like something out of a mystical storybook. She stared into its yellow eyes before it took off into the forest, beckoning her to follow. She obliged immediately, pushing tree limbs away from her face.

"Drew?" Piper jumped up. "Drew! Where are you going?"

Piper's holler reverberated behind her, but she didn't turn back.

Eight

Drew continued through the trees until they cleared along the riverbank. The owl wailed louder from somewhere ahead. The rush of water drowned out the calls from her friends back in the clearing. Mist dampened her hair, freezing into icicles. Her hands and face were numb with cold. Branches snapped underfoot as she clawed her way through the forest following the ball of light.

A voice spoke. *His* voice.

"It's an estuary, Drew. Where the river meets the sea."

Shane.

She spun around, but all she saw was an endless expanse of tree trunks. A memory played in her mind like a movie she could watch over and over. It was the last time they'd been in this exact spot, only it hadn't looked the same back then.

"Aren't they cool?" Shane said. He was pointing at a cluster of lotus flowers floating on the surface of a still pool of water. "They grow out of muddy water and rise to bloom like that. Beautiful things growing out of such a dark place."

The memory faded and darkness returned. Shane was gone, leaving her again. But the flowers—the flowers remained. She moved closer to the water's edge in disbelief. Hundreds of them floated in the water. Wind from a sudden surge of water took her breath away. The flowers were pulled under creating a clear path to the other side.

There he stood. The old man. He glared at her from across the river, his body unmoving while his hair whipped his face from underneath a hat.

She wasn't sure what the hell he expected her to do. Walk on water? That wasn't a talent she possessed.

Out of nowhere, a girl's voice spoke. Drew recognized it as Enid's.

"It's a magical place. If you're not forced to stay here, that is."

Surprised, Drew whirled around. Despite her sweater and jacket, goosebumps crawled across her skin. Had Enid followed her out here?

Enid stepped closer. "I was going to talk to you earlier, but you had people around."

"I could've introduced you—"

"Come on. They couldn't be friends with someone like me. Not the way you can." Enid didn't have on a jacket, only the same heart-covered sweater.

"Aren't you cold?"

Enid laughed. "I don't get cold."

Her entire body stiffened and the hairs on the back of her neck bristled. She turned back to the river. The flowers were gone. Of course, they'd never been there. They weren't real, they couldn't be.

The ball of light disappeared. She strained to see the old man, but he no longer loomed on the other side. None of it was real. She was losing her mind. Yet Enid *was* here. Scanning around in desperation she realized there was no clear path through the trees to get back to the fire.

"There isn't a way out. Not really. Believe me, I've tried," Enid said.

Every muscle inside her wanted to bolt through the dense forest, but she couldn't leave Enid here alone. What if this girl was suffering some sort of mental break? Drew knew the feeling of being locked in your own mind without a key.

"Come with me. I'll have my friend drive you home," she said.

"I *am* home."

"This place isn't home to anyone, Enid. Seriously, where do you live? My friend can give you a lift. I know he won't mind—"

"You saw the old man across the river."

"Did *you* see the old man?" Drew asked.

"He's like a gatekeeper here. He wants you because you're the only one who can see him. At least that's what I think. You can see me." Enid's deep-set eyes surveyed her for a reaction and warning bells went off in her head.

Holy shit.

The truth smacked Drew in the face. Hard.

Enid was one of them.

She couldn't believe she'd missed the signs. Even now, she was trying to dismiss the truth about Enid, and it was right in front of her. Because if this was happening, the wandering souls could cross an invisible line and appear as human as anyone. Fear gripped her just thinking about what that could mean.

"Who—who are you?" she asked. "Why are you here?"

"I don't know why I'm here, but I am." Enid reached out a hand. "Come with me."

Drew backed up. "Where?" She eyed Enid suspiciously.

"Across the river. Aurora. Both. There are secrets there and I need your help."

"Now? Are you crazy?" Curiosity pulled at her, but she still didn't know if she could trust Enid.

"Why not now? We're here, aren't we? We need each other," Enid said.

"I can't, not now. My friends will freak out if I leave and they can't find me."

"Come back then. I don't know if I can keep coming to you. I have no idea how I did it in the first place."

Branches snapped as swift footsteps echoed through the trees behind her. Flashlights beamed through the cracks. Piper and Cole called out her name.

She turned back to face Enid, but the strange ghost girl had disappeared. How could she not have known? The wind picked up and she shivered pulling her hood up to block the cold.

Piper burst through the trees first. "Drew! What the hell happened?"

Curious stragglers followed, with Nico and a

smug-looking Claudia among them. She wished the ground would open and swallow her up. Anything would be better than the judgement that would follow. There would be questions, questions she didn't dare answer. They already thought she was crazy. Even she was starting to agree.

Calm down and think!

She needed something clever to say to get her out of how ridiculous she must look.

Nico stood in front of the small group that gathered around the river's edge. His expression held concern over anything else, or so she hoped.

Forcing a smile, she said the first thing that came to mind to divert everyone's attention.

"Everything's fine. I, um—I thought I saw something running in the woods. I wanted to check it out."

Piper jumped on board. "I saw it too! A wolf or coyote." She squinted her eyes and looked past Drew into the wooded area. "It's gone. The shows over, I guess."

Claudia marched past everyone, coming to a stop inches away from Drew's face.

"Is that what you saw, Drew? A wolf? Because I was there the whole time and saw nothing. And besides, if you knew anything about animals, you'd know they would never come so close to a large group of people. What's really going on?"

Chatter rose above the swift river. She wondered if she should take her chances and jump in, letting it carry her away from here.

Piper pushed in between Claudia and Drew. "Back off, Claudia. I saw an animal run into the woods and Drew followed. That's what's going on. Why do you always have to start shit?"

"Oh, I'm the one starting shit? Why don't you ask your friend here why she felt the need to track my father down and interrogate him in our driveway about her dead boyfriend?"

Nico stepped in between them. "Woah. Enough, Claudia."

"We're done," Drew said. She leaned to the side to address the crowd watching. "Did you hear that? We're done here! Start walking back!"

There were mumbles of protest. Cole, who'd been hanging back, waved his hands to push them out and they started to retreat. Claudia's mean-girl army held their ground.

"I don't know what you're up to going to the police and digging for information that doesn't exist but leave my father out of it."

"Just go, Claudia."

"Whatever, Drew." Claudia turned to leave flashing her middle finger behind her.

"Wow. What was that all about?" Nico asked.

"A rich spoiled brat who thinks she can tell people what to do," Piper said.

"I've known her for a long time," Nico said, "but she's no friend of mine. She hits below the belt. Doesn't care who she hurts. Don't let her get to you."

"Easier said than done." Drew had whispered it, but he still heard.

Things had gotten so crazy lately. If people hadn't noticed before, they would now. She'd heard comments around school after Shane's accident. Theories of what really happened and mutterings that he'd committed suicide.

She'd tried hard not to let it get to her, but Claudia's comment and the gossip hurt more than she cared to admit.

Piper draped an arm across Drew's shoulders. "I swear to God, I'll fight her for you."

"My money's on Piper," Cole said grinning at his girlfriend.

"I don't need anyone to fight my battles but thank you. She's just angry because I got her in trouble with her father."

Nico leaned against a tree angling a flashlight through the trees. "Did you really chase something through the woods? You look spooked."

There was no way he could ever understand her world. Not a chance. "It was just an animal. I'm sure it's gone now."

She exchanged a look with Piper. She didn't believe her but said nothing.

Oblivious, Nico kept talking. "You tracked down Claudia's dad? What does he have to do with anything?"

"I didn't *track* him down. I was at Piper's and happened to see him in the driveway. I just…I had a question for him. Can we drop all this and go back to the fire? I'm freezing."

"Sure. Let's go." Nico aimed the light on a

makeshift path allowing everyone to step ahead of him, including Drew. "I'm pretty resourceful, you know, if there's anything you need…"

She halted and he bumped into her. They were so close she could feel his breath on her face. Her stomach fluttered. "I don't know what I need. Not yet anyway."

"Well, when you figure it out, let me know."

"I'll keep that in mind."

His intentions were good, but no resource of Nico's could help.

She picked up the pace to catch up with the others. They entered the clearing with the bonfire, rock music blaring from a speaker. Flames burned into the starry sky shining on Piper's pink hair like a neon light. Someone puked by the woodpile. Drew stepped over beer cans and cigarette butts that were strewn along the ground marking a territory that didn't belong to them. She sat back down on the fallen tree. The owl was gone, the branch empty. All she could think of was how Enid was one of them. Like the Crimson Lady. Like the old man. She wondered what secrets were buried here.

Nico hadn't left her side and she hated that she liked having him nearby so much. After she'd reassured Piper that she was fine, and Claudia would in fact not look better with a black eye, Piper and Cole refocused on each other.

"I'm heading out in a minute. I can give you a ride home if you want," Nico said.

The adrenaline vanished leaving her with overwhelming exhaustion. Home sounded wonderful, but she couldn't bring herself to leave with him.

"I'll wait for Piper and Cole. Thanks, though."

"Okay. I'll message tomorrow?"

"Sure. Bye, Nico."

She was torn between wanting to see him again, and her fear of falling for him. She hadn't come here for Nico or anyone else. She didn't have time for any of it. She came to find answers and she'd gotten a tiny piece of a complex puzzle. Enid wasn't real—at least not in the human sense.

The chatter diminished as the crowd thinned and the music stopped. Flames no longer danced high, rather they smoldered into a glow of embers and ashes.

Cole was talking with friends and Piper approached. "Do you want to talk about the real reason you took off into the woods because I know it wasn't to chase coyotes."

"No," Drew said, "but I'm fine."

"You don't look fine."

"I've got this."

"See, that's what I don't understand. Got what?" Piper lowered her voice. "Was it another ghost?"

Piper knew the truth. She'd seen her experience it before. Drew wouldn't lie to her. "Yes."

"I thought so. Is there another reason why you wanted to come tonight? Other than Nico that is." Piper smiled at her.

Drew's cheeks flushed again. It was frustrating the mention of his name did that to her. But it was out of her control. "First of all, I didn't come here for Nico. He's just—"

"A *friend*. For now. But maybe he could be more

than that! And if that's the case, it means you're finally moving on. How could that be a bad thing?" Piper crossed her arms. "After what I just saw, I can't help but wonder if you came back here for some other reason. I just have no idea what it is. Am I wrong?"

"You're not wrong."

"Alright, good start. So, what is it? You said the lighthouse creeped you out. What else could it be? Coda River? That boarded-up house?" Piper gestured around her. "Haven? Drew, nothing's out here."

"I'll tell you everything that I know, but not here. Not now."

"Are you guys ready to go?" Cole emerged from the dark and turned on a flashlight.

"Ready if you are," Drew said.

As they walked back to the parking lot, she surveyed the trees on each side for a sign of Enid or the old man. Nothing.

Waves rumbled as they pounded the rocky shore. Aurora's beacon rotated, cutting through the fog. Headlights cast shadows as people scrambled to their vehicles.

Heat blasted from the vents, warming the car, and she took her hood down. They drove away from Neptune Point, Aurora—and everything that went with it—leaving it behind. But not for long. All she could think about was Enid; she'd told her they needed each other. Maybe Enid was the clue she'd been waiting for.

The rest of the way home, Piper did something unusual for her. She dropped it, not mentioning another word about what had happened. Drew got out of the jeep and waved goodbye before entering the house. She tiptoed up the stairs to her bedroom, careful not to wake Gran. Tiredness weighed her down like a winter coat. She dug for clean pajamas in the dark, changed, and crawled into bed.

Enid is a ghost. How didn't I know?

She promised herself she would go back and find Enid first thing in the morning.

Nine

Drew awoke to pouring rain hitting her bedroom window. A dull ache pulsed like a drum from the nape of her neck to the top of her head. She yanked the covers over her head and closed her burning eyes.

Thoughts from the party flipped through her mind like pages in a book.

The creepy owl.

The old man.

Floating flowers that could not exist in that cold, fast-moving river.

Enid—who was not of this world! How could Drew have missed that?

She had to go back to Neptune Point. But this time she'd go to the abandoned house by Aurora.

Sitting up, she swung her legs off the side of the bed as her phone started vibrating on the nightstand. Unknown caller showed up on the screen. She wondered if she should even answer it. What if it was the detective calling with information?

She cleared her throat. "Hello?"

A pause.

"Who is this?"

This time her father's gruff voice answered. "It's me."

Hearing him brought her back to the last good memory she had of him. Her five-year-old self crying on the ground over a skinned knee. He'd scooped her up and calmed her with that same voice. That memory also marked the end of his trips back home.

"Drew? Don't hang up—"

She held the phone with a shaking hand. Talking to him stirred up pain that she'd rather keep buried. "I'm here."

"I need to see you," her father said. "I'll be…town…month."

"You're cutting out." She held the phone closer to her ear straining to hear him as noise filled the background. Her stomach was in knots. "Where are you?"

"I'll be back home in a couple of weeks, and we need to talk. Can you hear me? Drew?"

"I hear you," she said. "Why didn't you call last week when you were in town?"

"You knew about that? There wasn't time. We left the same day."

"Sure. Well, next time you should at least check in on Gran. She needs you." She suppressed the building anger. He didn't deserve one ounce of emotion from her.

"I'm coming back. I've got a contract at the shipyard. I'll be sticking around for a while."

The anger won. Years of frustration over empty promises and betrayal poured out. "Let me get this straight. Now that I'm all grown up, you plan to *stick around for a while*. For the last decade, I've meant nothing to you, and suddenly you need to see me? Is this why you're calling? Because if so, I'd say we're done here."

He didn't even know her anymore. How could he think his coming home to stay was anything close to what she needed? All that would do is complicate her life more than it already was.

"We need to talk. I have…important…tell…"

"You're breaking up again! I can't do this. Goodbye, Gabe."

If she could slam the phone down, she would. She resisted the urge to throw it against the wall. Fuming, she got up and opened her closet door to find something to wear. She shoved hangers aside and they scraped along the metal post. How dare he call her and try to come back into her life now! Where was he a year ago? Ten years ago? She yanked on a pair of jeans and searched for a sweater.

At the very back hung a navy hooded sweatshirt. Her heart sank like a weight to her stomach. This was Shane's sweater. Tears pricked her eyes. With trembling hands, she reached out and touched the worn fabric. One moment she stood in her bedroom, and the next her mind took her to the day he gave it to her. It was also the day he showed her the pocket watch for the first time.

***

Night fell. Stars dusted the sky bringing it to life. Rocks knocked against each other with every wave that rolled to shore. She walked along the beach with Shane holding hands, fingers intertwined. The sand under her feet was cold as summer had come to an end. A rush of air whipped off the water and she shivered. It hadn't gone unnoticed by Shane, as nothing ever did.

"Are you cold?" he asked.

"Freezing." She turned to meet his face.

He'd pulled his sweater off and handed it to her, causing his black undershirt to lift revealing his lean torso. She knew him intimately. He ran a hand through his dark, wavy hair, pushing it from his eyes. Those sincere, blue eyes. He looked at her so differently than anyone else. He loved her. Like *really* loved her and she'd never been so sure of anything. Being around him made her feel like a butterfly— everything fluttered in the best way. She slipped into the sweater and breathed in his intoxicating scent.

"I have to tell you something," he said.

"That doesn't sound good."

He stopped walking and looked her in the eye. "I think my mom was keeping something from me. A secret." He reached in his pocket and took out a watch. Opening its round casing, he used his phone's flashlight to show her. "Look at the engraving. *Morana*. What does that mean? Why would she give this to me and take off never to be heard from again? It doesn't make sense." He turned it, revealing the back of the watch, and held it out so she could look closer. "There's a map on the back."

She took the watch from his fingers and examined it. "I can't make it out. It's too faded."

"Look at the way the lines curve." He pointed at a rectangular shape. "Right there, that's a lighthouse. I think it's Neptune Point."

"Really?" She turned it around in her hand. "I don't know, Shane. It could be anything."

"There's more." He unclasped a key from the chain.

"What's that for?"

"I have no idea," he said. "I've searched every inch of the house, but there's nothing with a lock."

"Weird. Did she say where she got it, or why it was so important?"

He dropped the watch in the palm of his hand and closed his fingers over it. "Nope, nothing. She said to hold it for safekeeping until she came back. That was six months ago."

"Has anyone heard from her? I don't know, a friend or family member somewhere?"

"No one," he muttered. "She hadn't been herself for a while, but my parents haven't exactly been getting along either. Maybe she really did just take off. She'd threatened it enough."

Drew knew that heartache all too well. "I'm sorry you're going through this. I wish there was some way I could help."

"My dad is talking about leaving town again. He's applying for a job near Boston where my uncle lives. He's given up."

He'd said it with a nonchalance that she didn't

understand. Did he want to leave too?

"What does that mean for us? Wouldn't you have to go with him?" She didn't know what she'd do if he left.

"Don't worry, I'm not going anywhere. I'll be eighteen in a few months. Time to move out on my own." He shoved his hands into his pockets and looked out on the horizon. A vein pulsed along his temple. "Drew, I just can't shake the feeling that something is very wrong. I'm missing something but I have no idea where to look."

She stepped beside him, and he wrapped his arms around her. She held him tight, closed her eyes, and breathed him in.

***

She stood shivering as the memory faded. She held the too-long sleeves of Shane's sweater against her nose and inhaled. She was desperate for his mix of cologne and deodorant—citrus and sandalwood—to surround her like it did that night. But too much time had passed. His essence was gone. He was gone.

How cruel to come so close to someone, to love someone, only to have them ripped away from her. She didn't think she'd ever be able to put those shattered pieces back together. Life was unfair. Now she was left alone to walk a thin line with the dead…or undead, as it were.

She knew what she had to do, where she had to go. Heading for the stairs, she glanced down the hall on the way by. There was no sign of the Crimson Lady, but Drew was sure she'd be back again.

Gran called to her from the kitchen, and she stopped only to mention the call from her father. She gave her a brief summary while Gran sat drinking coffee. Drew didn't stick around to talk about it further. This was how it always went: her father promising a noble return and Gran disappointed in the end, making excuses for him.

On a mission, she shoved her feet into her boots and threw on her jacket at the same time. She bolted from the house and ran through an onslaught of icy rain to her car. Her phone buzzed inside her coat pocket with a message from Nico. There would be no convertible ride today, but he hoped to see her later. She could ditch this crazy plan and hang out with him, but the sweater against her skin reminded her of why she couldn't do that. Not today. She'd find out what happened to Shane so that once and for all she could move ahead with her life—whatever that meant.

She backed out of the driveway and accelerated to Neptune Point. Rain pelted the windshield, melting, as the wipers cleared it away. The last remaining leaves tumbled across the road, their vibrant colors gone. They blended with the dark clouds and even darker thoughts swirling in her mind. She didn't even know what she was hoping to find. Enid had told her to come back... Would she be there waiting for her?

She stretched her neck from side to side trying to relieve an ever-present tension. Her fingers clutched the steering wheel so hard they hurt. The speedometer read ten miles too fast, so she slowed as the road wound along the cliffs. Releasing a hand, she turned up the radio. Maybe music would help, even though her head still hurt. She should've taken ibuprofen before she left the house or maybe even eaten something.

A debate raged in her mind. It was like those old cartoons with an angel on one shoulder and a devil on the other. The dark side told her to give up and let it go. She'd fail if she tried, looking ridiculous in the process. On the other hand, a lighter voice with a determined whisper told her to push forward. But there was no choice. Not really. There was a mystery here that lay right in front of her and somehow it involved Shane.

She bit down repeatedly on her lower lip to stifle the sorrow. As hard as she tried, she couldn't keep tears from escaping. She blinked fast and wiped them from her cheeks with the back of her hand. Her options were limited to ignoring all the shit happening to her, which was impossible, or doing whatever it took to find answers.

She had to get to Neptune Point and find Enid. She'd have the answers Drew needed.

She kept driving. Her phone buzzed, but she ignored it and kept driving, pressing her foot down heavier on the gas. Rain turned to sleet, the wipers having a hard time keeping up. The windows fogged and despite blasting the heat, she had to crouch down to see where she was going through the clear bubble along the bottom.

She coasted along, winding turns faster than the weather allowed, and she knew it was dangerous, but she couldn't help it.

The same message played in her mind on repeat.

Aurora. She's there. Help her.

She hated that the wandering souls didn't just say what they meant. She didn't want to piece together more mysteries than she had to. She'd already given in and was well on her way back to Neptune Point, that had to be what the old guy wanted. There was nothing else she could do.

She strained to see ahead through rain and swaying trees as a section of highway narrowed to a two-lane passage. Her momentum sped up as though floating over the pavement. Standing on the side of the road was the old man, his wet hair hanging like ropes under his hat. His long coat blew in the wind.

The steering wheel shook under her tightly gripped hands, and she knew at that moment she was going to crash.

She hit the brakes with too much force. She was losing control and didn't know what to do. The car fishtailed back and forth and swerved sideways toward a guardrail. She shrieked as the car spun, throwing her head against the wheel. Hideous sounds of shattering glass and crunching metal deafened her. The airbag smacked her in the face and knocked the air out of her lungs as her body jerked against the seatbelt. Warm fluid oozed from her head to her chin. A high-pitched sound rang in her ears.

And then everything went black.

***

She walked barefoot along the twisted path toward the old man.

He called to her, *Come back. Don't go.*

Cobblestone steps led to a place deep into the earth. The shrill call of an owl rang in her ears. A rush of water sounded nearby, but all she saw were shadows.

A woman appeared in front of her and moved in close.

The Crimson Lady.

This time her dress was clean and free of blood. She leaned close, observing Drew's face before touching her cheek.

"You'll be okay," she whispered.

***

Drew drifted in and out of consciousness. A metallic taste caused her stomach to lurch, and she swallowed bile. Smoke wafted around her, and she smelled the rancid odor of burning rubber. It was hard to breathe, and every inhale hurt. Frantic voices sounded close to her, but she couldn't make out what they were saying. A stabbing pain shot from her head to her toes, and her muscles ached with a soreness she'd never felt before. She tried to move but warm hands gripped her arms with a comforting gentleness.

"Try to be still until help arrives, dear."

Sirens wailed jolting her to a hellish reality. Why were there sirens? She opened her eyes to flashing lights swirling around her. A brace was secured around her neck before strong hands lifted her onto a hard board. Her whole body shook. Ice rain blew violently at her face.

I'm so cold. Am I dying?

She closed her eyes as the hard surface she lay on moved up slowly and gently pushed. A burst of warmth hit her, burning her frozen skin. She tried to sit up but couldn't move. She opened her eyes again to find the rain outside had been replaced with ceiling lights. Everything looked so white.

I'm in an ambulance. Why?

Something tightened on her arm and released.

"What's your name?" a man's voice said.

"Drew," she whispered.

A man in a uniform stood over her. He looked at her with kind, serious eyes.

"Hi, Drew. I'm Pax. You've been in an accident. We're taking you to Silver Boulder Hospital. I'm going to ask you a few questions on the way, okay?"

Pax? Accident?

The man's head turned to a woman wearing a similar uniform, who handed him something. He fitted a mask over Drew's nose and mouth. Air seeped into her lungs, but she couldn't take a deep breath without pain.

"How old are you?" he asked.

"Seventeen." She tried to move the mask, but he stopped her.

"It's just a little oxygen to help you catch your breath." He smiled at her and something about him was recognizable. "Do the best you can. I'll hear you."

"Do you know what town you're in?" he continued.

"Atlas Cliffs." Tightness in her chest made it hard to talk. "Am I going to die?"

"You're not going to die," he said and patted her arm.

Pax. She thought about it again. She knew him from somewhere.

"We were able to get your cell phone and a backpack from your car." This time the woman spoke to her, but Drew couldn't see her face.

If she died, would she be a ghost like the others? Gran would be broken and alone. Hot tears ran down the sides of her face. Her chin trembled and her head throbbed. A sharp jab pierced her arm, and a bag of clear liquid was hung on a metal post. The man spoke to someone in the front seat and broken voices sounded through radio static. Sirens howled as they picked up speed. Every bump sent her body into agony, and she thought she might throw up.

The woman said something to the man, calling him Paxton.

Paxton. A paramedic. Shane's father.

She couldn't keep her eyes open any longer and felt herself slipping away. The next time she opened them it was a struggle to focus.

How much time has passed?

She was moving, but not in the ambulance like before; this time she was being wheeled through doors. People spoke on each side of her but sounded muffled. She tried to move her head, but it didn't budge, still braced against the hard board underneath her. Her eyes watered as she squinted at the fluorescent lights above her. One of them flickered. A baby cried. A voice blared over an intercom announcing codes she didn't understand.

Paramedics parked the stretcher in a very bright room. Desperate to see Paxton's face again, she tried to speak—just a squeak sounded through her rattling teeth.

His face appeared as he leaned over her. "Drew, we've gotten a hold of your grandmother. She's on her way. We're leaving you now, but the doctors and nurses here will take good care of you."

She reached a shaky hand out to him. "Shane's dad?"

He bent down closer. "What did you say?"

"Shane?" She coughed and grabbed at her mask trying to pull it off.

He gently pulled the mask down for her. "He was my son. I remember you. I'll check in on you. You're in good hands." He readjusted the mask, released her hand, and walked away.

She wanted to scream at him to stay. Ask him about the bag and if he knew anything about the watch. She wanted to know if he'd heard from Shane's mother.

She couldn't stop crying and it made her head hurt more. A woman with soulful eyes placed a hand on her arm. She wore a lab coat with a tag clipped on the pocket, but Drew couldn't focus enough to read it.

"I'm Doctor Wymond. We're going to run some tests." She smiled, causing her hairline to pull against her tightly wound bun. She carried an authoritative presence despite her small stature as she gave commands to the people around her.

All sense of time became lost to Drew as people bustled around her. Machines beeped. A warm blanket covered her. The chills calmed. The pain eased. Darkness wrapped around her in a cocoon.

Ten

Drew swatted away a tapping at her arm. Gran never woke her up for school. What was going on?

"Let me sleep."

Sharp pain flashed in her skull. Her eyes flew open. No one was tapping her. The overhead light was on, although dimmer now. Cold metal rails lined each side of her bed and a tube trailed out of her arm, limiting her reach. She followed the tube to a bag of clear fluid suspended on a pole.

She was in the hospital. She never made it to Neptune Point. She'd lost control of her car and crashed into…What? She couldn't remember. There weren't any other vehicles on the road. None she recalled, anyway. She hoped no one else was hurt. She remembered flashing lights. Riding in an ambulance. Shane's father.

The old man in the pouring rain.

Enid.

She could not stay in this room for long; she had to find Enid.

She licked her dry lips and flinched at the motion. Raising her hand, she felt a bandage stretching from her cheek to above her lip. Her body ached terribly like she'd been beaten up. A wave of nausea surged, and she breathed deep to get through it.

Her lungs burned a little, but at least the mask was gone. So was the brace around her neck. She wiggled her toes against the crisp sheets to make sure they moved. They did, thank God. She was alive!

If she'd died and became one of the dead wandering aimlessly for eternity—No, she couldn't think like that. It terrified her too much. She didn't know if everyone who died wandered aimlessly without purpose, but she sure as hell wasn't okay with doing that herself.

There was another light tapping on her bare arm. She propped herself up on shaky elbows and squinted around the room. A shudder crawled over her skin, and the fine hairs on her arms crept up. A gust of icy air brushed over her and she rubbed her arms. Sitting up made her head pound in her ears.

Staring at her from the corner of the room was a boy. If he could even be called a boy. Luminescent and glowing, he sat, sort of—yet somehow not quite—on the chair. Hovering.

"Jesus Christ!"

"Hi," he said.

She pushed herself toward the top of the bed and tried to catch her breath. The boy's wide, luminous eyes watched her. The throbbing in her head intensified. She'd never seen this one before. Maybe if she closed her eyes and ignored him, he'd go away, like they used to. But she knew better. They didn't leave her alone anymore.

Dizziness forced her to lie back down and be still for a moment.

Lifting her head, she dared to look. The boy's dark hair curled around his face, framing doe eyes that glimmered as no humans could.

"What do you want?"

The boy moved closer until he hovered over her. Despite the sudden chill from his presence, sweat dripped down her back. She bit her bottom lip and winced.

"I'm Ezra." His raspy whisper drifted to her ears.

The black writing on the bag. *Ezra.*

"Where did you come from? Do you know someone named Shane?" As she said it, she couldn't believe she said that out loud—especially to a dead boy.

He laughed. "You met my sister."

Her exhausted brain and sore head caught up with his words. "Enid? Is Enid your sister?"

He inched closer to her face, and she stared at him with blurry eyes.

"He doesn't want to hurt you," he said.

The image of the old man standing on the road flashed in her mind.

"The old man? Do you know who he is? What does he want?"

The boy's head snapped toward the closed door for a second before his shadowy face turned back to her. He held a finger up to his lips and like air releasing from a pinhole said, "*Shhh!*"

He faded into nothing as the door opened.

Gran shuffled in and closed the door quietly behind her. "You're awake!"

Drew was left with more questions after meeting this new ghost boy. He left before she could get an answer about the old man; he had to have known something that could help her.

"In all my years on this Earth, I've never been so scared," Gran said. Bracing herself on the bed rails, she leaned down and kissed her on the forehead. "How are you feeling?"

Like death.

But she wouldn't tell Gran that version. The poor woman looked terrible, so damn weary. Her hair was parted at the side and dangled in a mess of frizzy waves, and her blood-shot eyes were puffy.

"My head hurts and my body aches a bit. But I'm okay."

"Should I get someone? The nurse said to call if you woke up in pain. What do you need?"

Good question. She needed to get out of the hospital, find a car, drive to Neptune Point, find Enid… The list was never-ending. For Gran's sake, she kept it simple. "I need to go home."

"Not until the doctor says you can. You're bruised and banged up. They had to stitch a gash over your lip. I didn't catch everything they told me, but the doctor will be back in the morning." The lines on Gran's forehead deepened as she talked.

"What time is it?" As she spoke, she realized what she should have asked was, *what day is it*? She didn't even know.

"Nearly four."

"Sunday morning? I've been here all night?"

"Yes. Are you sure you're alright? Maybe I'll go get the nurse—"

"I didn't hit anyone, did I?" She was nervous to hear the answer but the thought of someone getting injured or worse because of her made her sicker to her stomach than she already was.

"The police said you hit a guardrail."

"My car?"

"From what I heard, it's not good, but it can be replaced. You can't. Focus on getting better and we can worry about the car later."

Not good.

After months without answers, she finally had momentum going. She was ready to find answers, ready to find out once and for all what was happening. What would she do now?

The pain persisted, moving to the side of her head into her temples. Rubbing her forehead, she swallowed and breathed deep to settle her stomach. This would be a problem. She had to get back to Neptune Point before Enid disappeared—now more than ever after the ghost's luminescent brother had visited her.

"How long have you been here?" she asked Gran.

"As soon as they called me, I came. I think it was around two o'clock in the afternoon. That nice boy down the road drove me. Where were you going in such a hurry? You could've been killed!"

"What nice boy, Gran?"

"Oh, you know. You were two peas in a pod back

in the day. Inseparable. Nick and Maria's boy."

"*Nico*? Nico drove you here?" Drew wondered if he had come in to see her. It had been a long time since he came around as much as he was these days. She didn't know what to make of it, whether he liked her as a friend or if there was something more going on.

"He'd still be here if I hadn't sent him home around midnight." She reached behind Drew and arranged the pillows. "You need to rest."

"Wait—How did Nico know about the accident?"

"His father's tow company was called to remove your car. I don't know what I'd do if something happened to you." Gran held the rails, her hands shaky. "You're all I have."

She put a hand over Gran's; she'd never seen her in such a bad way. "I'm sorry I scared you. I'm going to be okay. Promise."

She felt the same about Gran. If something happened to Gran, she'd be a true orphan with no family. She was all she had.

"I want to get a call to your father. He should—"

"Absolutely not. Please don't."

"Drew," Gran admonished. "He's still your father, and the only one you've got. His insurance was still active. He has not abandoned you."

Drew chewed on her lower lip. They cracked and peeled under her teeth. She wanted to yell out all the reasons why she had no father, how blood wasn't enough to bond you to someone, and that yes, in fact, he had abandoned her a long time ago.

"I don't want to see him. Please respect that."

But Gran only shook her head. "This anger you hold onto isn't good. It'll eat you alive."

"Hasn't yet; I'm still here. And I'm not *angry*. I'm…" Disappointed. Hurt. Lost. "It doesn't matter."

Gran rubbed her face and yawned. Drew pointed to a reclining chair laid out flat against the wall with a pillow and blanket. "Get some sleep. Everything will be okay. We don't need him."

Gran brushed a piece of hair from Drew's face and limped to the chair. It didn't take long before hushed snoring sounded in the corner.

Drew wished she could fall asleep snoring too. She thought of calling out to a nurse for pills or something, anything, to knock her out so her head would stop hurting and her stomach would settle. She drifted in and out of fever dreams. Dreams where she was searching for the ghost boy, but he never came back.

She must have slept because the next thing she knew light broke through the curtains and the door swung open. A nurse entered with a machine on wheels. His hair looked crunchy, held in place with too much gel. The makeshift bed where Gran had slept was gone and the blankets folded. Drew hadn't heard her leave.

"Hi, Drew." He held up a plastic bag before plopping it down on the chair beside her. "I found your things from yesterday. Your phone is in here too, but I have no idea if it works. I might be able to find a charging cable somewhere. I saw your sweet grandmother in the hallway on her way to the cafeteria. How are you feeling?" His name tag had a small happy face sticker above his name. Danny. He was way too fresh and cheery for her mood.

"Been better."

"You're lucky. Someone must've been looking out for you." He clamped a tiny device on her trembling finger and secured a cuff around her arm. It inflated and squeezed tight, numbers appearing on a screen. He asked questions about her pain and how bad it was, and she answered them the best she could, but all she could think of was how this was not part of her plan. She should have made it to Neptune Point where Enid would have been waiting for her just like she'd said. Drew had been prepared to ask her what she knew about the old man, and about Shane. But no. She was stuck in this prison.

After ensuring the hospital gown was tightly fastened so she wasn't exposed for all to see, the nurse helped her to the bathroom rolling the IV pole behind her. She closed the door for privacy and got a good look at herself in the mirror.

"Sweet Jesus."

She held onto the sides of the sink to steady her shaking legs. Her red hair spilled over her shoulders in a tangled mess. Dark circles under her eyes blended with a bruise across her cheek. The bandage above her lip came unstuck and she lifted it to see three tiny stitches—the skin swelling around them coated in dried blood.

She looked as bad as she felt.

Walking took effort but she made it back to the bed with Nurse Danny's help. She was in rough shape, but it could not stop her from getting out. She wasn't sitting back waiting anymore!

As she was planning a way out, nausea returned with a vengeance. She'd tried for hours to not throw up, but she couldn't hold back anymore. She leaned off to the side desperate for a garbage can and threw up, almost missing it. With every retch, hot fluid burned her throat. The nurse was by her side to keep her from falling off the bed. She hovered over the bucket, gagging when the stench hit. She dry-heaved so hard she thought she'd burst blood vessels in her eyes. Once she was sure nothing else could possibly come out, Nurse Danny helped her sit upright and handed her a cold washcloth. It had been a long time since she was this sick.

"What's wrong with me?" she asked, pressing the cold washcloth to her neck.

"You've got a concussion. Unfortunately, vomiting can be a part of that."

"Will it go away soon?"

"Hang tight. I'll get you something to help." He gave her an energetic smile and checked the IV drip before leaving the room. He returned quickly with a syringe in one hand and a blanket in the other. He talked as he worked, depressing the syringe into the IV tube. Whatever he injected would settle her upset stomach quickly but might make her sleepy. She didn't care; anything to calm her churning stomach. He gave her pills to swallow with a little water for her pain. After covering her with a warm blanket, he tied the cord of the call bell to the bed rail.

"I want you to ring if you need anything. I'm going

to get you some toast. It might help to have something in your stomach. The doctor will be in for rounds soon."

He patted her leg, wrote something on a clipboard at the foot of the bed, and dashed out of the room.

The heat radiating from the blanket warmed her sore body. Attempting to prop herself up on her elbows proved to be too difficult and she fell back on the pillows. Lying still, she stared at the ceiling. Her thoughts rolled out of control like a train off the track.

She wondered if Nico would return. He couldn't see her looking like this—what would he think of her then?

Shane's dad. He might know something about the watch.

She still wasn't done with Dominic Sloan; people didn't react like that unless a nerve was hit.

The Crimson Lady.

It started to come back to her. She remembered her body slamming into what felt like a wall. The deafening sound of crushing metal against cement and shattered glass flashed in her mind, and a sharp ringing sounded in her ears. That blood-soaked woman had appeared at the accident afterward, but Drew had no idea why.

And now instead of meeting Enid at the lighthouse, she was stuck in a hospital bed. She had to get back on her feet and fast. There was so much to figure out.

Her eyes were heavy, but the pounding in her head faded to an idle ache and the nausea eased as the medication kicked in.

A knock at the door sounded and the doctor—the same doctor from the night before—walked into the room with Gran following her. The looks on their faces gave nothing away.

"I'm not sure if you remember me, Drew. I'm Doctor Wymond."

Of course, she remembered her. "I do. Are you here to tell me I can go home?"

"Not quite yet. Your CT results came back good, there's no fracture or bleeding on the brain. You do have a mild concussion so I'd like to keep you here one more night, but I see no reason you can't go home tomorrow."

Tomorrow! That wasn't the news she was hoping for. She couldn't stay another night here.

"What about school? Work? Can I drive?" Drew felt desperate.

"You'll be able to drive but give yourself a day or two and see how you feel. Gradually resume your regular activities. In the meantime, eat well, drink lots of water, and limit screen time as much as possible. Most importantly, rest."

Rest? *Not going to happen.* "So basically, I'm going to be okay."

"You might have headaches, dizziness, and some nausea that linger for a bit, but I have no concerns about a full recovery."

Gran sat on the foot of her bed and smiled. Her eyes didn't look as red or puffy, but her face was so pale it matched her sweater. Drew worried about her.

The doctor stood poised beside her exuding all the patience in the world. Her features were familiar, although Drew had never met Dr. Wymond before the accident. The sparkle of a nose ring caught her eye, and she noticed a scar along her cheek. It reminded her of Enid's.

How strange.

"Do either of you have questions for me?"

"What if I promise to take it easy? Are you sure I can't go home today?"

Dr. Wymond smiled. "Even if you promise, I'll still recommend one more night. Your guardian can sign you out, but it would be against medical advice. Tomorrow is better. I will have my office book a follow-up in a couple of weeks unless you need my assistance before then."

From the look on Gran's face, she wasn't even considering letting Drew leave until the doctor said it was okay.

Piper peeked around the corner. "Is it alright if I come in?"

Gran stood and winked at her. "I'll let you all catch up. Be back in a bit." As she left, Drew couldn't help but notice the loose fit of Gran's sweater. Either the last twelve hours did a number on her, or something else was going on. Maybe it was just a baggy sweater.

Piper entered the room with a duffel bag draped over her shoulder. Dr. Wymond stopped to exchange small talk with her before leaving.

"How do you know her?" Drew said.

"Blythe—Doctor Wymond—is Cole's mom. I thought you knew." Piper held the bag up before placing it on the floor, "I stopped by your house and threw some things together for you." She took her jacket off and draped it over a chair. "I want to hug you so bad, but I'm afraid I'll hurt you!"

Drew opened her arms to her friend. "You won't hurt me." She tried to reach out, but with the IV tube stuck in her, her motions were limited.

Piper leaned down to her and hugged her carefully. "It's good to see you. I was so scared." Piper let go and sat on a chair pulling it as close as possible. She looked from the IV pole to Drew's bruised face.

"Don't worry. It's not as bad as it looks."

"Nico called late last night. He said you'd been in an accident and were okay, but I had no idea…What happened?"

Drew told her, at least everything she could remember, which wasn't a whole lot. It still came out sounding more graphic and horrendous than she meant to. Maybe the doctor was right, and she had more brain trauma than she realized. The more she talked, the more Piper just gaped at her, shaking her head.

"I don't get you, Drew. What the hell were you doing? What was so important out there that you almost *died* trying to get to it?"

Drew shrugged and looked away from Piper's imploring eyes. She had wondered earlier if she still would've crashed if the old man hadn't been standing on the side of the road. It was raining hard, and she was driving fast. She'd lost control and was veering off the road, regardless of if he was there or not.

Maybe Ezra was right, and the old man wasn't trying to hurt her.

But if he wasn't out to harm her, what *was* he

trying to do?

Nothing made sense.

"What's going on, Drew? I've been by your side through everything. Please. *Talk* to me."

"I want to tell you, I do. But if you don't believe me…Piper, my own mother and father don't want to be around me, I can't lose you too."

"Is that what you think? You're like a sister to me, Drew. You can tell me anything. You're not going to lose me. I promise you."

Piper knew more than anyone—alive, anyway. Shane had known her secret. He found her interesting, not crazy. Drew was an anomaly. An exception to the norm, whatever normal was supposed to be, but it wasn't normal to see dead people. In the movies maybe, but not in real life. The few times she'd said the words out loud only solidified how much of a misfit shy was.

But Drew told her. It was like taking the stopper out of a bottle and letting everything pour out. She told Piper about how the old man in her dreams had stepped into her reality, and his message to go to Aurora. She talked about Enid, and that more than anything, she was desperate to go back and find the ghost girl again. If Piper thought she'd gone crazy, she didn't show it. She talked until fatigue took over and she was having a hard time staying awake.

Piper wanted to help her. She probably had hopes of seeing something extraordinary, but Drew assured her she would be disappointed. There would be no fireworks, just spirits stuck in limbo.

When Gran returned looking extra tired and pale,

Drew insisted she accept a ride home with Piper. She felt like hopping out of bed and throwing a tantrum, begging them to take her home too, but she was so tired she couldn't move. Her eyelids heavy, she gave in and let them close. This time, sleep came fast drowning out her thoughts.

Eleven

Drew awoke, and for a moment forgot where she was. Low voices and squealing wheels whirling by sounded from the hall. A lemon antiseptic aroma hung in the air. The intercom announced codes just out of earshot. She was alone in a hospital room.

She remembered trying to talk to Shane's father about Shane, but he wouldn't elaborate on anything. She had to talk to him again and find out if he knew anything about the watch and if it had been found the night of the accident. If she could get out of here and find a vehicle…She sat up and looked at the clock on the wall. Four o'clock; she'd slept the afternoon away. If only she could make the night go as fast. That was doubtful. Especially if the old man came back to finish what he'd started.

The duffel bag that Piper had brought for her sat untouched against the wall. With weak legs, she shambled over to grab it and propped it up on the bed. The IV tube handing from her arm trapped her in the hospital gown and made moving difficult. Inside the bag was a mishmash of clothes and toiletries. Piper must've been in a rush, but at least everything was there. She resisted the urge to rip it all out and settled for clean socks and underwear for now. After discovering a hairbrush, soap, and deodorant, she headed to the bathroom on a mission with one hand on the IV pole like a zombie dragging its leg. At least she'd smell good.

Closing the door behind her, she faced the mirror. Sleep sure hadn't helped to brighten her appearance. The bandage over her lip had loosened and was starting to come off, so she pulled it the rest of the way, wincing as it ripped her skin. She held a washcloth under hot water until it was soaked and steam rose. Holding it over her face with one hand, she gripped the sink with the other to steady herself. Careful not to tear at the cuts and bruises, she washed off days-old traces of makeup. Dried blood transferred to the white cloth as she dabbed at the exposed stitches. Would she have a scar like Enid or Dr. Wymond? She wondered how they got theirs and why theirs looked so similar. She hoped Enid hadn't given up on her returning to Neptune Point.

She turned off the tap when condensation misted over the mirror. Her image blurred and shifted in the slow-building haze. Wrenching paper towel from a wall dispenser, she wiped the mirror, but vapor continued to cloud over. Her eyes must be playing tricks on her, maybe a weird side effect of the medicine she'd been given. Yanking more paper towels into her hands, she scrubbed the mirror and leaned in for a closer look. The thick smoke-like fog twisted like the funnel of a tornado. She rubbed her eyes and blinked, holding her breath as though it would make a difference. It never did. Her legs wobbled, forcing her to sit on the edge of the toilet. Gripping the sink with both hands she pulled herself up as the tornado funnel formed words.

Go back.

This time her legs gave out from under her. Grabbing the IV pole for balance, it rolled toward the wall with a crash. Nothing like that had ever happened before. She looked around in the claustrophobic bathroom. What was happening? Who was the message from?

A knock thudded at the door.

"Drew? Is everything alright in there?" Nico— She'd know his voice anywhere.

"Yeah."

She looked back at the mirror. The storm cleared and all that remained was her horrified reflection staring back. Nico couldn't see her looking like this. She tried to brush the tangled mess that was her hair, but her efforts were futile. A hair elastic had been wound around the handle, so she pulled what she could up into a ponytail. She'd have to face him. Hiding out in the bathroom wasn't an option.

Another knocking at the door, this one louder.

"Did you fall? I can get someone—"

She swung the door open to face him. His hair had been neatly textured and styled, and he wore blue jeans and a gray sweater. He looked good. Too good.

"Um. Sort of? I did—fall, I mean. I'm okay, though. I was just washing up." She rolled the IV pole in front of her a little too fast. "I haven't quite figured out this damn thing."

"I can see that. Let me help." He took hold of the metal pole and extended his arm for her to hold as she stumbled toward the bed like an old lady in a nursing home. As she leaned forward, the sides of her hospital gown slid forward and she had to use her free hand to grab at them, trying to pull them back. It was bad enough that she looked like she'd been in a brawl and lost, she didn't need Nico seeing her pink cotton panties too.

Holding the gown closed, she sat on the bed. She might as well be naked given how vulnerable she felt with him watching her, but worry was the only thing his face gave away.

When she struggled to pull the blanket up, he swept in and did it for her. His signature scent of clean laundry with a subtle hint of citrus dominated the room, and she couldn't help but inhale deeply. It calmed her.

"Better? Do you need anything? Tell me what I can do."

He couldn't help with what she needed. A headache she'd been keeping at bay as a subtle thrumming escalated into mind-numbing pain.

"Actually, can you see if a nurse or someone can give me something for this headache?"

She'd barely finished speaking before he was running out the door. Within a matter of minutes, Nurse Danny sauntered into the room with a glass of water and a tiny cup of pills looking as fresh as he had hours earlier. He bustled around her with a swagger checking her vitals using little machines that beeped. Once he finished applying a fresh bandage over her stitches, he informed her that his shift would be over soon, and he'd been instructed to remove her IV. He peeled the clear adhesive from her skin and removed the tube from her arm in one smooth motion. The whole thing was painless compared to everything else she'd been through. She rubbed her arm and stretched it above her head.

Free at last! Well, almost.

Nico waited in the hall and entered only after she assured him it was okay to come back in. The nurse glanced at Nico and back to Drew with a wink and a smile. "Have a good night. Someone will be around later, ring if you need anything, and I'll be back in the morning."

He sashayed out the door. He was so light and happy; she wondered what his life was like when he wasn't on duty. She pictured him at a dinner party wearing something stylish. It was an existence she wished for—not the dinner party, but the light and happy part.

Nico pointed to the chair beside her. "Can I sit?"

She caught herself staring at him and her cheeks flushed with heat. Friends. They were *friends*. She shook it off.

"Of course. What are you doing here?"

"I can leave if you want to be alone. I messaged and tried to call but your phone goes to voice mail."

She'd forgotten about her phone and glanced at the plastic bag against the wall. "I think it's in that bag, dead probably." She paused and then spoke quietly. "I don't want to be alone."

"Piper said you were doing okay, but I had to see for myself. I keep looking at your car sitting in the yard all smashed in and I can't stop thinking about you."

His words touched her. He cared about her, and she had to admit, his company was nice. The thought of being alone for the night made her nervous. She couldn't even use the bathroom without being tortured.

"Once I convinced Gran to go home for the night, I wasn't expecting anyone to be honest. You surprised me. I'm happy you're here."

He smiled. "I'm happy to be here. It's so good to see you."

She covered her face with her hands. "I look awful."

"No way! Don't even say that. You survived a hell of a car wreck! Are you in a lot of pain?"

"My head hurts. Concussion, apparently, but I'll be fine. You have my car?"

"What's left of it, yes," he said and handed his phone so she could scan the photos.

The front of the car had crunched into a jumbled mess of metal and the windshield was cracked like a massive spider web. The picture of the airbag remnants brought forth flashbacks from the accident and pain seared through her. People yelling and rushing around her. The lights. Sirens. She was lucky.

Or maybe luck had nothing to do with it. She recalled the Crimson Lady showing up to tell her everything would be okay. Drew needed to figure out what was going on, especially if a ghost woman had a hand in her survival.

Nico didn't say a word as she held his phone with both hands examining each picture again. The silence between them was comfortable, unlike the awkward kind she found among most other people. She didn't have to fill the void with mundane chatter. She tried to ignore the fact she was more herself around Nico than she was with Shane, at least in the beginning.

She handed Nico his phone. "Thanks for showing me these, I didn't realize how bad it was."

"I figured you'd want to see them."

"I guess I'm without wheels for now." She tried to joke but it fell flat.

"I know, it sucks. But what matters is that you're okay. Find out what your insurance company will give you for it; it shouldn't take too long. My dad has lots of contacts for second-hand cars, and I've always got something to drive if you need a ride."

"I might take you up on that offer."

"Anytime." He smiled and reached into his jacket pocket. "I found this in your car. On the passenger seat."

He held out a watch with a chain dangling from it. *The* watch. She thrust the blanket off her legs and shot up from the bed. The blood drained to her feet, leaving her dizzy. She reached her hand out, and he dropped it in her palm.

"This was in my car?" The last time she saw it was in the bony hand of the old ghost man.

"Yeah. Is it not yours?"

She turned it over. *Morana.* Flipping it open, she ran her finger over the engraved lines that Shane swore was a map. It was Shane's pocket watch! But who left it in her car? And when? The key that used to be attached to the clasp was gone.

"What is it?" Nico asked.

"This belonged to Shane. Remember the bag Claudia told you about? This was in that bag! The police didn't know what I was talking about, but it was in there at some point. I think someone stole it. But how did it end up in my car?" She thought about all the ghosts that had appeared to her recently. The Crimson Lady, the old man, Enid. Even Ezra. It had to be one of them... No other explanations made any sense! But ghosts stealing jewelry didn't either.

"Could it have fallen out of the glove compartment or something?"

"No! I didn't have it. I swear this was not in my car before the accident. You don't understand. Something weird is going on."

"Weird how?" Nico sat back in his chair and folded his hand together. "Fill me in, I told you I'm resourceful."

She *could* tell him her theory about a ghost entity placing it in her car during an accident to send a message. But she didn't know how to define this relationship with Nico—opening up about her deep, dark secrets didn't seem part of it.

"What do you know about Neptune Point?" Drew asked instead. "Or the lighthouse?"

"Like the history?" Nico said.

"Anything."

Like her, Nico had been born and raised in Atlas

Cliffs. He was as much a part of this town as Drew was, but they never talked about the rumors that circulated.

"Um. The lighthouse was built in the late 1800s and named after the first lighthouse keeper's wife— Aurora. She died in a fire and the burned part of the house was rebuilt with brick. The combination of wood and brick gives it character but represents the tragedy to this day, even though the wood is rotting and falling apart. It's too bad the place couldn't be restored. I think it's always been in the same family. Anyway, you probably know the other stories. People say the place is cursed, haunted, whatever you want to call it."

He spoke matter of fact but the way he lit up telling her what he knew made her smile. She hadn't realized how passionate he was about the topic. It reminded her of how painting used to make her feel.

Drew laughed. "You just sounded like a history textbook. I'm impressed."

"It's probably the only class I enjoy. If I wasn't getting my mechanics license when I graduate, I think I'd take it at university. Be a teacher or something."

"If you love it so much, why not just do it?" she asked.

"It's not that easy. Dad's counting on me, and I don't want to let him down. I can't do that to him. Not after my brother left for school two years ago." He looked down at his hands. "Why do you ask? I mean, what's at Neptune Point? You've heard it all, I'm sure."

"Do you believe what people say?"

"If you're asking if I believe in ghosts, I…" He scratched at the back of his head. "Well, I'm skeptical.

How many times have we hung out there and never seen anything? Sure, it's a lonely place and sad shit has happened, but that doesn't mean it's haunted." He looked at her more closely. "Did you see something?"

Her skin crawled and her stomach reacted again. She couldn't tell him the truth. He told her all she needed to hear with that one word. *Skeptical*. He would think she was crazy.

"I thought I did, but it was only an animal."

He didn't look convinced but dropped it. She stared at the watch in her palm. "Do you know who owns the place now?"

"Claudia's father."

Interesting. That was news. Why Dominic Sloan owned the lighthouse was beyond her.

"She was bragging about how he bought it from the city," Nico continued. "She wanted to change the hangout name to *Claudia's Haven*. I'm surprised there wasn't a banner hung up when we arrived to be honest."

"Why would Claudia's father buy a run-down lighthouse? It doesn't make sense."

"Maybe because he owns half the town, and it was just another piece to conquer. He's horrible. And the way Claudia lost it on you the other night showed me all I needed to see. I'm done talking to her."

Nico might be… but I'm not.

"Why do you say her father is horrible? Do you know something?"

He looked at her and down at his hands. "No. What I do know, I don't like. He isn't to be trusted. I know you went to see him, but if I were you, I'd stay away."

"It sure sounds like you know more than you're saying," Drew said.

"I don't."

A bag surfaces months after Shane disappears, bearing the name of someone else—a dead boy—and Shane's missing watch is found in her car. Everything had to be connected. She could feel it with every fiber of her being. All she had to do was solve the puzzle.

"Drew?"

She looked up. Nico sat at her side, staring at her.

"Are you sure you're okay? Look, I know you want answers. I can't imagine how hard it's been losing him. But if you're up to something and it involves Claudia's family—"

"I'm just tired. I can't wait to get home."

A half-truth. She couldn't wait to get out of there. Too many questions needed answering, and now, she had one more: should she give in and tell Nico everything?

Nico leaned forward in the chair toward her, sliding his hand close to hers without touching. He hesitated, resting it on the bed instead. An uncontrollable flash of heat rose to her cheeks, and she was sure her face reddened. Hyperaware of how close they were, she could hear every breath. Only an inch of space remained between their hands, an electric current palpable, but he didn't close the gap. His head was turned down as though contemplating. If only her ability was mind reading.

She released the watch from her palm letting it fall beside her on the bed and squeezed his hand. In contrast to her own soft skin, his was rough and calloused beyond his youth. He turned his hand over to link his fingers with hers. Her pulse thrummed in her ears. She'd never held Nico's hand before. Certainly not like this. The troubles around her melted away like wax on a candle. When their hands parted a moment later, neither of them said a word about it.

In that blink of time, she got a break from constant fear and anxiety. When she'd been with Shane, it was an adventure. Unpredictable. The perfect storm of two people in chaos searching for their match.

Nico's calm settled her storm in ways that Shane never could, and she wanted to hang onto him, if only for a little while.

And as if knowing that she was buzzing inside and needed a piece of calm, for the next few hours Nico didn't leave her side.

Twelve

Drew had been home for two days, but it felt more like a week.

Late morning sun filtered in through the curtains casting light across her bedroom, and she pulled the blanket over her head to block it. This was not part of the plan; she hadn't meant to stay in bed for so long, but the doctor's warnings had proved correct. She'd continued to have headaches, and when the dizziness hit, her stomach rolled. What she hadn't expected was the exhaustion. She couldn't bring herself to do anything, least of all go back to Neptune Point, but the last thing she wanted to be was a caged animal who'd given up.

Money from the insurance company would take weeks to arrive, which meant no car. But she wasn't giving up—she would have to fight through it, get up and go.

She popped open the cover on the pocket watch and studied the engraved lines. Shane believed it was a map of the area at Neptune Point. There was a rectangular object with three lines and a circle at the top. Aurora, maybe? The lines extended beyond

Neptune Point into the woods toward Haven.

The old man weighed on her mind. If his intentions weren't to kill or hurt her as Ezra said, she had to find out what it was he was trying to do and if he was behind putting the watch in her car. He must have been trying to get her to go back to Aurora… But why?

She hadn't seen him since the accident, but he was always waiting for her when she fell asleep. Sleeping more the past few days than she had in the last year meant a buffet of nightmares. She woke up terrified and covered in sweat more times than not. She wondered what a dreamless sleep felt like. If he had no bad intentions, he sure had a weird way of showing it; he scared the hell out of her.

She wished Ezra would come back. She couldn't shake the boy from her mind. The black lettering on the bag bearing the same name was weird. Enid must have been his sister, and Drew knew she had to see her again, but she'd never tried to go out of her way to contact the dead. If anything, she wanted them to leave her alone.

Piper had been stopping by after school with homework and an appetite for ghost stories and adventure. But Drew knew what was to come would not be thrilling in the way Piper hoped.

Her phone buzzed with another message from Nico. He'd even left a voice mail. He sounded nervous; unlike the confident Nico she knew. They hadn't seen each other or spoken since Sunday night in the hospital. If she was being honest with herself, she was avoiding him. With every encounter, her feelings for him deepened, and it was unnerving. She couldn't let herself deviate from finding out what happened the night Shane disappeared, yet here she was, still in bed, doing nothing about it.

Drew turned on her side and a fizzing sensation hit like someone opened a soda can in her head. She squeezed her eyes shut and opened them to stabilize herself. She had been lying down for too long.

Throwing back the covers, she sat up slowly. If she let fear keep her hostage, she'd be stuck in bed forever. She was going to get up and visit Paxon Bishop. Enid would be next.

Her unfinished painting still stood in the corner gathering dust. The one she'd rage-painted after Shane's memorial service before collapsing on the floor, wailing like a wounded animal. The deep blues and blacks churned to create a storm wave surging against a rock wall, seagulls perched on top, overlooking the dark abyss. It served as a constant reminder of that horrible night—the police showing up at her door with news that changed her life. She would go the rest of her life knowing that she would never see a message from him, hear his voice, or hold him in her arms again.

Enough.

Jumping out of bed, she grabbed the canvas from the easel and tried to break it in half. When it refused to snap, she tossed it under her bed. The heaviness of that dark place threatened to pull her back down and she refused to let that happen again. It rendered her useless to Gran, her friends, and Shane; if she didn't find out what happened to him, no one would.

She'd shower and borrow Gran's car. A visit to Shane's father could turn up information about the watch and where it came from. The watch showing up after all this time could mean something, especially if Shane had it the night of the accident.

Drew examined her reflection in the bathroom mirror and waited for a tornado cloud to appear, but nothing happened. The past couple of days had been quiet. Too quiet. She opened the bathroom door and peeked down the hallway. Empty.

Closing the door again, she stared in the mirror. The swelling above her lip had diminished, but the stitches would dissolve and leave a scar. It was a small price to pay for not dying. She stretched the neck of her t-shirt, yanking it downward. Grotesque gold and faded purple bruises cascaded from her left shoulder tracing the seatbelt line. Every part of her injured body knew how to heal itself. If only it was that easy for the rest of her.

She stood in the shower and let the hot water soak into her skin, easing her stiff muscles. The throbbing in her head subsided, finally, along with the dizziness. *Progress.* By the time she turned the water off, the entire bathroom was filled with steam. After one last look in the mirror for a message that never came, she hurried to her room to put actual clothes on instead of pajamas.

In the hospital, the words in the mirror had pleaded with her to 'go back,' and that was exactly what she planned to do.

As she placed a hand on the railing to go down the

steps, a draft surrounded her. The door to Gran's room was ajar and the window closed. The sky had turned from sunny to an ominous gray. The dropping temperature had nothing to do with outside air. Blood thumped in her ears like a metronome, and a shiver tickled her arms. She could break free and run downstairs, or she could turn and face the storm.

Do not look away. Show no fear.

A shadow flew down the hall before materializing. The Crimson Lady floated back and forth. The dress twirled in the air as she moved in jagged steps along the corridor. But this time it was different—there were no blood stains, and Drew wasn't sure why the change.

The lady whisked in and out of the bedrooms as though searching for something.

Remembering the accident and her reassuring words, Drew decided to speak to her. There was no way The Crimson Lady wanted her dead, unless 'everything will be okay' translated into, 'you'll be dead soon and join me in my messed-up ghost world.'

Ezra talked to her. So did Enid. Maybe she could talk to all of them.

"What are you looking for?" It came out more of a whisper, but she did it.

The ghost spun around and froze in place with a vacant stare. Her mouth opened and a deep moan escaped. It faded into a crackling, like dry leaves under feet. The lady rushed at her, and they were face to face. Drew stepped back and flattened herself against the wall. Pressure heaved over her bruised chest. She inhaled shallow breaths as her stomach tightened with fear. They'd never hurt her before, but anything was possible. If the lady did something to her, no one would know what happened. She heard Gran in the kitchen and was about to scream for her until The Crimson Lady's eyes changed from hollowed sockets to a more human look.

For a split second, Drew caught a glimpse of her—the woman she used to be. No longer scary, she appeared light and kind. This woman *loved* someone. Suddenly, gut-wrenching heartache poured from the lady like water. Drew could feel her death; emotions of torment and denial that were not her own flooded through her. The woman's last moments flashed in seconds before fading to black. This poor woman had been murdered.

"What do you want me to do?" Drew breathed.

"Find him." She reached her hands to wrap around Drew and started to fade away.

"Find who? I don't know who you're talking about!" Drew tried to reach out to her, but she vanished.

Did the lady mean Ezra or the old man? Maybe it was someone she hadn't met yet. Or maybe it was Shane.

"Drew? Are you okay up there?" Gran's voice pierced the dead air.

The floorboard creaked as she peeled herself from the wall and caught her breath. She held the railing and treaded downstairs to the kitchen.

"You're awfully pale, dear." Gran sat at the table with a spread-out newspaper sipping coffee.

"I'm fine, feeling a lot better." With shaky knees,

Drew stood at the counter and in small bites, ate a muffin that Nellie had made. She poured herself coffee with too much sugar and milk to help it go down. It wasn't something she usually drank, but she needed all the help she could get.

"Are you going somewhere?"

"I need a favor," Drew said. "Your car, just for a little bit. School stuff."

"Aren't you supposed to be resting?"

"Gran, please—" Drew couldn't let Gran stop her. Not now. "I gave it a couple of days, just like the good doctor said. But I'm done resting. I need to get caught up."

Gran tapped the coffee cup looking up from the paper.

"Gran, I'm good. Please."

"Fine, take it. But it started making a noise. I'm not sure what's wrong with the damn thing. I'll take it to your friend down the road this week. He's a nice man. Always has time for an old lady." Gran tucked long strands of frizzy hair behind her ears and returned to her paper.

Guilt hit her at the mention of Nico's place. She would have to talk to him eventually.

"Thanks." She started for the door and spun around. "Do you need it later? I won't be late."

"Don't worry about it. I'll have Nellie drive me home after work today."

She said goodbye to Gran and was already barreling for the door when she realized it was snowing. She pulled on boots and a jacket before grabbing the keys for the Buick, a boat of a car. Stepping outside was walking through a snow globe. November and already the first snow of winter. It carried a warning of what was to come.

***

She drove along Adam's Ale Road past the embankment on her right that held back a dark, angry sea as waves broke around rocks. Snow fell fast in big flakes that melted on her windshield and the road. She held the wheel of the car steady with both hands as the memories flew through her mind, screeches of metal against cement filling her senses. She shook her head as though it was an etch-a-sketch, hoping she could forget. Easing her foot off the gas, she plowed along the road as powder whipped away to the sides.

Shane's father had always been pleasant to her. She hoped that he would continue the conversation they'd started in the hospital. The smallest detail he might be able to offer about Shane or the accident could help. If he refused to talk about it, this little excursion would be for nothing. For all she knew, he might not even be home.

Hills replaced ocean cliffs with patches of brown and white as the snow accumulated. A small sign that read 'Juno' came into view, as a large, predatory bird flew overhead. The wingspan was too vast to be a raven or crow. It looked like the same massive owl as the night at Haven, only this time it flew during the daytime.

Her eyes blurred and she blinked a few times to clear her vision. Ringing sounded in her ears and faded out—remnants from the accident. The car veered to the other lane, and she turned the wheel swerving back on track.

Focus.

Ending up back in the hospital was not an option.

Rows of leafless trees lined the valley. A farmhouse stood at the top of a slope and a rusted tractor with a missing wheel leaned on its side. The heat in the car suffocated her and she turned it down. She reached into her bag for a piece of gum and popped it in her dry mouth. As she opened the window a crack, the rustic smell of wet earth seeped in, taking her back to the winter before Shane disappeared. It followed the most amazing summer she'd ever had. After his death, she had vowed to never return to this place, yet here she was, wandering back because Paxton Bishop might have answers.

Houses were scattered through the village center as she got closer to Shane's home. She remembered it well from the few times that he had taken her here. Turning a corner, she pulled onto a street of houses set farther apart from each other until she saw the bungalow log home.

Gravel crunched under the tires as she drove into the driveway, and she eyed a truck that was parked off to the side. There were porch chairs stacked in a corner of the wrap-around deck. This was the spot where she had shared a few intense conversations with Shane. He'd been so worried about his mom. She wondered if

Detective Porter knew anything about her, or if Shane's mom was mentioned during the investigation.

Drew got out of the car and paused, holding the door for balance, as a wave of dizziness surged. Snow danced around her in a flurry of white, but her insides burned, and she rubbed her sweaty palms on her jeans.

She closed the door, careful not to slam it, and stepped onto the wooden steps. They shifted underfoot with each advance. Drapes covered the large living room window, blocking her view inside. She had no idea if Shane's father was home. She stilled at the front door; black paint had chipped away revealing the metal underneath, and when she glanced at the porch railings, she could see some were broken. This place had been neglected.

She pressed the doorbell and waited, hearing slow footsteps from the other side. The door opened.

Paxton Bishop looked different than what she remembered; she hadn't gotten a good look at him during the chaos a few days ago. He looked older now, older than a year should age someone. He wore dark sweatpants and a gray sweater with what looked like a coffee stain on it. His facial hair had created a shadow along his jawline, and his eyes were half-mast. He sure didn't resemble the gentle paramedic from a few days ago and she questioned her choice to come here. What if he was a serial killer or something sinister?

Stop being over-dramatic, Drew.

This was Shane's father. He was a paramedic and took care of people. He didn't hurt them.

"What are you doing here?"

A hint of alcohol hung on his breath, and she recoiled.

"Um, I'm sorry to show up like this, but I need to talk to you."

"What about?"

Hesitating she bit her lip. He should know the reason she would show up at his door. What other reason could there be?

"Shane," she said.

She shivered under her jacket and waited for him to shut the door in her face, but he didn't. Instead, he opened it wider and waved her into the foyer.

Drew had only been inside a handful of times, but it looked like time stood still. The living room held the same worn sofa and loveseat as before, and the same old television sat in the corner. Photos in dusty frames lined the floor-to-ceiling shelf and a dying plant adorned the mantle, orange coals burning in the fireplace.

She took her boots off and followed him into the kitchen. Dirty dishes filled the sink and black spotted bananas sat in a wired basket on the counter. He unscrewed a bottle of whiskey and generously poured it into a glass that already had half-melted ice cubes.

"Have a seat, Drew. Can I get you anything?"

"No, thank you," she said, pulling a kitchen chair from the table and sitting down.

He sat across from her, sipped the amber fluid, and placed the glass down. "It's good to see you well. I asked about you before my shift ended Monday and found out you'd gone home and were recovering nicely."

"I am." The chewing gum helped her nerves. She resisted snapping it with her tongue.

"You wanted to talk to me about Shane?" he said.

Where did she start? She shoved her hands in the pockets of her jacket and felt the watch. "I did. I mean, I do. I went to the police station and talked to Detective—"

"Let me guess." He sat back in the chair, and it creaked. She hoped he didn't fall back. "Valerie Porter?" he said.

"Yes." She leaned forward. "You know her?"

He shook his head slowly. "I do. I've had more than enough conversations with Detective Porter. Why were you speaking with her?" He slurred his words.

"Did you know a bag was found and turned in to police?" She hesitated when he didn't answer. "It's rumored to belong to Shane," she said.

"I'm aware of a bag with some other kid's name on it. The rumors are wrong and you're wasting your time, Drew. It isn't Shane's, can't be. Shane's dead." He sipped his drink.

His words hit her like a punch to the chest. She might be in denial about Shane, but she couldn't let go of the nagging feeling to keep searching for answers.

"Shane had a pocket watch," she said, "I heard it was in that bag. Do you know anything about it?"

She didn't tell him she had it—he might want it back. She wasn't ready to hand it over. Not yet.

"His mother gave it to him. She said she'd found it in a thrift store. I have no idea where it ended up. At this point, I don't even know why it all matters. I've answered the same questions more times than I care to. Shane is dead. The sooner you accept that the sooner you get to move on. Because you're young and have your whole life ahead of you and that is what you should be doing. Not sitting here across from a shell of a man who's lost everything."

His eyes glassed over, and he wiped them with the back of his hand. He was broken. She knew she shouldn't push it, but she needed to know more.

"That's just it, Mr. Bishop. I am trying to move on, but I need to know what happened. Something isn't right."

"Pax. Call me Pax," he said before sighing. "We might have to live with the painful truth that we will never know what happened. Trust me, I've gotten pretty goddamn good at it. This isn't my first rodeo."

His wife. The man had lost his wife and his son in less than a year. He must think her horrible showing up like this.

"I'm sorry," she said, "Maybe I should've come to see you right after it happened. It's just...you showed up when I had the accident and I...I've been wanting to talk to you ever since."

"Why? Because I might know something?" he asked.

He was right. She wanted to find out what he knew. But seeing Shane's dad like this made her sad.

"No. Because you were kind. After everything you've been through, you're out there working and helping people. I wanted to say thank you."

He softened. "I've been to scenes that…change a person. But work is all I have left. If I didn't go back to work, I don't know where I'd be. It's kept me alive. Gives me a purpose to keep going."

She thought of Shane's mom and how she'd left without a trace. She might be pushing it, but she couldn't leave without asking him about her.

"What about your wife?" she said carefully. "Have you heard from her at all?"

He spun the crumbs of ice in his glass before gulping the last of it. "Nope. Nothing. It's so unlike her. She loved her son more than life. There is no way she would've left him. I reported her missing the next day when she hadn't returned my calls. I can't help but think something horrible happened to her, but no one knows anything."

"Shane said she left when you lived in Boston and that she'd sent a text message."

"She did. The only reason I came back here was for Shane. His mother was from Atlas Cliffs, and he had it in his head that she might be here. Her message said she was returning home. What else could that mean? He begged me. I rented this place and gave him a year with a promise that he attended school. He struggled to stay in school before. Got into some stuff. It started so well until…well you know the rest. I wish we never came back." He looked at her. "Sorry, but it's the truth."

She figured his apology was for the pained expression that must have spread across her face when she considered never having met Shane. On one hand, she wouldn't be going through this agonizing heartache, but on the other, she never would've gotten to live the love story they'd had. "That's okay, I understand. It hurts but has nothing to do with you. He mentioned you wanted to move back to Boston."

"I did. Now more than ever. I'm leaving after the holidays."

"You're giving up?" she asked.

"What else am I supposed to do? I'm miserable! My wife is gone. No one knows a damn thing, but I believe something happened to her. Her son is dead. There was no way he survived that car accident. You were fortunate that you're still alive yourself. Don't let this consume you." He shook his empty glass. "Trust me."

"Why did you say *her* son?"

"I didn't mean it like that. Shane was *our* son." He stood up and brought his glass to the counter with his back to Drew. "He wasn't my biological son."

Shane never said a word about that. Not once. She thought he had told her everything.

"I had no idea," she said quietly.

"Shane didn't know. I couldn't bring myself to tell him. Even after he read his mom's message that she'd left. I was scared I'd lose him too. Maybe that makes me an asshole."

"Who is his father? Do you know him?"

"Iris never told me. As far as I know, she'd never told him about the baby. She just left town. We met at the hospital where we both worked."

"So, Shane's biological father lives in Atlas

Cliffs?" She tried to think of who he could be.

"He was from here, but who knows where he is now? I thought maybe she returned home to confront him; you know? Let him know that he had a son. Who knows? Maybe they ran off together after all these years." Hanging onto the counter, he turned to face her, and his face was full of sadness. "Look. One thing you need to understand—Shane was *my son*, in all the ways that matter. Iris was pregnant when we met. I fell hard for that girl, and as far as I was concerned, he was *my* baby." He rubbed his face with both hands. "I don't mean to be rude, but is there anything else you need from me?"

"The text message. Do you still have it?"

"From Iris? Yeah. I printed it. Why?"

"Can I see it?" she asked.

"You can have it. The police already have a copy. It makes me feel sick to read it. I just don't get it. I've come close to burning it too many times to count." He headed out of the room with a stagger in his walk. She wondered if this was how he spent his days off, drinking alone in his misery. She thought of her father and his alcoholic days. Never violent, but always troubled.

She stood and wandered into the living room to the shelf of pictures. Some she recognized from before, like Shane's old school photos, his father in uniform receiving an award, and the family dog who passed a few years earlier.

An added photo sat alone on the top shelf; one she'd never seen before. Standing on tiptoes, she reached for it and dusted off the glass with her sleeve. A woman in a flower-printed sundress appeared to be dancing on a beach. She faced the camera smiling as she held her hair from her eyes. Drew gasped and the frame nearly slipped from her hand. The woman was younger, but there was no mistaking that face and those eyes.

The Crimson Lady.

All this time Shane believed his mom left them. She never abandoned her family—someone had stolen her from them. Any hope Drew had of finding his mother for answers dissolved and, in its place, a new plan formed. Solving his mother's death might lead to the reason behind Shane's disappearance.

Paxton returned and nodded at the frame. "That's one of my favorite pictures of her. I took it at Crane Beach. She loved the ocean. I asked her to marry me that day."

His eyes glazed over again. He shook his head and handed an envelope to Drew. "Here's the note she'd left us. It doesn't make sense, none of it makes any sense. That's what's so hard. I'm a good man. I work hard. How did I end up here? I've lost everything."

She placed the frame back on the shelf. She couldn't do it to him. Look him in the eye and tell him she knew without a doubt that his wife was dead. Murdered.

She knew there was something big here, but she couldn't burden him with any more pain. Not until she knew more. Not until she was sure.

And she would be sure.

She took the envelope from him and put her boots on to leave.

"Take care of yourself, Drew. I know you think there is something to solve here, but when it comes to Shane, it's clear. My boy died the day his car crashed into that water. All that matters is you keep his memory alive. Don't go looking for something that isn't there to find. It'll take over your life, and that would be a shame."

"Thank you for talking to me. If I find out anything, I'll let you know." She wished she had something else to offer him. "Don't worry about me, I'll take your advice to heart."

She trekked to her car, starting it up to defrost the window. Not only was she going to find out what happened to Shane, she was going to find Iris's killer.

Thirteen

A good three inches of snow had fallen, and it was still falling, but the road looked clear enough. Drew left Shane's father and Juno in the rear-view mirror as she drove back to town in a state of highway hypnosis. The Crimson Lady had a name.

Iris.

And that wasn't the only thing she'd learned. Shane's mom—*Iris*—was dead.

Murdered.

Drew almost pulled the car over to throw up. Almost. Instead, she forced herself to breathe through the waves of sickness. Why would anyone want his mom dead? Shane's last message to her was that he had something to tell her, something about his mom having a secret.

Maybe Shane had found out his mom had been murdered and went looking for her killer… And then her mind thought it before she could stop herself: what if Shane had been—

Weight pushed in on her chest and her throat choked up.

No. She couldn't let herself go there.

The only proof she had was unbelievable! If she told anyone she could see his mom on the other side they'd probably lock her up.

Paxton thought his wife had left him, which gave him a motive. The man was shattered. The look on his face when he'd watched Drew with the photo… He was either a brilliant actor or he was a psychopath.

But no. She didn't believe he'd killed her.

She had to find more information. Maybe Enid knew something, seeing as she was part of the ghost world too.

She reached for the envelope on the seat beside her. Ignoring her pounding headache, she balanced the wheel with her knees and opened the envelope. Inside was a folded piece of plain white paper. Feeling dizzy, she signaled and pulled off the road.

A few simple lines in type were on the page.

I'm returning home for a bit. There is something I must do, and I can't explain without hurting you. Please give me time. You and Shane are my world.

Forever my love,

Iris

She reread it five times before her eyes went blurry again. She leaned back in her seat and closed her eyes for a moment to ease her aching head. Had Shane's mom returned to Atlas Cliffs looking for the man who'd fathered her child? Shane had begged his dad to move here. Something was off, and Shane knew it; he'd driven out to Neptune Point the night of his accident. That place had to be connected to all of this. And who knew more than they were willing to say? Claudia's father.

Dominic Sloan. Not only had his behavior been super weird, but he also owned the lighthouse at Neptune Point. He had to know something.

She wasn't far from Marble Gate Estates, and it was late enough in the day that Piper would be home from school. Maybe she'd knock on Claudia's door while she was there. She pushed her plans to drive out to the Point aside. For now.

Drew rang the doorbell at Piper's and waited. Piper opened the door and when she saw Drew, a look of surprise crossed her face.

"What are you doing here? I was going to come out and see you. Come inside." And when she saw the look on Drew's face she asked, "What is it?"

Drew didn't answer. She didn't have to. Not with Piper. Piper just nodded and pulled her inside, leading her up the grand staircase to her room.

When they were inside and alone, Piper closed the door, leaning her back against it.

"Alright, Drew, what happened? Spill it."

There was no point in hiding anything. Not with Piper. She handled everything else in stride, this should be no different. Still, the thought of telling her everything left her queasy. "I—I went to see Shane's father."

"You did? Why?"

"To find out what he knows. About Shane. The bag…the watch."

Piper's black-lined eyes widened. "Shit. What did he say?"

Drew told her about the conversation and the photo.

"He really has no idea where she is? That's weird. Do you think something happened to her?"

Drew breathed deep.

"Her name was Iris and she's dead. Murdered."

Piper sat cross-legged on the bed, staring at her. "How do you know?"

"I've seen her, the woman in that picture. Only she's not alive."

"She's one of them?" Piper looked around the room. "Is she here now?"

"No. It doesn't work like that. This morning she spoke to me."

"What did she say?"

"'Find him.'"

Piper scrunched her face. "Find him? What's that supposed to mean?"

"I think—I think she means Shane. It's the only thing that makes sense."

"Well, first of all, none of this makes sense. And second, *find Shane*? Does she mean his ghost? Have you seen him?"

Drew plopped down on a bean bag chair. "I know how it all looks. But if Shane was dead, he'd have visited me somehow. I've had memories…flashbacks of him that feel so real. But no, I've never seen him in that way. Piper, what if he isn't dead?"

"Drew…"

"I know what you're going to say, but Piper, Shane would've done everything in his power, living or dead to find his way back to me. Iris's words were cryptic, so I could be wrong, but I think Shane knew. I think he knew she was murdered, and I think he knew who killed her. I'm betting if I find that out, if I find who killed her, it'll lead me to him somehow."

Piper looked confused. "So, what? You think he faked his death? Drew, this is crazy."

Drew rubbed her temples. "I don't know. But if there's a chance at all that he's out there—"

"You're going to find him." Piper leaned forward and propped her chin in her hands.

Drew nodded slowly. "I think I have to."

Piper's brows knitted together as she worked to grasp all this—not that Drew herself was doing much better.

"Maybe he, I don't know, went somewhere else?" Piper said. "Like the ghosts you see are stuck, but he wasn't? I know you want to believe he's out there alive somewhere, who wouldn't want that? But if all this falls apart, I don't want you to get your hopes up only to go through his loss all over again."

Drew had to admit she didn't know much about the other side or how it all worked. She got up and sat on the bed beside Piper. "I don't want that either, but I can't ignore what I know about his mom. She deserves the truth to come out. She needs to be at peace and I'm the only one who can give that to her."

"This is heavy," Piper said. "If someone in this town killed Shane's mom, they sure won't take it well when you start digging up information. Why don't you go back to the police? Detective-What's-Her-Name?"

"Valerie Porter. And say what? 'I see dead people and Shane's mother was murdered'—come on, Piper. I'm just a nobody teenager from the edge of town. You know they'd laugh me out the door or into the psych ward." She'd never let that happen; one hospital stay was plenty! "Do *you* believe me? I need to know that you're not sitting there thinking I've lost it. You're the only person I trust with this and I'm telling you the truth!"

"I believe you! I promise."

Drew studied Piper's face, but as far as she could tell, Piper was all in. There wasn't even a hint of doubt. Drew gathered her into a bone-crushing hug, only relenting when she remembered the rest. More to tell, more complications.

"There's more. Shane's dad isn't his *actual* dad. His mom got pregnant in Atlas Cliffs. I need to find out who the guy was."

"That's a needle in a haystack," Piper said. "Impossible."

Nothing is impossible.

Drew showed her the letter and regurgitated what Paxton had told her about the situation, that he wasn't sure if Shane's biological dad even knew.

"You think she came back here to tell him, and he killed her?" Piper said.

"I don't know but I'm going to find out. I think it's all connected to Neptune Point; I'm going back."

"Now? No, it'll be dark in an hour. Better if you can wait until tomorrow. I'll skip school and go with you."

Drew looked at the window. It was getting dark earlier by the day. Her head had its own heartbeat and pain seared behind her eyes. "I've got to find Enid."

"Ghost girl? See? I listen." Piper swung her legs over the bed. "This is like something out of a movie."

"Only it's real. Too real."

Piper leaned forward. "You don't look well. Please go home and get some rest. I'm begging you to wait until tomorrow at least."

"Tomorrow." Drew's voice trailed off. She couldn't make that promise to her friend. She'd done nothing but sit around and wait. Tomorrows were turning into weeks.

She got up to leave. As Piper walked her out, she noticed a stack of papers and pamphlets for various schools. Drew hadn't even thought about more school. She was lucky to get through each day. A pang of envy hit her. Piper would be able to escape all of this, unlike her.

"Are those the applications your mom was talking about?" she said.

"University for next year. I'm going to pursue law."

Piper would be leaving Atlas Cliffs. She'd always known this day would come but hadn't thought it would be so soon. What would she do without her?

Piper hugged her. "You can always come with me. Escape this place. Get a job until you figure things out."

"I wish! I'll worry about that later. I've got to solve a murder first, but maybe when the dust settles, I'll be able to run away with you."

"Damn, girl. I didn't mean it like that—"

"I know you didn't." Drew hugged her. "I should go." She walked toward her car with Piper at her heels.

"Drew. I'm going to help you. Those applications have been consuming me. The truth is I'm terrified! My parents expect perfection. They want me to go into criminal law but I'm going to be a human rights lawyer. I want to help people; pro bono isn't in their vocabulary. I'll never give them what they want, but school is my ticket out of here."

"Believe me, I get it. Take the opportunity and run. You're the smartest person I know. You see past all this." She waved her hand toward the grand house. Drew would never have the luxuries that Piper had, but Piper's mom was hard on her, and Drew saw the fights firsthand. Money did not equate happiness.

As if on cue, a pristine sedan crawled along the street and pulled up the driveway. Drew recognized Claudia's fancy, white car. The window slid down and Claudia leaned her head out the window.

"Ladies. So lovely to see you both. I've missed you, Drew. Heard you had an accident? You look no worse for wear."

"Go home, Claudia," Piper said.

Claudia turned the car off and stepped out. Her tall black boots had been shined and she wore a jacket trimmed with fur.

"I have a bone to pick with you, Drew. Since you're in my territory and all."

When had they become animals? It wasn't as though Drew was going to pee on the ground.

"You're currently on *my* territory if you want to play that game. Go home!" Piper looked at Claudia with fire in her eyes.

Drew put a hand up to calm her. "Actually, Claudia, I've been wanting to talk to you. This just saves me a trip."

If Claudia thought Drew was some wallflower, she had another thing coming. She could stir the family pot to her advantage. Claudia's father knew something about Shane that he wasn't saying.

Claudia crossed her arms. "This should be good. Please, be my guest."

"The other day I spoke with your father—"

"Oh my God. You're obsessed! Let go of your dead boyfriend! And leave my father out of it!"

"Open your eyes! He's hiding something. You don't believe me? Fine, go ahead. Ask him about Shane. Even better, he knows a lot of people in this town, ask him if he knew Shane's mother, Iris. I'd be curious to know what sort of reaction he gives you. Because all it took was a simple question and he lost it on me. It wasn't the other way around like he wants you to believe."

Drew straightened her back and pain shot across her chest, but she refused to back down or let Claudia see weakness.

"What's wrong with you? Do you need a team of doctors to fix whatever mess is going on in there?" Claudia waved her hand over Drew like a magic wand.

"You can hate me if you want," Drew said. "I don't care because I've done nothing wrong. You said your father talked to someone about Shane's pocket watch. He knows something, Claudia."

Claudia's perfectly made-up face turned red, and her nostrils flared with each breath. "You're insane. I'm done with you."

She flipped her hair as she got in her fancy car, slammed the door, and sped down the street. Drew let her shoulders relax and rubbed her bruised chest.

"Wow." Piper chuckled. "She wasn't impressed with you."

"Maybe I should've been more careful, but I couldn't help myself. And she's not done with me. She doesn't let things go so easily." Drew was definitely not done with Claudia.

Piper tilted her head and stared down the street toward Claudia's house. "You really think her father is hiding something? Maybe he's just a crotchety guy."

"Hell, yeah, I do! I'm going to find out what it is."

"Don't get too close, Drew. You asked him a couple of questions and look how he acted! Imagine if you keep poking around? I bet the public doesn't see that side. If he's got an agenda, I guarantee he won't let some kid stop him. I just worry about you."

"I know what I'm doing," Drew said, but she knew she didn't.

"I hope so." Piper pulled her sleeves over her hands. "I'm freezing. Did you want to come back inside?"

She did, of course, but there were too many things she needed to do. She was getting close; she could feel it. "I better head home."

"Don't do anything stupid. Remember. Wait until *tomorrow*." Piper hugged her and went back to the house.

Drew drove toward home as the sun went down. A sliver of orange spread across the sky and a full moon brightened. Fatigue seeped into her bones and ringing sounded in her ears. As she approached her house, she debated on continuing along the road to Neptune Point. It would be dark and the only light she had was her phone's flashlight. It wasn't that long of a drive. She could go and walk the path to Haven in hopes of seeing Enid. If only she could communicate with her somehow. Ghosts took care of that on their own; usually unwanted.

She pushed her foot down on the gas and almost flew by her house when she noticed a green truck parked in the driveway.

Who is that?

Slowing down, she angled off the road and grabbed her phone. There'd been no missed calls from Gran.

As much as she wanted to, she couldn't ignore it. She navigated the big car up the driveway, past the truck. A bumper sticker in the shape of a fish on a hook that said, 'bite me' was stuck on the back.

She got out and cupped her face against the driver's side window. A suitcase, a backpack, a coat, and a pack of cigarettes lay on the passenger seat. Her stomach knotted.

Gabe.

He'd come back. And after she'd told Gran specifically not to contact him! She could run back to the car and drive away, but all that would do was prolong the inevitable. She knew it.

Opening the front door, she stepped inside. A pair of work boots sat on the floor. She heard faint chatter coming from the kitchen.

"Drew?" Gran called out. "Is that you?"

"It's me."

Here we go.

In the kitchen, her father sat across from Gran at the table. Time hadn't been kind to him. His pale green deep-set eyes were unreadable as he looked up at her. Gray was scattered through his red hair and lines in his weathered face moved as he smiled tentatively at her. She hated that she looked like him. He stood with his arms out and she stepped back. He better not try to hug her. He must've taken the hint because he sat back down across from Gran.

"It's good to see you," he said.

Her body stiffened blocking herself from showing any emotion toward him. "Why are you here? I told Gran I was fine. I don't need you."

"She didn't tell me anything. You'd been admitted into the hospital. I'm still a next of kin. The insurance company let me know. Don't get mad at her."

Her body tensed. "When do you leave?"

"Okay," he said, "It's going to be like this, I see."

"Like what?"

He turned in the chair to face her. "You're still my daughter. If anything happened to you…you're all I've got. And I need to talk to you."

"You lost your daughter the day you left." Her eyes

pricked but she refused to cry. He could never see the hurt he'd caused.

"I fucked up. I know that. Let me try to fix it."

How could she forgive him for abandoning her? He'd made her an orphan. She had no parents. There would never be a father-daughter or a mother-daughter anything. "That's not possible."

"I've changed. I'm gonna do whatever it takes to prove that I can be trusted." He sounded sincere, but too many people threw that word around. *Trust.* And she wasn't buying it from him.

She gripped the counter with both hands to steady herself. "It's too late, Gabe. Don't waste your time."

"Don't say that. Look, we can talk about this later. I've got to tell you something and I don't even know where to start."

Now he was wasting her time. She wasn't going to give him the benefit of the doubt for anything.

"I've got somewhere to be," she said. "You're not staying here, are you?" This was Gran's house. Not his. She looked at Gran hoping she wouldn't argue and beg him to stay, but she sat in silence. "Gran, can I take your car again tonight? I promise I won't be long."

"Drew, please sit down?"

Gran gestured for her to take a seat. "Listen to what he has to say first. You're going to want to hear it."

Nothing he could say could interest her. But she paused, breathing slowly to calm herself. She sat beside Gran and crossed her arms.

Gabe looked up at her. "Your boyfriend, Shane? He's alive."

Fourteen

Drew couldn't believe what she was hearing. At the same time, she wanted to scream from the cliffs.

I knew it!

"How do you know?" she demanded.

"I saw him about a few weeks ago in South Carolina. He was working on a fishing boat. I wanted to tell you over the phone, but the connection was bad, and I figured you'd just hang up on me anyway."

"South Carolina? Are you sure it was Shane? Could it have been someone who looked like him?" Thinking back, she only recalled Gabe meeting Shane once or twice at most. How could he remember what Shane looked like?

"I wondered that too at first, but I have proof." Gabe stood and took his phone out of his back pocket. After a few seconds of scrolling, he held it up to show her a picture. She grabbed the phone and brought it close to her face, staring hard. A young man leaned over the rail of a boat, smoking a cigarette. Patchy hair filled in on his unshaven face and his sun-tanned skin made him appear older. Overgrown dark hair hung over his eyes, but the piercing blue was still visible through the messy strands. She ran her fingers across the screen. It wasn't a clear shot but without a doubt the person in that photo was Shane.

As she stared at the phone, the months gone by, and the space of a thousand miles swept over her. Memories played through her mind. Every intimate moment. Walks on the beach, talking. Laughing. All this time she'd spent mourning for someone she'd loved so deeply, and he was on a boat somewhere? The belief of who he was—*is,* that she'd held onto for so long, crumbled into pieces. He was alive, but she didn't even know him anymore.

Her head pounded behind her eyes, and she felt dizzy like she might be sick. What was he doing in South Carolina? He didn't think to call her or send a message? Something simple like, *hey, I'm not dead!*

Gran leaned across the table and placed a hand on her arm. "Are you alright, dear? You don't look so good."

Drew was hearing a lot of that lately. She held the phone tight and slumped in her seat. Gabe sat across from them, watching her face intently. She wanted to run out of the room screaming. Part of her wanted to find Shane. Squeeze him and kiss his face. But another part wanted to know how he could leave her with nothing! How he could leave and allow her to believe he was dead!

She loved him. Missed him so much her insides hurt. She'd been so angry at his death, mad at the universe for taking someone so precious away from her. But there was always a nagging feeling that something wasn't right, especially when she never saw him the way she could see the others.

Before handing back the phone, she texted the photo to herself. She needed to have that picture at her fingertips.

"I don't understand. Everyone—the police, his dad, me—knew he'd died that night. Why would he run away and let everyone think he'd died in a car crash?"

"I don't know," Gabe said, "all I know is something clicked when I saw him. I snapped the picture and looked up the news article from after the accident. I knew it was the same guy. It's him, Drew."

She'd set out to find him, but never dreamed he'd fled of his own free will. This changed everything. She was searching for someone who didn't want to be found. Now, what was she supposed to do?

"Did you talk to him?" she asked.

"I tried. Even followed him. He looked right at me, got all skittish or something."

Skittish. That didn't sound like Shane. Maybe something, or someone, forced him out of town. Maybe there was a reason why he couldn't reach out to anyone. She thought about Shane's last message, his knowledge that his mom had a secret.

She leaned forward and gripped the edge of the table. "Did you call out his name or try to get his attention?"

"I yelled and he ran. He boarded a boat. It hauled anchor and left before I had a chance to do anything."

"Do you think he recognized you?" Her mind raced trying to figure out exactly what happened to Shane.

"I don't know. I think he panicked." Gabe sat back in his chair and folded his arms across his chest. "Look. I know you don't want to hear this, but from what I saw, he doesn't want to be found."

The throbbing in her head was so bad she thought something might burst inside. She put her fingers through her hair and rubbed her scalp. She couldn't imagine Shane wanting to be hidden away somewhere.

"Where was it headed?" she said.

"No idea. I wish I had more, but all I got was that picture."

"How do I find out the name of the boat?"

He leaned forward and folded his arms on the table. His face was serious as he focused on Drew. "I know this is a lot. When I found out about your accident I got off at the next port and flew home. It's all I've been thinking about. I don't know what this kid…Shane's deal is, or why he took off, but you deserve to know. I know you've been through—"

"You have no idea the hell I've been through. This is someone I love. Do you understand how that feels? To love someone?"

"That's not fair," he said.

"Do you know what's not fair? A little girl whose mom abandons her and the only person in the world she thought she could count on dumps her like garbage." She looked at Gran's solemn face and softened her tone. "If it weren't for Gran, I'd have no one. What would you have done then? Did you really expect she'd raise me alone?"

Gran touched Drew's hand. "I'd do it all over

again. You've kept me going. You're all I have too."

Gabe sat back in his chair and crossed his arms. "It didn't start like that. I was coming back, I just…"

"You just didn't care," Drew muttered.

Everyone she'd ever loved left her. The one person she'd never dreamed would hurt her faked his death to get away from her! As hard as she tried to stop them, the tears flowed. "I just—I need to know how to find that boat."

"You can't go on some fool's errand! What if something happens to you?" Gran said.

She ignored Gran and fixated on Gabe. "What do you know about the boat? You must've noticed the name!"

Her father scratched the stubble over his jaw and tapped his fingers on the table. She wanted to reach out and shake the truth out of him.

"*Aurora*," he said.

The old ghost man's words echoed in her head. "The lighthouse? The boat is named after the lighthouse?"

"It's called *Light of Aurora*, so who knows what it's named after. What you do with this is up to you, I guess."

Gran snapped her head toward him, her eyes filling with tears. "What are you doing? Do you see what you've started? We agreed to you telling her the truth about Shane, nothing more! That boy left her and you're sending her on a wild goose chase! She'll never let this go now. You better stay close because I won't be able to stop her from getting hurt."

Aurora.

She rubbed her eyes and pulled herself together. Gran was full-on crying. Drew reached out and wrapped her arms around her.

"Nothing's going to happen to me. But I finally have validation that Shane's alive, I can't ignore that."

Gabe curled his fingers into a fist against the table, almost hidden by the frayed cuffs of his work coat. "If there's anything I can do to help—"

"I've got this." Drew slid her chair back and it screeched along the tiled floor. She wasn't sure yet where she was going, but she had to get out of there. "I need some air. Gran, I'm borrowing your car to hang out with Piper for a bit, okay?"

Gran waved her hand, defeated. "Take it. Go."

"Is your car in the shop?" Gabe asked.

"My car is dead. Broken." Standing she faced, Gran. "I'll figure something else out soon."

He had no idea. But how could he? He didn't know anything about her. She resented his ability to still cause her anguish after all these years without even trying, but without him, she wouldn't have the proof she'd needed that Shane hadn't died that night.

Drew charged out of the kitchen and through the front door with her shoes and coat half on. The sun had long set, and clouds obscured the night sky. Nearly slipping on the icy driveway, she climbed in the car and fired up the engine.

Using her phone, she opened a web browser and typed the name of the boat. She found a vessel query site and searched further, only finding a number listed instead of a company or name. She cross-checked the number on a different page; the boat was a fishing vessel registered in Atlas Cliffs.

It might be somewhere in South Carolina, but the *Light of Aurora* had originated here. She wondered if she could find information at the shipyard. What did she have to lose? She left the driveway and sped through town to the docks.

At this hour the place was quieter than usual. Floodlights positioned at the entrance of each building sliced through the darkness. The area could be under surveillance and the last thing she needed was someone questioning why Gran's car was lurking around the dockyard. She turned her headlights off and drove at a crawl along the far side of the main building, labeled Atlas Cliffs Shipyard, and parked under a canopy of trees.

Wind swirled around her as she got out of the car and zipped her jacket, the air cold and biting. The main building would be a good place to start; she'd simply ask about the boat. She jogged up to the front door of the main building to find it locked and empty. She looked around, taking in her surroundings. She hadn't noticed the empty parking lot.

She crept to the back of the building to find a barrage of ships set amongst the rows of cargo cranes. Smaller boats were docked a little farther down. She pulled her hood up and shoved her hands in her pockets, checking the back of each one for the name. She wasn't sure what she was looking for, but if Shane was on a boat called *Aurora*, it had been here before. And if that boat was docked here, she swore to herself she'd board it and refuse to leave until she found Shane. There had to be a good reason for him to run away and let everyone believe he was dead. Something horrible must've happened. She couldn't help but think of his mother—but if he'd found the killer, why hadn't he gone to the police?

An outside light flickered on near a smaller warehouse close by causing her to duck behind a truck. A black sedan parked directly in front of the warehouse door. She had seen that car before...

She snuck around the truck and darted closer, the darkness covering her, squatting behind a garbage bin. Three men in suits exited the vehicle. Drew had to cover her mouth to keep a gasp in when one walked into the light: Dominic Sloan.

She knew he owned the shipyard, but he had a hand in a lot of companies in town. The local news station, the dying newspaper, and even a local pharmacy. That was a known fact.

But what was he doing here so late, after everyone had gone home?

She strained to hear them talking but their tone was too low, and the high-pitched ringing started in her ears again. She plugged them with her fingers, but it was no good. She ignored it and snuck closer, keeping hidden in the shadows as they entered the building. A gut feeling screamed at her, *danger!* She ignored it. They were up to something, and she was going to find out what it was. Claudia's father had threatened her— people didn't do that unless they had something to hide.

She crept over to the door, reached for the handle, and waited. She couldn't hear anything. They could be on the other side of the door or farther into the building. With her thumb on the latch, she pressed down and pulled as carefully as she could, opening the door a sliver. She peeked inside but was met by darkness and silence.

She yanked it open and stepped inside with both hands behind her to keep the door from banging shut. Gruff voices came from somewhere, echoing off the walls, but they didn't sound close by. She edged along the wall, using it as a guide until a flicker of light shone through a window at the top of a set of stairs. It looked like an office.

Sneaking behind five large containers, she reached the bottom of the steps. She thought about bursting inside and confronting him as she'd done before. But what if he got angry and lashed out at her? What if the men he was with were dangerous?

One careful foot in front of the other, she stepped up the first few steps. A loose metal stair clanged under her feet, and the voices silenced. She could hear the blood pumping through her head in a loud, steady thump. She waited. Heavy footsteps thudded closer and as the door began to open, she bolted back down and hid behind a tool bench. An exit sign shone red across the room, but she couldn't remember if that was where she came in, or another door.

A stalky, bald man stomped down the stairs. "Who's there!"

She crouched lower.

Who the hell are these people?

"No one's out there. Get back inside!" another voice called from the room.

Footsteps echoed, but this time the door stayed open. She moved from her hiding spot to get closer and listened.

"It'll be torn down."

"They can't touch it. It's mine."

"The lighthouse belongs to the town—"

"That house—the property, belongs to me. My family. I will protect what is mine at all costs."

She recognized that last voice as Dominic Sloan.

"If someone tears down that house, we're fucked. I told you back then, it was a bad idea to take her out there." Another voice now, sounding frustrated.

A crash sounded and she darted back behind the tool bench.

"Question me again and those will be the last words you speak. Where is he? They're getting sloppy."

"They left him. No issues. They leave port tomorrow."

"I want someone on him."

"Done."

The voices spoke back and forth so fast, that she lost track of who was saying what. She stood up quickly, hitting her head on a pipe. She covered her mouth with both hands to contain the squeal that wanted to escape. Footsteps slammed down the stairs again and she took cover in a crawlspace between two barrels. Flashlight beams poured around her.

"Who's in there?"

"It's probably rats. I told you, there's no one here!"

The men moved around her searching like snakes looking for prey. She curled into a ball, hoping they wouldn't find her. She could run, but she had no idea which way was out! What would they do if they found her? Maybe they'd show her the exit. Or maybe...

A hand touched her arm and she almost screamed.

"It's just me," the voice whispered.

Enid!

The ghost girl stood beside her scanning the room. "Don't say a word. I see them and they're off your tail."

How did Enid get here? Not wanting to risk them hearing, she didn't dare speak.

Another door slammed and shook the building.

Enid's hand relaxed on her arm. "It's alright. They've left."

Drew wriggled from the corner she'd been squished in. "How did you find me?"

"I wish I knew. It just happens sometimes. You never came back. And now..." Enid smiled. "...Now I'm here. You were gone a long while."

"I know. I had a little accident. Who are those men?"

"Good question."

"You don't know?"

"No." Enid headed for the stairs to the still-lit room above. "Wanna find out?"

Drew stood, rubbing her dirty hands on her jeans. She pulled her phone out and used the light from the screen to scope out the place before moving. A car engine rumbled to life outside; the men were leaving. She tried to remember everything she'd wanted to say to Enid, but her mind was elsewhere; Shane was alive, and she had to find that boat.

She followed Enid up the steps into the room. A fluorescent light dangled over a desk with blueprints spread across it; they didn't resemble anywhere Drew knew of. Cabinets lined the back wall and she quickly pulled on each one, but they were all locked. A few stools were scattered throughout the room with a larger armchair behind the desk.

"There's nothing in here," Drew said.

"Oh yes there is. Look here."

At the wall, Enid moved a black and white picture of the lighthouse at Neptune Point in its early days aside. Behind it was a safe.

Drew pulled at the handle. It was locked with a padlock. It wasn't a typical padlock, like on her locker, this one required a key. Not just any key, she realized. A very *specific* kind—and not just one; there were two keyholes.

Enid leaned closer as if considering the lock. "Do you think you can pick the locks?"

"No," Drew said, "but I don't think I have to."

The missing keys on the pocket watch Iris gave to Shane flashed in her mind. Why would she have the keys to this safe?

"I know the key that will open it."

Enid looked at her and smiled. "Good. Let's see it."

Drew winced. "I don't have it. It's missing."

"Missing? That's not going to do us much good."

"No," Drew said, her disappointment mirroring Enid's, "but I think I know who has it. Dominic Sloan."

"I don't know that name," Enid said, trying to open the cabinet drawers. She appeared as human as anyone. She still wore the same clothes and had the same hairstyle, but she didn't look like the others.

"How are you so...human?" Drew asked.

"It's all I've ever been. Alive. Dead. Human." Enid shrugged.

Drew didn't know what to think. She'd never experienced them like this before. Even Shane's mother appeared like stardust rather than a human being.

"You can touch things without going through them. Can't you use magic powers or something to pop it open?"

Enid made a face. "It doesn't work like that."

"How does it work? How did you know I was here?"

"I don't know. It's like I'm...nowhere...but suddenly I sense your fear. Next thing I'm beside you. It was the same way at school. Only that emotion was different."

"How so?"

"Sadness. But not like I'm sad it's raining; it was more painful than that. I don't know what you want me to say. I've been sixteen years old forever. What do I know?"

Something about Enid's words struck Drew. The Crimson Lady was Shane's mother, an adult. Enid was a girl—a possibly very old girl, but a girl, nonetheless.

These weren't just ghosts she was seeing. They used to be people. Real, live *people*. Enid had died as a girl, never getting the chance to do anything.

"I'm sorry, Enid."

"For what? That I'm dead?" Enid smiled. Her human-like self faded a little into the translucent being Drew had become accustomed to. "It's not how you think. I'm not the same as when I was alive, but I would like to get out of this *place* I'm in. My brother and I are stuck in between worlds, kind of, I can't explain it, and I don't know how exactly I know, but I *know* you can help us with that. In exchange, I'm going to help you with whatever all *this* is."

"Your brother is Ezra?" Drew asked.

"Yes."

I knew it!

"Enid, I saw him! I saw him at the hospital. How did he know where to find me?"

Enid crinkled her nose and tilted her head. "I should know the answers to your questions, but it's strange…I don't!"

Drew eyed the door and listened to make sure they were still alone. If those men returned, she had no idea how they'd react to finding her here. She had to hurry and get the hell out.

"Enid, do you know of the accident that happened in the Coda River last January?"

Enid shook her head silently.

"So, I'm guessing you have no clue who Shane is, do you?"

"I'm sorry, but I don't," Enid said.

"Okay. That's okay. Have you seen a woman wandering around? White dress...sometimes covered in blood?" As she was asking the question, Enid's silhouette twitched, and her head turned downward as she frantically pointed at a cabinet in the corner behind the desk. It had been left open a crack, a lock hanging from the handle.

"Look, Drew!" Her voice cracked like static, and she lit up with the light of a hundred fireflies before fading into nothing.

"Don't leave me here! Enid!"

But it was too late. Enid was gone.

Drew crouched down to examine the contents of the drawer. Envelopes with elastics around them were stacked inside, 'Sloan Enterprises' stamped on the front. She opened one labeled *CS*. Unfolding a thick piece of paper, she held it up and turned it around. It was a blueprint of the Casting Spoon! She pulled more papers out of the envelope. Numerous bank transactions filled the pages. One bank statement was addressed from Zurich. If a bank in Switzerland was involved, Dominic Sloan wanted to hide something big. She flipped through the other envelopes. Some were labeled with initials, and others with numbers.

And then she saw it.

At the very back of the drawer was an envelope titled 'Aurora'. Tugging the elastic off so hard it snapped, she opened it and removed a stack of documents. There were more bank transactions and blueprints, and she recognized one of the blueprints as the lighthouse. Another sheet of paper was a title for land at Neptune Point. But it wasn't in Dominic Sloan's name.

Jack Morana.

Reaching in her coat pocket, she pulled out the watch and flipped it open. *Morana.*

A creaking came from below, startling her, and the door swung open. Dominic Sloan's broad figure filled the door frame.

Fifteen

Dominic Sloan loomed in the doorway. He looked at where she sat on the floor with papers and documents spread around her.

"You shouldn't be in here." He advanced toward her, and she scrambled to stand as he snatched the papers from her hands.

"This is private property!" he yelled.

She stepped back to move away from him. "Why do you have a land title for Aurora? Who is Jack Morana?"

"None of your goddam business!"

"Does this have anything to do with Shane Bishop? What do you know about him? You found that watch somehow, didn't you?" Her voice shook as the questions poured out. "Claudia was right. You were talking to someone!"

His eyes turned on her like a shark and he gripped her arm. "I didn't want it to come to this, but you give me no choice. I told you to stay out of my business!"

One of his associates charged up the stairs and stood leaning against the door frame. The only way out was through that door, and that was precisely where she intended to go. *Now!* Snapping her arm free, Drew broke through the space between the man and the frame, only to stumble to the floor. The man grabbed her, pulling her to her feet. Two more men charged up the stairs. She was surrounded.

She screamed as a huge hand clamped over her mouth. She kicked her feet trying to make contact, but the grip on her was too tight.

"Got her!"

"Bring her inside."

Enid!

She tried to will the ghost girl back for help. If Enid could sense her fear, surely the terror ripping through her would be enough to send a message.

They dragged her back into the small room. The man holding her captured her muffled shrieks into his hand. His pudgy fingers smelled of metal and rust. Her stomach lurched—maybe if she threw up, he would let her go.

Dominic Sloan gathered the papers from the floor and dropped them on the desk. Sitting in the armchair behind it, he leaned back and linked his fingers together. His calmness terrified her.

"I cannot allow him to release you unless you're willing to cooperate. And this—" He gestured toward her. "...Is not conducive to cooperation. Tell me, Miss Harlow, are you going to continue screaming? Because if so, I have ways to silence you. Your choice. Sit and talk, or scream. Your choice." He reached down and placed a gun on the desk.

He was a psycho, and he wanted her dead. She had

no other choice but to play his game. She nodded her head.

Yes, sit and talk. No more screaming.

"Let her speak."

She coughed as the hand released from her mouth. "You're crazy!"

Dominic Sloan nodded to the man, and he carried her to a wooden chair, plopping her down with a thud. He stood over her and reached for a gun from inside his suit jacket. They were going to kill her. She looked around for an escape route. It wasn't looking good. She faced her captor. He sat there like he was at a dinner party. Did Claudia know this side of her father? Did anyone?

"What do you want—"

"I will ask the questions." He picked a piece of lint from his suit. "First, you trespass on my property. Now, you trespass in my office. This is a problem. Tell me: why are you here? And before you think of lying, remember...." He tapped the gun. Gold rings adorned his hand, and she imagined him punching her and how much damage they'd cause. She shuddered. "Your choice."

"I...I'm looking for a boat. I believe it's from here."

"Which boat might that be?"

She studied his face. He stared at her with a hardened expression of a hawk. He wasn't going to let her out of here alive now that she saw him for who he really was. A monster. She'd become like Enid on a quest to solve her own murder from the other side.

There was no way out of this. No turning back.

"The *Light of Aurora.*"

His eyebrows raised and he glanced at the man standing beside her. He knew exactly what she was talking about, it was written all over his face!

"I see. What makes you think you would find it here?"

She was here now. If she was going to die tonight, she'd find out what he knew before he killed her.

"It's the same name as the lighthouse. It's registered in Atlas Cliffs, so it had to have docked here at least once before. I asked you about Shane in your driveway, and you threatened me. I know he's alive. He's on that boat."

She bit her lip. A tingling sensation covered her legs, and she shifted in the chair. The man beside her moved in ready to react and she swayed to the side. She wasn't going to go down without a fight.

"You're playing with fire, little girl." He stood up and stalked around the room before perching on the desk in front of her.

She scanned the room again; she had to get out of there. Sloan's men blocked the exit. There was no way out. If he killed her here, no one would know. Dominic Sloan was a pillar to the community and beyond; nobody would ever suspect him of murder! They would think she ran away to chase the boyfriend who was found alive.

Think, Drew!

"I don't want any trouble. I promise I won't tell anyone about those papers, or the boat. Just let me go."

Begging was the only thing that she could think of, even if begging this man for anything made her sick.

He laughed and her skin crawled. Seconds later, the maniacal laugh stopped, and he turned serious. Dead serious. He reached for the gun on the desk holding it with his finger on the trigger, examining it like a precious gem. "Your father is Gabe Harlow. He recently took a job here in the shipyard. Asked to stay in town for a while. He was the one who told you Shane is alive on the *Light of Aurora*, no?"

He knew her father. She might not feel love for the man, but she didn't want harm to come to him either.

"No. It wasn't him—"

He slapped her across the face with the back of his hand. It was a sharp blow, hard and stinging, and her cheek was on fire. A shrill buzzing filled her ears.

"I told you not to lie to me! Your father told you about Shane Bishop, didn't he!"

Staring up at him, she dropped her hand from her face and balled both into fists at her sides. "Yes! Is that what you want to hear? Jesus Christ! What are you hiding? Why do you care about Shane? He was no one to you!"

And then it hit her like his slap.

Iris.

She couldn't stop herself, the words coursed out. "You knew his mother, didn't you? Where is she!"

Bracing for another slap—or worse—her body stiffened. Instead, he crouched down beside her, gun in hand. The man beside her gripped her shoulder and she winced. This was it. At least she'd hugged Gran one last time.

Dominic Sloan's clenched jaw spasmed as he spat his words. "Never mention that name again or I *will* kill you."

She wanted to yell in his face, 'Iris is dead! Murdered!', but she couldn't do it. If he killed her, the truth would die too. Shane and his mother would be forgotten. Claudia would never know the beast her father was, and Atlas Cliffs would continue to hold him on a pedestal. She couldn't bear that to happen.

Fight. Stay alive.

Feeling like she might faint, she spoke through shallow breaths as little stars clouded her vision. "Tell me what you want me to do, and I'll do it."

"What I want is for you to stay the fuck out of my business. As far as you're concerned, these documents don't exist. Your search for Shane ends now. He doesn't want you; do you hear me? He's gone."

If she survived this night, she would never stop searching for Shane. Dominic Sloan killed his mother, and she would find a way to prove it. She held herself together.

"Can you at least tell me if he's alright? Wherever he is?"

Dominic grinned. "Shane ran away. He wanted a new life, and he came to me for help. He lives a life of luxury now. Why would he ever want to return? It's how he wanted it."

She didn't believe him. Shane wouldn't have anything to do with this evil man. She was cracking. Losing it. Tears pricked her eyes.

His lips curled and he nodded to the man standing over her. A gun clicked against her head. She closed her eyes as her stomach tightened and her chest constricted. She tried to catch her breath.

"It would be a shame if your father had an accident here at work, don't you think?"

"My father has nothing to do with this!"

"Or perhaps your grandmother on her way to that bakery of hers?" He tapped the barrel of his gun on her chest. "And the other woman that works there…Nellie Quinn. Has she taken the place over yet? I hope the wiring is up to code—"

"Stop it!" Tears streamed down her face. "I told you I won't say anything. I'll do whatever you want. Leave my family alone! Kill me if you want, but please don't hurt them!" She was at his mercy, and she knew it. She couldn't let anything happen to them because of her.

He knelt in front of her and grabbed her by the chin, pinching her skin. One of the stitches above her lip let go. "I will protect what's mine. Do you understand?" He snapped to the man standing beside her. "Stand her up."

The man pulled her from the chair, holding her in front of Dominic, his hands on her shoulders like a vice.

"Wherever you go," Dominic said, "someone will be watching. Listening. If you so much as utter a word or make a move, I *will* know. And next time, you will not be walking out alive. Do you understand?"

She stared at him, wishing he'd implode, wishing he'd burn to death. Or perhaps Enid would come to her.

Or even the Crimson Lady. Of course, nothing happened. Nothing would. She was alone and powerless.

"Yes! I won't say anything."

He let her go, nodding to the goons behind her. "Get her out of here."

"Move," the bald man said, gesturing with the gun.

They shoved her down the steps and to the back door. The cold wind had turned to rain, icy droplets pelting her. Drew shivered.

"Get out of here," the man said. "Run. Before he changes his mind."

She didn't wait, turning and running as far and as fast as she could. She glanced back to see the man watching her leave, but no one chased her. Passing boats and equipment she bolted to freedom. Her lungs were on fire as she reached the main building, but she refused to stop until she was inside the safety of Gran's car.

She fumbled with the keys and started the engine. Gripping the steering wheel, she erupted. Crying until she hyperventilated. Shane was gone, but not dead. He just ran away. Leaving her alone. Without answers, without a reason. And she couldn't do anything about it.

And anything she did, any questions she asked, any answers she sought, would put her family's lives at risk. She couldn't go to the police. If she talked about what happened, someone would find out. Was her phone bugged? Her house? The *car*? She flipped the visors back and searched around her looking for a microphone or camera, finding nothing.

She left the shipyard and drove around checking the rear-view mirror. She didn't want to go home yet, and someone could be following her.

The sign for The Tough Cookie came into view and she pulled up alongside the building. At nearly eleven o'clock, everything was closed, but a light was still on inside. She caught a glimpse of Nellie walking with a clipboard in hand. It wasn't unusual for her to work late sometimes. Gran had done the same thing. She longed for the old days when she could run to the bakery, plop herself on a stool and talk to Nellie over cupcakes. Those were simple times.

A cold chill made its way down her spine.

What if someone followed me here?

Drew glanced in the mirror. She didn't see anyone around.

Positioning the car back in gear, she pulled onto the road.

She passed the entrance to Marble Gates Estates. Piper was working tonight, and her house wasn't an option either. She drove by Claudia's house and wondered if the key to the safe was inside somewhere, or if Dominic always had it on him. She needed to get into that safe. She also had to find Enid again. To do that, she'd have to get to Neptune Point undetected.

Driving away, she pulled onto the cliffside highway for home. Little stars cascaded around her vision again and she felt light-headed. What had only been days since the accident seemed more like weeks, and she couldn't tell whether she was getting better or worse. That slap Dominic had given her across her face hadn't helped! She touched her sore cheek.

Asshole.

He couldn't get away with this!

Gabe's truck was gone, and the house was dark except for the porch light. Her mind raced; she didn't want to go inside just yet. The rain had stopped so she parked Gran's car and walked down to the beach. The surf curled into the shore, bringing the familiar rattle of pebbles against the sand.

Dominic had told her that Shane was living in luxury and wanted it that way. Could it be true? He let her believe he'd been dead for months! She tried to remember every conversation she'd had with Shane hoping all of this wasn't one great big betrayal.

Sitting on a piece of driftwood, she picked up a handful of sand that the snow hadn't touched and let it slip between her fingers as the wind carried it away. A new kind of loneliness ached inside.

It was so cold.

A branch snapped, and she heard rocks slide downhill. She sprung up and ducked against the cliff wall.

"Drew?"

"Nico?" Drew saw him and moved away from the shadows of the cliff. "Is that you?"

"Yeah."

With a black beanie on his head, and his face red with cold, he walked toward her with his hands shoved in his pockets. She remembered holding those hands in the hospital. She'd missed being around him. Desperate for someone to hold her and tell her everything would be okay, she almost ran and hugged him.

Almost. The last thing she wanted was to pull him into her nightmare.

"What are you doing down here?" he asked. "It's freezing!"

"I could ask you the same question."

"I was at Maze with some friends, I wasn't ready to go home yet. Claudia was there," he said and his face soured. "It was weird though. She hardly said a word to anyone. She kind of looked like she'd been crying."

"Crying? Really?" She had no clue what Claudia would be crying about.

He nodded. "She stayed about half an hour then took off alone."

Normally, the idea of Claudia crying would have pleased her. Normally, she'd make a rude comment about her. Normally. But not this time, because for the first time, Drew pitied her. She'd rather have a father that was in and out of her life than a monster. She wondered what, or who had made her cry.

She caught Nico looking at her.

"Drew, did I do something to make you uncomfortable?" he asked.

"What? No! Why?"

"I don't know… The last time I saw you was in the hospital, and you haven't returned any of my messages. I guess I thought maybe I'd done something wrong."

Drew flinched. She had been avoiding him, but not out of discomfort. Quite the opposite.

But now Shane was alive somewhere.

When she thought of him, she felt betrayal creep in. How could he have been alive this whole time with no contact? It hurt. Her eyes filled again, and she tried to hide her face. But when she stepped forward, she was as much in the light of the full moon as Nico was.

"You're bleeding!" Nico reached out and cupped her face. "What happened?" He used the cuff of his sweater to dab at her face. "Drew, did someone hit you?"

Drew pulled away, reached up to touch the cut, and ended up with her hand on his. This time she couldn't hold back her tears, the floodgates unleashed.

"What's wrong?" He hugged her tight. She let him.

"Everything is such a mess. I don't know what to do."

He put his arms around her holding her close while she sobbed into his shoulder. It was all too much; Shane, his mother's ghost, Enid, the awful headaches that wouldn't let up, and the torment—the violation—she'd just experienced left her more vulnerable than she'd ever felt in her life.

When she managed to catch her breath, she pulled back, sniffling, and wiped her face with her sleeve. His arms remained around her, keeping them face to face. Their breaths fogged from the cold curling around them. He was so gentle and kind. Safe. He blocked the rest of the world out without even trying.

He moved closer. Good God, he was going to kiss her! She should pull back, move away, stop this. Kissing Nico would only complicate things. They were just friends! Except—she didn't want to pull away from him. She wanted this. She needed it.

She met him halfway and put her arms around his neck. The kiss was soft, and sweet. It didn't feel wrong, at all. It was comforting. It felt right, and she wanted to *let* it keep feeling right. She wanted to shut out the world and stay here with him.

But that was impossible.

She released him and stepped back, taking a deep breath. His arms dropped to his sides as he studied her. He seemed unsure of what to do next, but so was she. A few seconds passed in silence. He stepped closer and held her hands. She never dreamed in a million years that she'd be having this moment with Nico.

"Why don't you tell me what's going on? Maybe I can help."

Surprising both of them, Drew laughed. *Help?* Where would she even start? If she told him what she knew—that Shane was alive, that he'd faked his death and left, leaving everything behind, that she could see his dead mother, that Claudia's father was a psychopath—she'd sound crazy.

More importantly, she couldn't put Nico at risk.

She looked down at her feet in the sand. "I can't tell you."

"Are you in trouble?"

"No. Yes—I don't even know." Taking her hands from his, she covered her face and rubbed her temples. "My father showed up earlier. He had some…news. I want to tell you, but I can't just yet."

"Whatever it is, you can tell me. I can keep a secret," Nico said.

"I know that. I trust you. I do. It's just…it's been a long day. I need sleep. I've got to go home."

No longer in Nico's arms, she shivered from the icy night air.

"I'll walk you up—"

"No, it's okay. I'll go alone." She glanced back the way she'd come, but no one was there.

"What are you looking at? You definitely don't seem okay. I'm not letting you walk alone."

Nico didn't let her turn him down and started walking toward the crooked stairway. She rushed in front of him and climbed first, not taking her eyes off the top.

The road was empty. Across the street, the porch light was still on, waiting for her return. No one was around and the only sound was the waves below. She faced Nico.

"Thank you. I'm good from here."

"Are you sure?"

"Positive."

"Will I see you tomorrow?" he asked.

The kiss flashed in her mind and heat flushed her cheeks. All this time, she'd tried to keep her distance, tried to stay focused on finding out what happened to Shane. Only to find that he'd left. Not murdered, not kidnapped. Not to hunt down his mother's murderer. He'd been the love of her life, and he'd just left.

And Nico was here. That kiss had changed everything. They'd stepped over the 'just friends' line. She was okay with that. More than okay. And that was the part that surprised her the most. Even if she didn't understand how she'd gotten to this place. She'd never looked at Nico as anything more than a friend before. But now…

"We'll talk tomorrow," she said.

Before she could change her mind, she kissed him quickly and ran across the road. She went inside and turned off the porch light. The house was dark and quiet; Gran must be asleep.

Moving the living room curtains, she peered outside, half expecting, half hoping to see Nico staring back at her. But he was gone, already having run down the road and out of sight.

She turned to go up to bed when she heard the slow pace of a car. She glanced out the window again as headlights passed by, stopping just past the house. It was a black sedan—the same sedan from the shipyard.

Dominic had warned her, hadn't he? They were watching her.

The car backed its way into the driveway.

She ran to the door and locked the deadbolt. She watched out the little window in the door with her phone in hand ready to dial 9-1-1.

A full minute passed with Drew's face pressed to the window, staring out. The car's low idle rumbled outside as if watching her—as if *knowing* she was watching them, *wanting* her to see them.

She grabbed the handle of the door, ready to run out screaming at them. If they wanted her to cower in fear, then they'd come to the wrong house. She was done playing the victim.

But the car moved again, leaving the property, this

time with squealing tires as it sped away. Good. Let them run from her.

All signs pointed back to Aurora at Neptune Point. She'd leave first thing in the morning.

Sixteen

Drew got up and snuck out of the house before Gran woke. She'd left a note apologizing for taking the car without asking—something along the lines that it was imperative she didn't miss an important assignment and was going to school. When it came to school, Gran would be more likely to forgive.

Blizzard-like flurries surrounded the car as Drew made her way to Neptune Point, to Enid. She'd thought of asking Piper to join her, but everything was different now after the Dominic debacle, so the fewer people involved, the better.

She plotted a route on a back road to avoid being followed. She couldn't stop checking the rear-view mirror though. The sedan from last night hadn't returned. They couldn't possibly be watching her every minute of the day. Unless they had bugged her phone or her house.

It didn't matter. She needed evidence, no matter the cost. If only she'd taken pictures of those bank documents and blueprints, but there'd been no time. If she could find proof—something tying Dominic to Iris, then her next step would be to contact Detective Porter.

Finding the key to the safe would be next, and that would mean talking with the one person she wanted nothing to do with—Claudia. She was the only way to get inside the Sloan house.

Shane had made his choice and run away. But she was still here. Had he even known that his mother was dead? She didn't understand how he could have just left the way he did. To leave and not even consider the unbelievable amount of pain he'd cause his father, or the heartache it'd bring her.

Thinking of it made her so angry.

Turning down a desolate road, she closed the gap to Aurora. Bifrost Bridge was ahead—the connecting section of road to Neptune Point. She didn't have a plan other than start at the keeper's house and work her way to the lighthouse. Dominic Sloan wanted this place so bad he was committing fraud and God knows what else to own it. She was here to find out why.

She was about to cross over it when a man stepped over the bridge, pointing toward the direction of the lighthouse. She pressed her foot to the brake, but instead of slowing down, the car careened forward, skidding on a layer of black ice, not stopping.

It was him! The old man.

She pulled on the steering wheel, turning into the skid, but it was too late. She had a brief, horrifying glimpse of ocean water to her right, then the ditch on the left, as the car weaved, bouncing down the embankment, before coming to a jolting halt at the bottom of the hill.

Her hands shook as she held the wheel. The man

stood on the bridge ahead, his long coat flapping in the wind. Maybe Ezra was wrong, and the old man did want to hurt her. It was like figuring out a cryptic message, and she was tired of not knowing his true intentions.

Still clutching the wheel, Drew stared right back at him, a new anger welling within her. She was tired—tired of being followed, tired of being chased, tired of being threatened. "Well? You got something to say, old man?"

Whatever he was going to do, he might as well do it and be done with it, but all he did was raise a bony finger. A finger he pointed at her before he vanished.

Drew blinked, shaking her head. She wasn't sure if she was angrier or relieved that he disappeared.

Climbing out of the car, she stared at the front tires stuck in the mud. There'd be no getting it out of this. She dug into her pocket for her phone and with frozen fingers, sent a message to Piper. She simply told Piper where she was and asked if she could pick her up at the end of the day. All she needed was a drive. When all of this was over, she'd owe her.

She scanned the bridge for the old man. She peered behind her and over the hill, but he was gone. She'd find out soon enough if he was waiting for her. She was done being afraid.

The cloud-covered sky made it look much later than mid-morning, and snow blowing sideways didn't help. She threw on a small backpack of supplies she'd brought with her—water, a flashlight, a pain reliever for the constant headache, and Shane's pocket watch.

She opened it, examining the engraved map one last time before tucking it in her jeans pocket. She tightened her bootlaces and shoved her hands in a pair of mitts before trekking across the bridge. A squawk sounded over her head; a swarm of black birds cluttered the tree-covered hill, staring at her as she walked by.

She leaned over the side of the stone bridge. The Coda River rushed beneath as it joined forces with the ocean. Waves crashed over boulders below. She couldn't understand how Shane had sent his car into the river on purpose that day, and then run away.

But she was going to figure it out.

Flinging her hood up, she continued until the lighthouse came into view. Stalks of foliage grew in tangles nearby, peeking through a layer of fog settled around it. Dried branches wrapped around each other, sticking out of a fresh layer of snow covering the grounds surrounding the keeper's house. The red paint on the lighthouse had peeled back, revealing a deathly gray underneath. Glass from the upper windows had fallen in jagged pieces to the ground, and every opening had been boarded up, isolated from civilization.

Drew trudged along a stone pathway to the front porch, avoiding the broken eaves hanging over the doorway. She misjudged a gaping hole where the middle stair was missing and tripped. She stood and brushed dirt off her jacket as she scoped out the area around her. A wave of dizziness almost took her down again; she grabbed the railing quickly, and when she did, a wooden floorboard snapped underneath, her foot plunging through. The sound of smashing waves against the rocks kept her painful scream from carrying.

She wrestled her leg out of the hole and pulled back her jeans to look. There was no blood, thankfully, and nothing seemed broken. She peered between the cracks in the boards covering the front windows, but curtains inside blocked her view.

The boarded front door loomed in front of her. She turned the rusted doorknob and pushed hard, but it wouldn't budge. She felt around for a weak spot in the boards to shove her way through and she slammed her body into it, but the door still didn't move. There had to be another way inside.

She wandered along the side of the house peeking through splits in the boards. When she trudged around back, she noticed one of the boards dangling loose, exposing a window. She tried to pry the window open, but she wasn't high enough. Flipping a nearby barrel upside down, she heaved herself on top of it and balanced as it wobbled. She put her face against the dirty window, but she couldn't see anything inside.

Drew had no idea what she would find inside. The Crimson Lady had wanted her to find someone. Maybe Enid was in there, or perhaps the old man was trying to lead her to this house.

She banged on the window, her mitts protecting her hands, smacking it as hard as she could. The glass cracked. She hit it one more time and it shattered into pieces. Boosting herself through the open space, she landed inside with a thud. Dust flew at her, choking her into a fit of coughing. She took a gasping breath and gagged as a putrid smell of mold filled the air. Narrow streams of light filtered in revealing yellowed wallpaper spattered with faded pink flowers and a door off the hinges on the far wall.

She stood unsteady at the window, holding the ledge for a moment before crossing the threshold into a grand room. The lack of daylight coming in made it difficult to see. She flipped light switches despite knowing they wouldn't work. She dug into her backpack and pulled out a flashlight, scanning the room.

An armchair lay flipped on its side with springs popping out of the seat cushion. Crumbling brick sprinkled the floor around a fireplace, and holes were scattered along the chimney that crept up to the ceiling. A grand piano coated in grime sat in the corner. The front door was across from her, and she could see the boards had been nailed on the inside frame as well. No wonder she couldn't get it open!

She walked through an archway that led her to a formal dining room with a large oval table, a bench seat, and four overturned chairs. Through a swinging door that creaked on its hinges was the kitchen that had been frozen in time. Red panels that had faded to pink lined the walls with cast iron pots dangling from hooks. The refrigerator door jutted open, and she peered inside finding it empty. Two of the cupboard doors were swung open, still stacked with plates. Black mold grew along the wall behind the sink. She pointed the flashlight inside a chipped mug sitting on the counter. Tiny bugs zoomed back and forth, and she jumped back, swatting the air.

A door was ajar beside the pantry. She glanced inside and a horrible smell of decay crept up from the darkness. She recoiled and pushed it closed.

What if evidence had been concealed down there? Like another cabinet of secret documents, or something more sinister—like a body. If Dominic killed people, it would make sense to hide them here. She couldn't turn back empty-handed; she'd come too far to let fear drive her away.

Gripping the doorknob, she yanked it open and swept the area with her flashlight. Uneven stairs descended into a basement, the sound of dripping water echoing from below.

Staring down into the black hole, she argued with herself.

One step at a time, you've got this!

And the rational part of her yelled back, *don't go down there alone! What if someone is waiting for you?*

Stretching her neck from side to side, she started down one step at a time, hoping they were strong enough to hold her. She strained to see into the murky void and held the light in front of her. The smell— death—grew stronger. If she found a dead body, she wasn't sure what she'd do. Run screaming, probably. She tried to prepare for the worst.

The last step was missing, and she hopped down to the mud floor. The windowless basement resembled an underground cave. Green, algae-like growth covered much of the stone walls. Water trickled over the back wall and down a drain in the floor. She dared herself to touch the spongy moss-like substance. Her finger came back damp and tinged with green. Buckets had been stacked in a corner and empty liquor bottles were scattered throughout. An old washing machine sat on a cement block next to a table. She opened the lid, but nothing was inside.

The smell of rot was worse here, and she covered her nose with her sleeve. She crept around the space under the stairs. A rusted furnace with pipes stemming from it sat silent and unused. She pulled on the rusted handle opening the furnace door expecting to discover bones or worse, but it was empty. Nothing in this basement got her any closer to answers, other than the last person who'd been here liked whiskey. Living in this isolated place laced with fog and cold would drive anyone to drink.

She took one last scan around the room. She'd had enough of the basement. Frustrated, she kicked a bottle. It rolled under the table with a dull clang as it hit something. She angled the light under the table.

"What the hell is that?" she muttered.

Crouching down, she tilted her head to see underneath. A curved door like something out of a fairy tale was built into the wall behind the table. Framed in colorful stones, the door had been painted green with a shiny black latch. She dragged the heavy table away from the wall inch by inch until it slid onto the floor. The door was barely large enough for a person to squeeze through. She reached for the metal handle and pulled, but the nails gave way, and it popped off. Throwing it aside, she tried to force the door open. She took her mitts off and dug her fingers in the nail holes, pushing through the rotting wood until the door finally gave, swinging open. She picked up the flashlight and aimed it inside, taking a step.

And stopped.

She knew this place—knew it far too well for her liking. She'd been here before, countless times. This was the endless tunnel from her nightmares. The same one she'd always been desperate to claw her way out of, but never could. Despite the cold, she found herself damp with sweat. There was no way she could go in there. If she got lost, or worse, how would anyone know where to find her?

What if the dream came true and she got stuck forever?

The flashlight slipped from her hands, but she caught it before it hit the ground. Shaking, she held the light up and looked around. It was high enough that she could stand up inside. She couldn't believe she was considering this.

Do it, Drew.

Panic rose from her gut to her throat. She had no idea what—or who—waited inside that tunnel. She only knew she was about to find out.

Taking one careful step, Drew moved through the door. The walls matched the basement, green stuff included. The tunnel was long, the air thick, and heavy, making it difficult to breathe. She was hyper-aware of how rapid and shallow her breaths were, but she held her light steady with every step forward.

"Get out of there!"

Drew stopped dead in her tracks.

Enid! Her voice sounded small and far away. But it was her.

"Enid! Where are you!"

The narrow tunnel extended beyond the beam of her flashlight and farther than her eyes could see. She turned the flashlight to the walls. The rock was streaked with pale green and gray. Dampness seeped into her bones, her head aching. A silhouette lit up the passage a short distance ahead. A swirling dress came to view as she got closer.

"Iris? What are you doing here?"

The woman arched her head around and twisted her grotesque body to face Drew. Blood streaked her dress and down her arms. She held up her hands, her mouth twitching like she was saying words.

Drew stepped closer, gasping for breath as the air thinned. A percussion of water sounded around her with every step closer. "What do you want from me?"

Iris moved in tortured, crooked steps. "My boy will come back. He will kill him. Like he did me."

Drew couldn't tear herself from staring at the woman's face. Compared to her body, it appeared so human. So...alive. "Do you know where Shane is?"

They were an arm's length apart. She reached her hand out to Iris. The woman watched with pleading eyes and touched Drew's cheek with icy fingers sending a shock through her.

"His father hurt you."

Drew couldn't imagine Paxton hurting anyone— unless she'd been wrong. "Paxton never hurt me. Did he do this to you?"

Iris' head twitched back and forth in hysterics. Her mouth opened and she moaned, gripping Drew's face with both hands in desperation.

"Iris, who did this to you?"

The flashlight flickered and buzzed before dying. Iris' face changed from its human form. Tiny holes covered her skin as she started to fade.

"Not Pax. Dominic is his father! Find me. Save him," Iris hissed—like she was speaking through static over a radio. Her hands dropped from Drew's face as she whirled around and disappeared into a fine mist.

Shane's biological father was Dominic Sloan—and he'd murdered Shane's mom! That would also make Claudia his sister! If he'd found out, why would he run away? Unless he'd been threatened.

She heard a creak behind her. She spun around, smacking the flashlight against her palm but it didn't work. A bang echoed through the tunnel, leaving her in complete darkness. *The door!*

She couldn't be trapped in here—she immediately felt lightheaded, her breath coming in short pants. If she didn't breathe in fresh air soon, she was going to pass out.

Running her hand along the fuzz-covered wall, she walked back until she smacked into the door. She knelt, feeling for the seam of the door, and pushed. It wouldn't open. Dropping to the floor she banged on it with clenched fists. It was stuck closed, trapping her in this underground hellhole. She screamed as she kicked it. The wood gave way with a crunch, her foot snapping through.

Frantic voices hollered her name from somewhere outside.

"Drew? Where are you?"

She put her face up the hole in the small door. "I'm inside!"

She brought her foot up and slammed into the door again. This time the opening widened enough that she could wiggle through. Panting, she rolled over and flopped on her back.

"Don't worry," a voice whispered.

She sat upright and dizziness hit so hard she almost threw up.

Enid's ghost-like appearance was shifting to a human one as she crouched beside her. "That woman with all the blood. What's her name?"

Drew wrapped her arms around bended knees and took deep breaths to stop the room from spinning. "Iris," she finally said. "She was murdered. Remember those men last night? One of them killed her. She wants me to find her, but I don't know how! Can you help me?"

"I don't know—"

"Please, Enid. I need you."

"I'm not sure how much help I am from this side of the line if you know what I mean," Enid said.

Drew tried to grab Enid's shoulders, but her hands went right through the girl's silhouette. "See? That's exactly why I know you can help! You exist in the same world she does! Can you find out where that woman goes?"

Enid tilted her head in thought. She looked unsure

of herself. "I'll try. But I don't have much control over what happens here. You've seen that yourself. I couldn't get to you before you went in there."

"But you did eventually! Whatever you did worked!" Drew said.

Enid touched the scar on her face. Drew didn't know if she felt pain, or if it was an instinctive reaction.

"How did you get that scar?" she asked.

"It's a birthmark. My sister had the same one. It tingles sometimes."

"You have a sister?"

"Yes, but she's still on your side."

"Does she live in Atlas Cliffs?"

If Drew could find Enid's alive sister, she could find answers!

"She does somewhere," Enid said. "I can't find her, but I've tried. It's so frustrating!"

"I can help you, Enid! You find Iris and I'll find your sister. What's her name?"

A crash erupted from upstairs.

"Your friends are here," Enid said. "Time for me to go."

"No, wait! They won't see you. Stay!" Enid held up her hands as they started to fade into nothing.

"I have no choice." She looked at Drew. "Blythe. My sister's name is Blythe."

And in a flash, she vanished. Drew wished she could ring a bell, snap her fingers, anything to bring Enid back. Every time she got close to finding out more, Enid disappeared.

"Drew! Where are you?" Piper cried out in

desperation.

"Down here!"

Drew stared at the emptiness beside her where Enid had just been. She touched her cheek thinking of the birthmark. She'd seen that same mark before...she'd thought it was a scar—*Dr. Blythe Wymond was Enid's sister!*

Seventeen

Footsteps thudded down the stairs into the basement. Beams of light lit the room and Piper and Nico's faces appeared over her.

"What in the hell happened to you?" Piper exclaimed.

Nico grabbed her hands and pulled her to her feet. "Are you okay?"

She nodded her head yes, wondering why Nico was there. And honestly, how could she be okay? How could anyone? The edges of the living and the dead blurred together. She could communicate with people who *died*. She couldn't turn it off or make them go away. They were in her head all the time. At this point, she was teetering on the edge of sanity.

Piper hugged her. "Why didn't you answer my calls?"

She hugged Piper back. "There's no cell service out here, and the last thing I wanted was for you to come out now. I only needed a ride home later. How did you find me?" She looked at Nico. "Why did you both come?"

"Have we just met?" Piper said. "You should know

better. You said you were broken down, so I asked Nico to bring his dad's tow truck. When you weren't by your car, I just knew you'd be in this damn house! Why didn't you take me with you? I thought that was what we'd decided!"

If she had known Gran's car was going to break down, maybe she would've asked Piper to come.

"I couldn't wait."

"I can see that! This basement is nasty!" Piper leaned down and looked past the broken door into the tunnel. "What's in there?"

"I was trying to find out, but my flashlight died."

"What are you doing in here anyway?" Nico said. "You could've called me if you needed something."

"I didn't want to put you out."

It ran deeper than that, but she couldn't bring herself to tell him the truth. Although, he might find out on his own soon enough.

"I meant what I said last night. Whatever all this is, I *want* to help. I'll bring the car into the shop and look at it."

All of this was more than he could imagine.

"Thanks. Gran's going to be pissed. I didn't exactly ask permission."

Nico gave her hand a gentle squeeze. From the surprised looks on Piper's face, it didn't go unnoticed. Drew let go and toyed with the button on the broken flashlight—busying her hands to keep him from holding or touching them. Not that she didn't want him to, but it would lead to questions that she wasn't sure how to answer. She headed up the stairs back to the kitchen and they followed.

While Nico poked around, Piper whispered gesturing to him, "What's going on there?" She was trying to be discreet, but Drew shook her head signaling—silently begging—Piper to drop it.

Piper smiled as they wandered into the dining room. "Look at this place! I mean we've seen it from the outside every time we go to Haven, but no one has been inside before!" She opened doors on a display cabinet. "Everything is so old. Who'd all this stuff belong to and why is it still here?"

"Piper, has Cole ever mentioned his mom's sister?"

"That's a random question. I'm not sure. Why?"

"I was just curious. She just reminded me of someone, is all," Drew said.

Nico picked up a half-melted candle sitting on the piano. Taking a lighter out of his pocket, he ignited a small flame on the wick. He tapped on the keys. An uneven, tinny clang cut through the room.

Piper clutched her chest. "Jesus, Nico!"

"Sorry." He sat on the bench in front of the piano. "Are we sticking around, or do you want to pick up your car and head home? It's your call."

Drew studied him. He didn't appear frustrated or angry, just matter of fact. He seemed unbothered by being here even though he had no idea what was going on. What he didn't know—what neither of them knew—Shane was alive. And that was only part of it. Now that she was inside this house, she couldn't leave until she found something tangible. There had to be proof connecting Dominic to Shane, or Iris, or both. *Anything*. The stakes were too high to leave stones unturned and she was running out of time.

"You can go back if you want, but I can't. Not yet." A decorative spindle rolled across the floor stopping at her feet. She bent down and picked it up, looking at the winding staircase. A space interrupted a line of spindles from the landing at the top. "I'm going up there."

Piper joined her at the bottom of the stairs. "I'm in."

Nico stood and leaned against the railing. He handed her his flashlight. "I don't know why you're in here, or what you're up to, but I'm in too."

The steps groaned under their feet as they made their way up the winding staircase.

"What's this about?" Nico murmured at her side.

"It's a long story."

"I look forward to hearing it."

Regardless of how this all turned out, eventually, he would know everything. When he did, the chances were high that this entanglement happening between them would end. That was the path relationships took in her life; they always ended, leaving her on her own. Her mom, her dad. Even Shane left her, faking his death to do it.

At the end of a long hallway, a shadow swept from one room to another, and Drew jumped. Whatever was up here could move through closed doors. Could it be Iris or Enid? She hoped it wasn't someone more hostile.

Piper grabbed her arm. "Did you see something?"

"Maybe. I'm not sure."

Drew couldn't afford to let ghosts scare her away now. The humans on her side were proving to be more threatening than the dead ones on Enid's. She stormed down the hallway, flinging the first two doors open. Both rooms were empty. Undeterred, she swung the next door open to reveal a small bedroom with a wooden rocking horse in the corner, and a canopy bed against the wall. The next one was a bathroom with a stench of death like the basement. It hit her as soon as she entered, forcing her to cover her nose with the neck of her jacket.

Pieces of broken tile littered the bottom of the bathtub where they'd fallen from the wall. Exposed pipes protruded from the wall.

She shone the flashlight around until she caught her reflection in a mirror above the vanity. Cracks in the surface, as though someone had punched it, distorted her face.

A chill curled around her. The flashlight dimmed and she shook it to keep the light from dying. What was with the lights dying in here? A glow crawled across the mirror. She reached out to touch it as words formed.

She's here.

A faint humming sounded close to her ear. The Crimson Lady's lullaby! She spun around, dropping the flashlight. It slammed against the vanity breaking off fragments of ceramic to the floor. She stared back into the mirror.

Piper strolled into the bathroom. "What are you looking at?"

Drew spun back to the mirror. "You don't see it?"

"See what?"

Piper stood beside her. Both of their warped faces reflected in the splintered glass. The words faded, the mirror returned to its normal damaged state, and the humming stopped.

"She's here. What does that mean?"

"What are you talking about?" Piper lowered her voice. "Did you see one? A ghost?"

"Shane's mother is in this house," she replied before fleeing the bathroom and tearing down the hallway past Nico.

"Where are you going?" Piper called out. "Drew!"

She burst into the last room at the end. A curtain rod hung off the wall and the drapes dangled to the floor. In front of the window was a dresser—the only furniture in the room. She marched over and gripped the knobs, pulling the drawers open.

And found nothing.

This is hopeless!

Clutching the sides of the dresser, she held in a scream. Her fingers ran over bumps in the wood. Initials had been engraved, but it was too dark to see. Her flashlight—Shit. She'd dropped it in the bathroom. She crouched down using the light from her phone to see.

E.M. was here.

It had to be a person, like when teenagers carve their initials into tree trunks. She thought of Enid and her brother, Ezra.

Nico walked in. "Would you please tell me what's going on? What is it with this old house? Because all I see is a bunch of junk left behind from God knows how long ago. I don't get it, Drew. Give me something, please!"

She didn't know what she should tell him. All of it? Nothing?

Piper handed the flashlight back to her. Somehow, it still worked. "Drew, what can we do? Maybe we should leave and get your grandmother's car loaded up. Go home."

She wasn't ready to leave, but she didn't know where to look next.

The tunnel.

"That underground tunnel in the basement. I couldn't see anything because my flashlight died, but what if something is buried in there?"

"Like what?" Nico asked, exasperated. "Why won't you just tell me? I'm getting all these little pieces, but none of it makes any sense."

She couldn't tell Nico about Shane's mother. He'd think she was crazy and making up wild stories! The chances were low he'd believe her. But if the underground tunnel led to Iris, she'd have no choice but to follow the path.

"Okay. I know you see—" Piper glanced at Nico, "*Know things*, but this has to stop. You're going to make yourself crazy. You've got let this—him go."

"Shane's alive."

"You think he is, Drew, but you don't know that—"

"I do now." She held up her phone with the photo. "He's on a boat called *Light of Aurora*."

Piper grabbed the phone from her hands. "What the hell? Impossible."

"Can I see?" Nico peered over Piper's shoulder. He glanced at Drew and back to the phone before leaning against the wall. Drew wished she knew what he was thinking. She watched his face turn serious as she filled them in, regurgitating what her father told her the night before. She mentioned the shipyard but left out the part about Dominic and his threats. She wasn't sure how to tell them without dragging them into it all with her.

"What are you going to do?" Piper said.

"I haven't figured that out yet."

"Gabe was at your house last night? Before I saw you at the beach?" Nico broke his silence.

"Yes," she said.

"Why didn't you tell me about Shane?"

If she'd told him on the beach, he would've closed off or left her alone. Maybe she'd been selfish, but she needed him. And she hated herself for feeling that way.

"I don't know. After the night I'd had...I didn't know what to think or what to do. It was too much. I was—"

"Ecstatic? Happy? After months of thinking he was dead, you find out your boyfriend is alive. It changes everything, don't you think?"

Nico was right; the impossible had come true. She should be floating on air! But she wasn't.

She shook her head.

"Shane left. He's alive, and he let me think he was dead. Who does that? When you saw me on the beach, I was terrified." She wanted to blurt out what had happened but stopped herself. If she told them about Dominic, there would be no way to undo her words. If they did or said anything to anyone, she knew he'd hurt them. "You don't understand."

Nico hugged her tight, right there in front of Piper. Every muscle tightened and she closed her eyes because she couldn't bring herself to look at Piper's face. What would she think? Why did it matter? His arms were pure, undemanding armor that gave her space to breathe. She let herself sink into him, indulging for this moment before pulling away.

"You're right, I don't understand. Last night..." Nico looked from her to Piper, who didn't say a word. He focused back on Drew. "Like I said last night. I'm here for you."

Drew shook. She was freezing and sweating at the same time—if that was even possible. There was still so much that Nico didn't know about her.

Piper screamed and jumped. They turned at once, Drew shining the light. It was just a mouse. It scurried across the floor, disappearing through a gnawed hole in the cracked and caved-in remains of the wall.

Nico drew a hand down his face. "Piper! For crying out loud!"

"Sorry," Piper said.

Drew lowered her light—and stopped.

There, just a foot away from where the mouse had disappeared, was another small door—the same as the one in the basement, with the curved angled frame and curled handle.

Drew shone the flashlight on it. They all saw it

now. Nico jostled the handle, but it was locked.

"Help me get this open!"

Nico leaned down and pulled a compact tool set from his jacket pocket. He was always prepared. After a few minutes of fidgeting with the hinges, he removed the door. Drew stepped inside and it opened into a room with a high ceiling with wooden ladder-like steps leading to another rectangular door at the top.

Icy breath brushed her cheek. "You're close," it whispered.

She spun around, watching as a shadow flew up and disappeared at the top. It was the same voice that had asked her to *find me, save him*.

Iris.

She handed Nico the flashlight. "Hold this for me. I'm going up."

"I'll follow," he said, holding the bottom of the ladder with one hand and aiming the light with the other.

She climbed up the staircase to the door. It was latched, but not locked. Popping it open, she leaned back as the door flopped down and hung in midair. She continued up into the attic room, brushing dust off her jeans. Light seeped in through a small, round window in between the sloped ceilings, illuminating a cloud of dust. Cobwebs full of dead flies coated the dirty glass and a spider cast a shadow as it dashed across the window.

Nico popped up behind her, and she took the light from him, scanning the large room. It must've spanned the length of the entire house. Whatever this room was, no one had been up here in years. A metal trunk sat in the darkness at the back. Drew walked toward it over creaking floorboards, hoping they wouldn't give out from under her. She wiped a layer of dust off and opened the lid. Clothing laid inside, smelling of must and stale cigarette smoke. A familiar coat on the top of the pile stood out. She handed Piper the flashlight—she had crawled up after them—and picked up the coat. Horn-shaped buttons lined the front. Her chest tightened.

She knew this coat—it was the same one the old man always wore.

Piper gave the flashlight back to Drew and set to work digging through the pile of clothes. At the bottom of the trunk, there was a small box. She handed it to Drew, who opened it and found a leather book. She cracked the spine and a newspaper clipping fell to her lap.

"What's that?" Nico asked, peering over her shoulder. "'Local lighthouse keeper dies at Neptune Point.'"

Drew read the words out loud. "'Aurora Lighthouse keeper, Jack Morana, presumed dead at Neptune Point...'"

Morana.

It was the name on the land title she'd seen in the warehouse, the one that Dominic Sloan didn't want her to see, and—

Sinking to the floor, she took the watch out of her pocket and ran her fingers over the engraving.

Why did Shane's mother have this?

A new pressure behind her eyes throbbed and queasiness rose in her stomach. As much as she tried to ignore it, her head hadn't been the same since the accident. It hurt all the time, but she couldn't let it get to her. Not here. Not now.

The flashlight flickered and dimmed. She smacked it against her leg, and it brightened again. She continued reading, but this time to herself.

The lighthouse had been automated since the 1960s when the Morana family obtained the property. On the evening of February 13th, 1987, in the middle of a blizzard, it was presumed that Jack Morana, who lived alone at the time, had fallen to his death while attempting to fix faulty equipment in the tower. His body was never found and is believed to have been swept out to sea off the rocky shore below.

Piper touched Drew's arm. "Can I see it?"

Drew stared at the article. She failed to see any connection between the name Morana and Dominic Sloan. How had the property come to be in his name?

Her friends waited. She was the reason they were here in the first place, but she didn't know what to say. She handed the page over to Piper.

As Piper read out loud, Drew turned the pages of the book, stopping on a black and white photo of Aurora lighthouse. The keeper's home looked fresh and maintained, quite unlike it was now. Nothing appeared out of the ordinary, and she pulled it out of its plastic sleeve to examine every inch of it. Another picture of Aurora was on the next page, but this time a man stood by the entrance. He wore a long coat and a hat. Blood pulsed in her ears, and she bit her lip. This wasn't just any man. She reached for the coat, touching the rough wool.

It was him.

She took the picture out of the plastic and studied it. Silver hair hung below his cap, whipping at his face. Lines creased around his eyes and mouth, deepened by his frown. The man in the picture, standing in front of Aurora, was the same one from her dreams, the same man who stood by the river that night at Haven, and who ran her off the road—not once, but twice.

She flipped the photo over. On the back was a name, and it didn't shock her to see it.

Jack Morana.

The old man had lived here, he'd *died* here.

But why was he stalking her from his grave?

She turned the pages, finding more pictures. One was of a man leaning on an axe by a wood pile; she'd never seen him before. A holiday snapshot of the living room downstairs came alive with a Christmas tree covered in tinsel in the corner. A woman wearing a red dress sat on the bench at the piano. On the next page, a young Enid sat under the tree. She wore a red barrette holding her hair back and held a gift on her lap.

Something fell from the album and skittered to the floor. Nico picked it up and gave it to her. "What's this?"

She held the chain, letting a heart-shaped pendant dangle back and forth. "I think it's a locket."

She propped the flashlight upright on the floor illuminating the space around them. Prying the pendant open she held it close to the light. The photo was small, but there was no mistaking Enid and Ezra.

"Do you know any of these people?" Nico asked.

"It's a long story."

"Right, back to that again."

She tucked the locket into the album and flipped to the last page. Not one, but two girls with dark hair grinned at the camera. The girls had matching birthmarks on their cheeks. One was Enid and the other looked a lot like her, but not identical.

Ezra was making a face as he crouched in front of them, but there was another young man standing behind them, wearing a dress shirt and a smirk on his face.

Drew held her hand out. "Pass me the flashlight."

Nico grabbed the light from the floor, and she held it close to the picture for a better look. She knew that face—that cruel half-smile. She turned the photo over. Names had been scribbled on the back.

Ben, Ezra, Enid & Blythe.

That young man named Ben grew up to be Dominic Sloan.

Why had he changed his name?

Eighteen

Drew stared at the photograph in her hand. Were they all related? It looked like they were siblings. If Blythe and Dominic—Ben? —were brother and sister, and lived in the same town, wouldn't Cole be aware?

She didn't know how the pieces fit, not yet. But a follow-up appointment with Dr. Wymond was in order.

The rumble of an engine sounded. Nico wiped the dirty window with his sleeve and tried to see outside. "I think someone's coming!"

"I wouldn't worry about it. It's probably just kids or something." Piper hovered over the trunk and held up the dead man's coat.

But Piper was wrong. If someone was there, they *should* be worried. Of course, Piper and Nico didn't know about Dominic, or that her every move was being watched now.

She stuffed the album in her backpack and grabbed the coat from Piper.

"Hey! What are you doing?"

Drew threw it in the trunk and slammed the lid shut. "We've got to get out of here." She flung her backpack on her shoulders and turned to Nico. "Where are you parked?"

"In the field by the entrance to Haven. Why?"

"I don't have time to explain. You're going to have to trust me. Let's move!"

The obscured area to Haven wouldn't be seen by anyone coming to Aurora. Escaping was possible if they hurried. Whoever followed her here would see her car in the ditch, believing she'd come alone.

Nico latched the attic door behind them as they barreled out of the small door to the bedroom, and down the stairs.

Piper stumbled into pace beside her. "Why are we running? Who's out there?"

The engine sounded closer, slowing down. Drew raced to the living room window and pulled the drapes aside. She couldn't get a clear view through the cracks in the boards, but a humming motor echoed from just over the bridge toward the house.

"Let's go out the window in the back. We can run for the lighthouse and cut through the trees toward Haven."

"Who's out there, Drew?" Nico said from behind her as she led them into the back room where they'd come in.

"Not now, Nico. Please!"

Drew leaned out the window. The barrel lay on the ground with a seagull perched on top. Its beady eyes gawked at her before it screeched and flew away. Waves crashed against the rocks. It had stopped snowing, but the wind sprayed mist on her face. The beacon of Aurora turned on, starting its dusk rotation.

Drew swung her legs over the windowsill and hopped down landing on a layer of snow below. She pressed against the house and peeked around the corner. As suspected, a black car was pulling off the road after crossing the bridge.

Piper glanced around the corner. "What are you looking at?"

Car doors closed with a bang like a gunshot. Drew pulled her back. "Hurry before they see us!" She nodded to Nico. "This way."

Drew was the reason they were here. If anything happened to them, she'd never forgive herself. She cut through dead grass bristling up out of the snow. Water surged over jagged rocks cascading below as she led them around the lighthouse; she was counting on being hidden by the lighthouse from whoever was tracking her.

Piper yelled as she skidded down wet rocks. Nico reached out and grabbed Piper's hands, pulling her back in step. Gasping, Piper gave her a thumbs up.

Nico stood pointed across a rocky field. "Through the trees over there?"

Drew motioned to a shed. The roof sagged in on one side, but it was big enough to conceal them. "We stop there first. Make sure no one is watching."

They raced for the shed and hunkered down behind it. This position gave her a partial view of the house. The bald man from the night before kicked the front door. Another man looked in the windows. She gestured for everyone to get low and wait. Nico huddled beside her, watching. The thumping in her head skipped beats and she couldn't catch her breath. She glanced at the sanctuary of trees ahead and back to the bald man. They had to make it to Nico's truck and get the hell away.

The bald man pulled out a gun and shot at the door. She jumped and Piper squealed, but the surf breaking over the rocks drowned out the sound. The men kicked in the door and stormed inside the house.

This was their chance. Drew signaled toward the trees before rising from behind the shed, breaking away for the forest path. Piper held pace with her, and Nico was right behind. As they made it to the concealment of the trees, she stopped to catch her breath—head pounding. She tried not to throw up.

"Who the hell are those men?" Piper coughed on her words. "And why do they have guns?"

"We're almost there. Keep going, okay? I promise I'll tell you later."

They raced through the woods of Haven toward the field where the truck would be waiting. It wouldn't be long before the men realized she was gone, and they'd come looking for her. The 'DeSarro and Sons' logo came into view on the tow truck as she scaled the hill. It was sweet relief as she got to the top. *Just a few more steps!* Her head pounded with a vengeance and her stomach hurt.

Don't pass out. Not here.

"Get in!" Nico said, firing up the truck. She and Piper climbed up beside him, shutting the door as he pulled onto the road. They turned a corner and drove past the black sedan and over the bridge, the house disappearing from view. She hoped they'd made it unseen.

Nico slowed down by her car in the ditch. "Do we pick up your car? Who's after us? Drew?"

"Don't stop. Keep going," she said and cringed at the thought of leaving Gran's car. She'd seen what Dominic was capable of. Getting back to town and away from Neptune Point was a priority.

"You can't just leave the car," Nico said. "What are you going to do?"

"I'll have to come back."

There were going to be questions, not that she blamed them. If the roles were reversed, *she* would demand to know too. When she'd started the day exploring Neptune Point, she never dreamed it would have turned into such a shit show. She mused how little information she could get away with telling them to appease but keep them from getting any more involved. Piper would say they were already ass deep, and maybe she was right.

"What do we do now? Go home and act like nothing happened? The police?" Piper asked.

Drew turned to look out the window. "I don't think they're following us, but we can't go home yet. Just in case."

"You want to tell me who those guys were and why they had guns?" Nico asked.

"I don't know who they are." This, at least, was honest. "Not exactly."

"But you knew to run from them," he said.

Drew squirmed in her seat. She didn't know where

to start. A man who had his hand in businesses all over town, not to mention was adored by the community, had it out for her. He was a criminal and evidence of that was all over those documents—and he knew she'd seen them. She knew that Shane was alive. His betrayal cut her deep, but she had to shove that anger down and find him. She knew that Shane's mother had been murdered. Piper was her best friend and it had taken her years to tell her that she could see what others couldn't, but how did she explain that to Nico? She didn't want to let him in just to lose him. Although, if he let it affect…whatever they were, maybe he was never really with her to start with. It would be a good test of trust. But at what cost?

"I'm not exactly an average person with regular problems, Nico."

"That much, I gathered. It's one of the many reasons why I like you so much." He glanced at her and back to the road. "But, what about the rest? What the hell is going on? We've known each other a long time. You know you can trust me. What are you so worried about?"

"You," she admitted. "What you'll think of me. Or that you'll talk, and something terrible will happen to my family or friends."

"I'd never do anything to put you or your family at risk. Jesus, Drew." His eyes darted to her again and back to the road. "I just want to find out why a couple of guys with guns were following you. Why would they want to hurt you?"

She touched her bruised face. She had to make sure

if she told them about Dominic that they wouldn't go to the police or let something slip around Claudia. She didn't doubt Piper's loyalty, and she knew she could trust Nico; she was just terrified they might go to the police and send Dominic into a rage.

She chose her words carefully. "Last night I found out some…things about a powerful man. Those two men work for him, and they'll do whatever it takes to keep me quiet."

"Like what? *Kill* you?" Piper said. "Who would do such a thing? You have to go to the police, Drew!"

"I can't and neither can you! He'll find out and do something horrible! He's warned me; if I say anything to anyone, he will hurt my family, my friends. Do you understand? That's the reason I didn't want to tell anyone." Tears burned her eyes. She was stuck and regretted ever asking for help. This was a nightmare! "You both must promise me that you won't breathe a word. Not one! I need to know that I can trust you with this."

Piper watched her intently, twirling pink hair around her finger so tight it cut off circulation leaving her finger pale. She released her hair and slapped her hands on her lap. "Okay. I don't like it, but I promise I won't say anything to anyone. Not yet. But I want to know who this guy is and if anything happens to you, I won't just sit back in silence."

"I've got this, Piper. I promise." She eyed Nico who was staring ahead at the road with a death grip on the wheel. His jaw tightened and he blinked faster than usual. Drew worried she'd made a mistake and already said too much. "What about you? Can you keep quiet? I'm so close to finding something I can take to the police, but if I go now, he'll have time to react, and I can't take that chance."

"Who's threatening you?" he said. "Look. You have my word; I won't say anything. But I'm with Piper. If someone tries to hurt you—" He took his eyes off the road to look at her and the truck veered off to the shoulder and back again. "Your face! The blood from last night! Where did you go, *really*? Did one of those guys hit you?"

She touched her bruised cheek. "Yes, but I'm okay—"

"Holy shit, Drew. You are clearly not okay." Piper observed Drew's face. "Who the hell did this to you? Was it those men back there? You said you were at the shipyard last night—"

"I was—"

"How—how in danger are you?" Piper turned in the seat to look out the window behind them. "Who's following us? Does this have to do with Shane? If he's alive, his father must be—"

"He doesn't know." Drew had to cut her off. The questions were spiraling. "As far as I know, the police don't either. That's what I'm trying to tell you. We can't go to the police yet. He'll find out—"

"What?" Nico shook his head. "Who will find out? And how can Shane's father not know his son's alive?"

Drew looked at her hands. It hadn't occurred to her to tell Shane's dad. Nico had a point. That poor man deserved to know, but she didn't want to put him in danger too.

"Gabe only told me last night," she muttered. "I…I've just got to find Shane. Find out what he knows about…" *Dominic Sloan.*

"Why didn't Gabe show the police that picture? Let them handle this! He's a piece of work, isn't he? Did he not realize he's putting his daughter at risk?" Nico brushed his hair back with his fingers. "Sorry. I know he's your father, but man…"

Drew had never seen him so pissed before. She spoke softly. "He's trying to get back into my life and thought by telling me about Shane he'd be able to…I don't know…swoop in and prove himself worthy or something."

Nico shot her a sideways glance. "Drew, if Shane's alive, people need to know about it. You've got to tell his father."

She shook her head. "I can't do that. Not yet. Paxton isn't Shane's biological father—"

"What does that matter? He's his dad—" Nico said, stunned.

"I know. You're right. But the man…the powerful man I told you about…he's Shane's real father." She reached over and touched his arm. "He's the man who killed Shane's mom. I think it all has something to do with why Shane left."

Nico pulled on the wheel, swerving into the parking lot behind the Book Nook. He turned to face her. "How do you know that? Drew, what happened? The guy who hit you and has men following you is a *murderer*? Who? Tell me who this person is!"

"Last night," she started, "I did go to the shipyard. I was trying to find information on the boat Shane was on. The *Light of Aurora*. The part I left out was…I followed those men into one of the buildings. I thought they left so I snuck into an office." She glanced over her shoulder at Piper. Drew almost mentioned Enid but wasn't ready to bring up the whole 'I see dead people' in front of Nico just yet. "They came back and found me. The man who hit me—he embodies darkness but hides it so well. No one would ever guess! It's terrifying. It's Dominic Sloan. He's got this whole town fooled, but I'm going to bring him down."

Nineteen

Nico turned the engine off. They faced the back of the building that held the Book Nook and Maze Café where smoke poured from a metal pipe sticking out of the roof. A woman threw a bag of trash into a bin and flicked a cigarette before going back inside the rear door.

Nico took the keys out of the ignition and spun them on his finger before gripping them in a fist. "He's a murderer," he whispered.

"Claudia's father," Piper said. She sat wide-eyed staring out the front window. "I *knew* there was something off about him with that fake smile plastered all over the news. So, he's Shane's real father?"

Drew nodded. "I believe so. No. I know so."

Piper squinted intently. "How can you be so sure?"

"Because he killed Shane's mom," Drew said, her irritation growing. Not with Piper, but with this—all of this! She looked at Piper. "Iris. Her name was Iris."

A knowing look crossed Piper's face. She hadn't forgotten the name from their conversation in her bedroom. "Maybe it's time you went to the police. What about that detective?"

"And say what? I have zero proof! It's my word against his and if he finds out that I'm talking…" She shook her head. Nobody knew what he was capable of! "No police. Not yet."

Drew turned her attention to Nico. Why wasn't he saying anything? He probably thought she was crazy. She was half-ready to believe it herself. "Nico, I'll understand if you want to walk away—"

He leaned on the steering wheel staring ahead. "I want in."

"Wait," Drew said, holding her hands up. "I don't want either of you to get sucked into all this. If it weren't for those two men at the Point, I wouldn't have told you in the first place."

But Nico only shook his head, his eyes full of a fierceness she'd never seen in him before.

"That asshole has been controlling my dad's business for the past two years. I had to keep my mouth shut. Dad had a choice: accept Dominic's help or let the business go under. Just like everyone else in this town, he had no idea who that man really is. One night I overheard them arguing—they didn't know I was outside—and I saw him burn dad with a welding iron. I'm still mad at myself for not stepping in. But I'm done being weak. He's using my family's business to hide behind, and I want to help you take him down."

"I had no idea," Drew said. "I don't know what to say."

"Say yes, and let's do this together."

"No. No, it's too risky. I can't let you or Piper be a part of this—"

"You're not *letting* me do anything. I'm ready to tackle him myself." Nico balled his hands into fists like a boxer. "Come on, let me help you."

"If Dominic finds out that you know…Nico, your family would be in trouble."

"No more than they already are. I have to do this," he said.

Piper unbuckled her seatbelt and faced Drew. "My parents are both lawyers. Why not let me talk to them?"

"No. Keep this between us, please!" Drew rubbed her neck trying to relieve the persistent headache. She had to keep them out of danger, but maybe they could help her. "If we're working together, it's on my terms. No one talks to anybody."

"Alright. Count me in." Piper smiled her 'ready for anything' smile.

Drew turned back to Nico. "Deal?"

"Sure. Deal." Nico reached his hand out and Drew took it.

Nico let his hand linger before pulling away. His warmth reached beyond her hand like electricity. The way he looked at her was magnetic. His eyes held hers. He *saw* her; the messy, the pain, and the softness beneath it all.

"Um. I hate to break this up," Piper interjected, "but I'm like pass-out starving. Can we finish this conversation inside over some food?"

When Nico smiled at her, she thought of the kiss. Alone time with him again wouldn't be terrible either.

"Sure. Let's go."

String lights zig-zagged and swayed above the

walkway as they hurried from the back parking lot to the front of the building. Drew scanned the road but there was no sign of the black sedan. She opened the door under a sign in the shape of an open book that read The Book Nook in gold lettering.

Inside, the connected Maze café was bustling with activity—typical for a Friday night. It was also the reason Drew had avoided coming here since Shane's death. No, his disappearance. She'd gotten so used to thinking of life with Shane before and after his death, but that wasn't the case anymore.

She led Piper and Nico to a table at the back of the room. Being inside Maze and seeing the painting on the wall again triggered memories of Shane. It was inevitable that they would meet again, but her feelings were different now. How could they not be? She'd trusted him with everything, and he left her.

She also couldn't ignore her growing attraction for Nico. Finding Shane was important because she needed answers and closure, but nothing he said to her could fix what he'd done.

She sat in a booth beside Piper with Nico across from them. After a waiter took their order, Drew excused herself and headed to the bathroom. She splashed water on her face and stared in the mirror waiting for a message that never came. She wondered if Iris's body was somewhere at Neptune Point, and if she'd be able to find her, even with Enid's help. What would Iris look like? Seeing a dead body wasn't something she'd ever experienced before, only the ghosts left behind.

She patted her face dry with dispenser paper towel. If it weren't for the bruise across her cheek, she almost looked like herself again. Her skin was healing; the scab had fallen off the cut above her lip. It might leave a scar but would blend easy enough, and it didn't bother her like it might have in the past.

One of the stalls opened. Shoes clicked on the tiled floor.

Claudia.

Drew frowned. Maybe if she was nice to her, befriended her even, maybe she'd find a way into that house. Her father had to have more information hidden there.

Claudia tightened her belt over a sweater dress. She looked up and their eyes met in the mirror. Claudia smirked. "Take a picture. It'll last longer."

Drew closed her mouth. So much for friendship—or fake friendship, in her case.

Claudia crossed her arms. "Well? What are you doing here anyway?"

"It's a bathroom, Claudia. Figure it out."

Claudia's scrunched her nose up making a face. "What happened to your face?"

Drew touched the bruises. "Car accident."

Claudia looked her up and down. "Wasn't that a week ago? I have make-up that will cover that up if you want."

Claudia didn't wait, opening her purse and taking out her makeup kit. Stepping closer, she set to figuring out how to tackle the challenges of Drew's face. For some reason, Drew let her. "Are you ever coming back to school?" she asked while she worked to cover the bruises.

"Since when do you care?"

Claudia stood with her hands on her hips. "You know, you could be a little nicer. I'm trying to help you. You're the one who started all this when you went after my dad."

Claudia's *dad*. The man who also fathered Shane. Drew was beside his sister, and she had no idea she even had a brother. Their father made Gabe look like a Saint! The anger inside her simmered to pity.

"I'll be back next week." Drew pulled away from Claudia and tossed the bunched-up paper towel in the garbage before turning to leave.

"I saw Piper and Nico," Claudia said. Drew stopped and turned back. "I thought she was with that doctor's son."

"She is."

"I see." Claudia's jaw dropped as if putting the pieces together. "Oh my God! Are *you* here with Nico?"

"No, not really. What do you care?"

"I don't. I'm just making conversation. Nico's a good guy."

Claudia was being nice, but Drew couldn't tell if it was genuine. "He is. We're just friends."

"For now." Claudia adjusted her belt again. "Maybe I'll stop by and say hi."

"Sure. Bye Claudia." Drew pushed the door open and walked out. She arrived at the table and sat down just as the food arrived.

"Do you think it's safe to go home?" Piper popped a fry in her mouth.

"If they didn't see Nico's truck. They'll assume it was just me out there. It's good we came here first."

"Will it be safe for you to go home?" Nico asked.

"I don't know. Gran might make things difficult. Once she finds out I put her car in a ditch and left it there..."

"It's not funny," Nico said. "They had guns."

"I'm not laughing. Look, I'll be fine. They aren't going to show up at my door and start shooting." The pep talk was for her benefit as much as Nico's. But those men did *not* want the spotlight and if they killed her, that's exactly what they'd get.

"So, what should we do next?" Nico asked.

It was a good question—one she was still trying to figure out. She didn't think Nico or Piper would like the only idea she had come up with. "I want to get inside Claudia's house and poke around for a key to that safe."

"How are you going to do that? She doesn't like you. Or me for that matter," Piper said. "Have you thought of the fact that if Dominic Sloan is Shane's father, that makes Claudia—"

"What are you saying about me?"

Claudia strolled up to their table. She didn't wait for an invitation, just slid in beside Nico forcing him to scoot over. She crossed her long legs to the side and propped her chin on a hand as she gazed at him. "I saw your dad's tow truck pull around back. Who did you rescue this time?"

Drew leveled a glare at her. She knew the nice girl

act wouldn't last long. "Go away, Claudia."

Claudia tossed fringes of hair out of her face, nonplussed. "You ran out of the bathroom so fast we didn't get a chance to finish our conversation. Or your makeup. You sure you don't want some concealer for that—"

"I have nothing else to say."

"I don't see your entourage anywhere," Piper said. "Did they finally realize how horrible their leader is and left without you?"

"They're well-trained," Claudia said. "They're smart enough to know when I need them and when to leave me alone." She eyed Piper's plate of fries, smothered with gravy and cheese, unimpressed. "Eating healthy, I see. Your mother won't be impressed when you can't fit into your prom dress."

Piper stood with her palms flat on the table. "Your mother won't be impressed when you can't show your face in public."

Drew put what she hoped was a calming hand on Piper's arm, easing her back down.

If Claudia was bothered, she didn't show it. She sat back stretching her legs out and crossing her arms. "Oh, relax. I'm just kidding. Our mothers are assholes. There's no pleasing them."

"Leave me and my mother out of this, or else—" Piper's hands balled into fists, and she held her stance.

"Or else what? You'll punch me? We aren't children." Claudia beamed a flawless smile. "Like it or not, our families are the same. It's all privileged bullshit."

Claudia picked up a fry. She examined it and nibbled it like a baby bird eating for the first time. "Anyone up for Haven tomorrow night? My father bought the property so you could say it's mine now."

Drew watched Claudia with a new perspective. All the beauty and attitude in the world couldn't detract from the loneliness hidden in that girl's eyes. She recognized it all too well; it might be the one thing she and Claudia had in common.

"Sounds like fun," Drew said. "I'll go."

"I'm happy to hear that. See what civility can do. Look at us." Claudia's smile could grow icicles.

She could feel Piper and Nico gawking at her, but she didn't dare look at them or she'd break concentration. It took every ounce of focus to make nice with Claudia.

"Why does your dad have interest in the property at Neptune Point anyway?" Drew asked as casually as she could.

Claudia plucked another fry, this time with more vigor.

"He owns lots of property. What does it matter to you?" Claudia shoved the plate and folded her arms. "You're inquisitive suddenly. What gives? Are you back on the bag thing?"

"That bag was nothing. I'm just making conversation. Trying to be nicer. Forget I asked."

Drew stood and put her jacket on. She gathered her things and shot a look at Nico and Piper. "I'm ready to leave when you are."

"I was ready five minutes ago," Piper smirked,

getting up.

"You're leaving already?" Claudia swung her legs out of the booth. She wasn't the type to be the last one sitting; she dismissed others, not the other way around. "Whatever. My friends are waiting. I'm out of here. I'll see you tomorrow. Don't forget!"

She sashayed away with her ponytail swinging.

"That was weird," Piper remarked.

"It was something!" Drew said. Though she couldn't figure out what exactly had just happened... Claudia was playing at something.

Just another mystery...

Nico got up and jingled his keys. "Ready?"

"You're going to make friends with her, aren't you?" Piper made that face she did when something grossed her out. "I can't believe she's Shane's sister. Both of their mothers had to be pregnant at the same time! They're close in age."

"Shane's a year older. He was behind in school, remember?" Drew shrugged. "And yes, I'm going to try and make friends with her. It's the only way inside that house."

Drew weaved through tables following Piper to the door. Laughter chimed around them, and soft music played through speakers. A few people waved at Nico, but he didn't leave them to chat. His hand reached for Drew's, linking their fingers. A flash of heat rushed to her face, but she didn't let go. She passed by the painting still hanging above the mantel. Nico was holding the rope, keeping her from falling like the swing in the painting.

The warm air from Maze fogged as it hit the cold outside. Dusk settled around them. Drew pulled her hood up as she stepped onto the slushy sidewalk, and they walked together back to the truck.

"Look!" Piper pointed to a black car at the other end of the parking lot. "Is that the same car?"

"Yup." Drew opened the passenger side door and climbed in, waving to Piper. "Get in!" They'd been followed.

Nico put the keys in the ignition. Instead of starting it, he pointed out the window. "They're getting out."

The bald man stepped out, tucking in his shirt before zipping his leather jacket.

"Get down!" Drew gripped Piper's arm, holding her below the dash.

"I'm not getting up. You can let go."

Crouching low, Nico pressed a button and the doors locked. "This truck isn't exactly discreet. There's no way they'll miss us. Let's just get the hell out of here."

Drew stopped him from turning the key. She watched as the men scrutinized the area. "Wait. I don't think they know we're here."

"What are they doing?" Piper lifted her head, trying to see.

The other man yelled something, and they marched around the other side of the building out of sight.

"Nico, start the truck. Go!"

He brought the engine to life and reversed. The truck beeped. Drew held her eyes on the sedan, hoping they didn't return. Nico went forward and pulled onto the street.

"What do we do now?" Piper sat up in the seat and hugged herself.

"We all go home." Drew turned Piper by the shoulders to face her. "Lock your doors and keep your phone close. I don't think they saw you or Nico today."

"How else did they know we were here?" Piper said.

Drew released her. "I don't know."

The truck rumbled and turned into Marble Gates Estates toward Piper's house. She hugged Drew before running inside. As they drove out of the neighborhood, they passed Claudia's house. It was dark except for a few lights in the upstairs windows.

Was Dominic in there now? Was anyone?

Nico caught her staring out the window. "Want to drop by for a visit?"

"Don't tempt me. I'm sure it's alarmed with cameras everywhere, but I'll get in there. Don't worry."

"That's the problem," he said, "I *am* worried."

Nico headed along the coast for home. He pulled into her driveway where an unfamiliar silver hatchback was parked. It could be Gabe's—unless Gran was so mad, she took the car without asking that she went out and bought a new one. But that seemed unlikely.

Nico sighed. "I'll go get the car in the morning. If anything happens in the meantime, don't text, *call*. We need a plan."

"You're not going alone! I'll go with you."

He faced her and the worry in his eyes made him look much older than he was. "It's not a big deal. I'll go pick it up and look it over in the shop. Once I find out what's wrong with it, I'll let you know, and we can take it from there."

"What if they follow you? Or…I don't know, put a bomb in it or something!"

He smiled that cute half smile that he did. "A bomb? Drew, I think it'll be okay."

He looked at her with such intensity that her skin tingled. He'd grown a lot from the Nico she used to know years ago. He brought passion to everything he did. Surfing. Fixing cars. *Her*. She reached out, closing the gap between them, and wrapped her arms around him. He dropped his arms from the steering wheel and returned her embrace. The barricade she'd put up after Shane's disappearance was crumbling a little every time Nico hugged or touched her…or kissed her.

She had to tell him. If this was going to work, he had to know her. The real Drew. If he couldn't handle it, she'd have no choice but to walk away.

She pulled back to face him. "There is one more thing you should know—about me."

"That doesn't sound good." He exhaled.

"When I told you that Shane's mom was murdered, I left out *how* I know." She took a deep breath. His eyebrows knitted together. She couldn't believe she was about to tell him.

He leaned an arm on the steering wheel as he looked at her. "Did you find something in that basement tunnel?"

"No, that's not it. Um…the thing is—you're going to think this is a little…a lot…out there." She couldn't say it.

"Drew," Nico said. "Just say it. I don't care what it is."

"I can see people after they die." She said it quickly, in a rush. Like pulling off a Band-Aid. "The reason I know about Iris—Shane's mother—is because she visits me. Yes, I realize how completely insane I sound right now!" She covered her face with both hands.

"Which is why you can't go to the police." His voice was quiet.

Drew dropped her hands and nodded, waiting for his reaction. The car was warm. Too warm. She reached out and turned the heat down. The engine rumbled in a steady hum. She sat back in the seat and stared ahead out the window. The sky had darkened, and a hint of stars cascaded through a mist of clouds.

"What do they look like—the dead people?" He finally spoke.

She hadn't been quite prepared for him to understand. Not this easily.

"Not like they used to. They *used* to look like a mist—like shadows. But these days, they're more real. Human-looking. And now they talk."

Drew waited, watching his expression, waiting for the inevitable *widening of the eyes.* The telltale *backing away from the crazy girl.* But it didn't come.

"Drew, did I ever tell you the reason we have a blue door?"

She shook her head, not having a clue.

"My mom did it to keep spirits away. I don't

know…it's supposed to look like water or something. She's superstitious and I don't think anything of it. I don't know what happens after we die, but if you can see even a little part of that…you've got a gift, Drew."

"You don't think I'm weird? You don't think this is all crazy and terrifying?"

"Maybe I'm the crazy one. But Dominic Sloan scares me more—and he's alive. I've known you for a long time. I've always thought you were awesome. I'm not going anywhere."

She cupped his cheeks with her hands and moved in close until their noses touched. She craved the connection building between them; there was such an ease about it. His lips met hers. This time their kiss was deeper than before, in tune with each other in a slow rhythm. She wished she could stop time and live in this moment for a while. His fingers curled in her hair and her hands slid from his face to around his neck. She didn't want it to end. The world was waiting to pounce as soon as she broke away from him…

But of course, it had to end.

And when she opened the door, cold air rushed in, clearing condensation off the windows. She grabbed her bag and hopped out of the truck onto the snow-packed driveway. Nico waited for her to get inside before driving away. She leaned on the door and closed her eyes.

Twenty

Drew hung her jacket on the hook and kicked off her boots.

"Drew?"

She followed Gran's voice to the kitchen, racking her brain for the best way to apologize.

Gran leaned on the counter and tightened her robe. "If you needed my car so bad, you could've just asked. Don't do that again."

"I'm sorry. How mad are you? Or is that even a question I should be asking right now."

"Oh, I was angry this morning. I had things to do, and you would've known that if you'd asked first." Gran put her cup in the sink. "Your father picked me up. He was helpful if you can believe it."

She didn't believe it. Helpful wasn't an adjective she'd choose for Gabe. "He hasn't left town yet?"

Gran started washing the few dishes in the sink. "He's working at the shipyard. Says he's not going anywhere for a while." She peeked over her shoulder at Drew. "Did you see the car in the driveway?"

Drew grabbed a towel and dried the dishes as Gran placed them on the rack. "I saw it. Whose is it?"

"Yours. He got it for you. Took care of the paperwork today. Even had it insured."

"Why would he do that? I don't need—"

"Yes, you do need his help. I need it. He's trying, so let him. Okay?" Gran took the towel from Drew and dried her hands.

She still had to drop the bad news. Gran wasn't going to like it. "Your car broke down. It's in a ditch but Nico's going to use his dad's tow truck to pick it up in the morning. He'll bring it to the shop, and I'll pay for the repairs. I know I should've called, and I'm sorry."

Gran sighed. "Were you hurt?"

"No. I'm fine."

"Alright then," Gran said. "I don't want you running all over town trying to find a guy who cares so little about you that he'd let you think he died. Let him go, I say. He doesn't deserve you."

Her words stung, but Drew knew she didn't intend to hurt.

Gran eyed her. "Thank Nico for me. Let me know what I owe him."

"Like I said, I'll take care of it. It was my fault for taking it in the first place."

"We'll talk about it later. I'm too tired tonight." Gran pointed to a set of keys on the counter. "Those are for your car. Please, give him a chance. Talk to him, Drew." She limped out of the room and turned back. "A woman called for you today. She left a voice mail with her name and number. I saved it for you… I'm going to bed. Goodnight." She hobbled upstairs.

Drew picked up the keys. If Gabe thought he could buy his way back into her life he was wrong.

She hated how much she needed this car.

Picking up the house phone, she listened to the message. She expected the insurance company, or maybe it was her mother trying to reach her again. Instead, Detective Valerie Porter's voice spoke with a vague message asking her to drop by and see her.

Drew deleted the message and hung up. Going to the police while she was being watched would be too risky.

***

Drew finished her first shift back at the Casting Spoon in over a week. With November in full swing, the chaos of the holidays was only beginning. The packed restaurant looked like Christmas had thrown up on it with boughs decorated with holly and lights hanging everywhere. It all had always depressed her. She couldn't wait until it was over.

But she was now in debt to Gabe and wasn't having it. She'd have to pick up extra shifts, give him the insurance money—anything to pay him back. Owing him money made her sick to her stomach.

There were a million places she would rather be than here, the house at Neptune Point being one of them—it was where she'd be headed as soon as she finished work. Regardless of where Shane was, or why he left, she had to find clues to what happened to Iris.

Her phone buzzed in her pocket, and she peeked at

it on a quick break. Nico picked up Gran's car without any bombs going off, and as far as he could tell, no one followed him.

She missed two calls from Detective Porter. She had no idea how the detective got her cell number. Ignoring them, she shoved her phone back in her pocket. A debate rolled around in her head: part of her wanted to know why the detective kept calling her, but the other part was scared to go anywhere near the station. If she told Detective Porter about Dominic's threats disclosing what she knew, would he find out? She couldn't take the chance. She brushed it away and set to work finishing up her shift.

The last hour crawled. Drew stacked trays and reset her tables, counting down the last few minutes until it was time to leave. She had to step out of the way as the door to the private room opened and the headwaiter—whose name was Jonathan, but everyone called him Nate—exited. As it swung closed, she glimpsed inside. Three men sat eating and laughing with Dominic Sloan at the head of the table. The sound of blood pumping swished in her ears. Her mouth went dry, and she poured a glass of water, chugging it like she had just run a marathon.

Seeing his smug face turned her panic into rage. Any practical thoughts left, leaving her with desperation for revenge. Her sweaty palms balled into fists. She slammed the glass on a tray and stormed into the room without a plan.

All three looked up from their meals with smirks on their faces. Two of them were the men who had been following her. And—sitting just out of her view—was none other than Claudia, along with a woman who had to be her mother.

Seeing Claudia threw her off and she lost her nerve.

"Can we help you?" Dominic scowled at her. Blood gushed from the steak on his plate as he sliced into it with expert precision. *Too* expert, like he'd done it a million times before in a million different ways.

"Daddy, this is Drew Harlow. She's the girl you met in the driveway. She's a friend of mine." Claudia's matter-of-fact tone made it sound true.

She wondered if this changed things for him—for her. If his daughter considered her a friend, would he still threaten her? Or would he back off?

He placed his fork and knife on the plate in perfect parallel and sat back in the chair. "It's coming back to me." He shook his glass. "While you're here, would you be so kind?"

She cringed and stood frozen in place. The other men chuckled.

Dominic glared at her. She couldn't let him see the fear creeping back in. Picking up the water jug with trembling hands, she filled his glass. What she wanted to do was dump it on him. As he sipped the water, she noticed the rings on his fingers and touched her cheek. She could almost feel them striking her all over again.

"Doesn't your family own the bakery by the boardwalk?" The woman with cranberry red lips matching her fingernails spoke, enunciating each word. She had to be Claudia's mother; they had the same fake smile.

"Um…yes. Sort of." Drew glanced at Dominic careful not to say too much. She couldn't let anything happen to Gran or Nellie.

"Sort of?" The woman chuckled.

"My grandmother owns it, but she doesn't work as much as she used to."

"Well, it is wonderful to see a local business stand the test of time. Do pass along my well wishes." This woman could've been cast in the Stepford Wives. They all deserved best actor awards, except instead of film, this was real life.

"I've got to go." Drew turned to leave. Being in this room was suffocating.

"See you later?" Claudia called from behind her, but she pushed the swinging door and exited as fast as she could. She'd agreed to go to Haven, and Nico and Piper were going to join her. She hoped Enid was able to come through for her and find Iris. Being friendly with Claudia was all part of the big plan—and it could fall apart at any moment.

Seeing Dominic with his family, sitting there like a king on his throne, sickened her. She rushed for the back room, untying her apron as she went. She changed out of her uniform and threw on her jacket. She left without talking to anyone. When she got to her car, she couldn't find her keys. She'd left her backpack behind.

Shit.

As she opened the door to run back inside, she almost slammed into Dominic Sloan. He held up her backpack. "Forget something?"

How did he do that? She snatched it from him taking steps backward. "Don't touch me!"

He put his hands up. "You're paranoid."

She backed up gripping her backpack. "You're psychotic! I'll scream!"

He looked around. "Go for it. I haven't done anything to you."

"You hit me! You threatened my family!"

Dishes clanged together from the kitchen inside. All it would take is for her to scream and someone would come running.

As if he sensed her thoughts, he let the door close behind him. "I have done no such thing." His voice was calm. Too calm. "No one will believe your accusations." He crossed his arms.

"Why did you follow me outside? What do you want!"

"You're friends with my daughter," he said.

"I'm not sure *friend* is the word you're looking for." She stole a glance behind her and saw her car parked. If she had her keys in hand, she'd run.

"Is it more like your relationship with Mr. DeSarro's son? Or the Arlott girl?" She'd been wrong. He did know of them.

"They don't know anything. Not unlike your daughter."

He shifted his crossed arms to reach up and hold his chin with a bent forefinger and thumb, not taking his eyes off her. "Why were you at Neptune Point yesterday?"

His gaze bore through her, and she couldn't help

but break eye contact. "My car broke down," she said.

"Not the answer I was looking for. Stay off that property or next time, I'll have you charged with trespassing. Or I'll just take matters into my own hands."

Anger returned with a vengeance, and she found some courage buried deep. "I know that Shane is your son."

"You know nothing," he seethed.

"Where is he? If you just tell me how I can reach him—"

"He wants nothing to do with you. You hear me?" He punched a fist into his other hand. "If you don't let this go, my hand will be forced. This will be on *you.* Remember that."

He straightened his suit jacket and went back inside. She stood in the cold shivering. What did he mean by that? His hand would be *forced*. She wondered how far his limits could go. If she pushed him enough, maybe he'd incriminate himself.

Shaking, she found her keys as she ran to her car and started to drive to Neptune Point. She'd get there before anyone else arrived and explore the underground tunnel. It terrified her, but she had to do it. She even packed a flashlight and extra batteries she'd found in a kitchen junk drawer. Her cell rang again.

Private number. It continued to ring as she hesitated. Assuming it was the detective, she wasn't sure what to say, or why Detective Porter was so determined to get hold of her.

"Hello?" Drew answered over Bluetooth.

"Hello, Drew?"

"Yes."

"Hi. This is Valerie Porter calling. I've been trying to get in contact with you since last night. Can you come to the station? I just need about half an hour of your time."

"What's this about?"

"New information has come to my attention. I might need your help."

"Look, I can't help you with something I know nothing about—"

"Please. It's about Shane's disappearance. It's important that I talk to you."

Drew peered in her rear-view mirror. Dominic and his men were back at the restaurant. How would they ever know? She could just go and hear the woman out. Besides, she had to admit she wanted to know what new information she was talking about.

"I'll be there soon," she said and hung up before Detective Porter could respond.

She swerved around toward the police station, driving down alleys to avoid being followed. She parked close to the building between two large vehicles and went inside, looking over her shoulder the entire time. She asked for Detective Porter at the window in the lobby and waited for what seemed like forever. Shifting in the orange plastic seat, she watched out the window. If Dominic had her followed and saw her here, he'd lose it.

Detective Porter opened the locked door and smiled at her. "Thanks for coming."

Drew followed her to an office. Certificates were framed on the wall with Valerie Porter's name on them, and a small photo with two young children had been pinned on a corkboard. It was different than the impersonal interrogation room from last time.

Detective Porter took a seat behind a desk and gestured to a chair on the opposite side. "Please. Have a seat."

Drew obliged and sat down. She fidgeted with a button clasp on the cuff of her jacket. "Why did you call me here?"

Detective Porter opened a folder and handed her an ID card with a photo. "Do you recognize him?"

Drew stared at the ID. It was Shane without a doubt, but the name was Ezra Morana. There was that name again! Her mind raced. She wondered where Shane got this obviously fake ID, and why Ezra's name was on it. She contemplated if the kids in the photo could be related to Jack Morana and if somehow, Dominic Sloan was related to him too!

Detective Porter spoke softly. "Drew? Do you know something?"

"No. Just that it's Shane."

Detective Porter placed another photo of Shane on the table. "And this one?"

It was the same one her father had shown her on his phone, except printed on glossy paper. He must've given the photo to the police after he showed her.

Drew glanced at it. She'd spent enough time examining that picture and it was only a reminder that Shane left her when things got hard.

"Yup. It's him," she finally said. "Is that all you needed from me? I have to go."

Detective Porter sat back in her chair. Maybe she was waiting for a grand reaction. Tears. Screaming. Who knows? But Drew couldn't pretend if she tried.

"You knew, didn't you? Shane's alive and you knew about it."

"My father works at the shipyard." Drew pointed to the printed one on the desk. "He showed that one to me on his phone, but this is the first time I've seen the ID."

"What about the name on the ID? Ezra Morana. You said before you didn't know the name. What about now? Has anything changed? Any idea who Ezra could be?"

Drew looked up from the ID and met Detective Porter's intense eyes. She couldn't tell her that the Ezra she knew was a young ghost boy who died years ago. "I have no idea who Ezra Morana is. The bag belonged to Shane, didn't it?"

Detective Porter raised her eyebrows. "Maybe. Has he tried to contact you at all over the past ten months?"

"Not once." Drew rubbed the back of her neck. "I really don't have information for you. He left town and let me, and his own father, think he was dead. I want nothing to do with him."

Detective Porter gathered the photos and placed them back in the folder.

"Have you told Shane's dad?" Drew asked.

"He was my first call."

She thought of Paxton and wondered if he was relieved or even more tortured than ever.

"Is he okay?"

"He's in shock. Shaken up as anyone would be." Detective Porter folded her hands on the desk. "We're searching for Mr. Bishop's wife, Iris. If you hear anything at all, or if he does reach out to you, we need to know. Our priority is locating Shane to ensure his safety and question him about his mother."

"You think he had something to do with his mother's death? There's no way! He was devastated when she left. He always felt that something horrible happened to her."

"Death?" Detective Porter echoed, her eyebrows raising.

"What?"

"You said, 'his mother's death'. Why would you say that? Drew, I can't help you if you won't talk to me. Whatever it is, I can help."

"I didn't mean that. I just meant—after Shane…I just assumed she was dead. I thought *Shane* was dead until a few days ago. I don't know. Maybe she is alive."

Detective Porter examined her, holding eye contact until Drew looked away, adjusting her seat. She folded her arms.

Drew met her eyes again. "Look. I heard he was last seen on a boat called the *Light of Aurora*. Find that boat, and maybe you'll find him." The only reason Drew told her about the boat was for her own benefit. The police would have the resources to find it more than she ever would.

Detective Porter wrote on a notepad and clicked the pen a few times. "You're sure you've got nothing else to say?"

"I am."

"Alright. Same as before. You have my number. If you think of anything at all, I don't care if it's what color shoes he had on, call me. Any time, day, or night."

"I will."

She walked Drew back to the lobby. "Detective Porter—"

"Valerie."

"Valerie." Calling the detective by her first name felt weird. It was more personal or something, and Drew didn't want to make this personal or let her believe she trusted her for a second. "If you find that boat or Shane…can you let me know?"

"I thought you didn't want anything to do with him." Detective Porter held the door open.

"I don't," Drew said, "but I need to know what happened."

"I understand, but I can't promise anything. We'll talk soon."

Valerie shut the door, leaving her behind in the lobby. Two officers walked by and nodded as they used their badges to gain entry into the back room. She wondered if Dominic controlled someone in the department. He had eyes everywhere.

She sat in her car with the engine going. A van on one side and the brick wall of the building on the other concealed her from view. Seeing that ID with the name Ezra Morana made her think of the album.

She reached in her backpack and dug it out, running her fingers along the leather before opening the cover. Turning the pages, she examined each with more attention than before. Flipping further into the album, she discovered more photos. Standing on a wooden walkway between the lighthouse and the keeper's home was a smiling family. The rocky cliff bordered the picture with the caption 'Morana's Moving Day 1987'. A man leaned in behind Enid and Blythe, and a woman's gloved hands laid on Ezra's small shoulders. Her dark hair escaped from underneath a knitted hat and stuck to her face. Dominic leaned against the railing, away from them. She recognized the scowl on his face. It was becoming a fixture in her mind, and she hated it. *Ben Morana* had been scrawled on the back of the picture.

He became someone else. Was Blythe Wymond in contact with him?

More pictures followed capturing happy moments and holidays, until halfway through when it ended. Another newspaper clipping was tucked in a sleeve. Unfolding it with care so as not to rip it revealed side-by-side photos of Enid and Ezra. Beautiful words described their short lives—they were so young. An ache in her chest brought a lump to her throat. She read the entire obituary for details about their deaths but found nothing.

She thought of being inside the abandoned house, recalling the initials on the desk, E.M. Ezra—or Enid—Morana. The same as the old man, Jack Morana. They were all Morana's. A family who lived in the house by

Aurora at Neptune Point. Including Dominic. When—*why*—did he change his name?

Using her phone, she searched *Morana*. It turned up news of Jack Morana's death. He'd been found inside the house, alone, no foul play suspected. Another article dated 1989 was about a boating accident in a small Maine town that claimed the lives of two children. Enid and Ezra Morana.

The only other detail was the driver of the boat. Ben Morana, who survived the accident. A pit formed in her stomach like a rock. Had Ben—*Dominic* done something to cause it?

When she typed in Dominic Sloan, a ton of information popped up. All good and full of praise, but nothing about his childhood, or a previous life.

She tucked everything back inside the album and stuffed it in her backpack. She held the pocket watch. The map curved and wound its way from the lighthouse into the forest represented by tiny lines with dashes that looked like trees. At the end of the line, past the trees, was a circle. She wondered what the circle signified but wasn't going to make any big discovery sitting here. She had to go back to Neptune Point. Back in the tunnel. And this time she'd have to follow it through.

She left the station and headed through town toward the coast. Smoke filled the darkening sky. Emergency lights flashed and sirens wailed. She slowed and pulled off a side street and parked. The Tough Cookie was only one block away.

No. It can't be.

She raced out of the car to where a small crowd had

gathered across the street. Her nose stung from the pungent smell of sulfur. She looked up. The 'Tough' part of the sign swung and snapped before hitting the pavement and the charred roof gaped open. Firefighters aimed hoses at the flames escaping from the front window. Caution tape created a barrier around the burning building. She advanced to an ambulance a safe distance away and stopped when she saw Gran. She sat on a stretcher crying, with Nellie's arm around her.

There was only one explanation for this, and it was no accident.

She'd forced Dominic Sloan's hand—and now he'd forced hers. She'd have no other choice but to defend herself and her family.

Someone lurked in the shadows across the street. Old man Jack Morana emerged from an alley and looked with his vacant eyes from the burning building to her. The streetlamp shone on his face. And for the first time, she witnessed something she'd never seen in him before. Despair.

Twenty-One

Police tried to direct Drew away from the scene until she yelled.

"That's my grandmother! It's our bakery!" She leaned over the stretcher and eyed the paramedics. "Is she alright?"

"We're taking her to Silver Boulder hospital," a man in uniform told her.

Drew squeezed Gran's hand and kissed her forehead as she was wheeled inside the ambulance.

Nellie wrapped an arm around Drew hugging her close. "It'll be okay. She has to be. Don't worry," she said through tears. "It happened so fast. I got out and she was nowhere. I ran back inside and found her on the floor—" Nellie covered her mouth and started sobbing.

Drew called Gabe to tell him the news as she ran back to her car and sped to the hospital. She couldn't believe Dominic would target Gran. She had nothing to do with any of this!

***

By the time Drew arrived at the hospital and found Gran's room, Gabe was already at her bedside. Gran was awake and fidgeting with tubes in her nose. She wouldn't stop rehashing the events leading up to the fire— every item she touched, what was put in the oven and at what time, and when she smelled something burning before seeing smoke. The devastation of losing a business she'd spent her life building would take more than whatever pill the doctor prescribed to help her sleep.

Gran blamed herself but Drew knew better: Dominic caused that fire, and his tracks were probably buried so deep no one would ever know. He could've killed not only her grandmother, but innocent people, and he didn't care. This would be the last time he hurt someone she loved. She would make him pay for this.

Gabe looked up at her. "I've got to tell you something."

"I'm not sure if I can take any more news tonight, Gabe."

"I gave the picture to the police. A ship docked and I was assigned to the repairs. Someone handed me an ID card they found on board. I was just going to return it to the office until I saw who was in the photo. No one was around, and the computer was right there, unlocked. I searched for the boat, the *Light of Aurora*. Dominic Sloan owns it, but I couldn't find a damn thing more on it. It's like it fell off the Earth. Do you know Shane's using a fake name? *Ezra Morana*, whoever the hell that is. You can hate me all you want, but I'm still your father. This is dangerous, and I don't want you digging around. That's why I gave the police those pictures. I'm only trying to protect you, even if you want nothing to do with me. I thought you should know."

A month ago, she would've been enraged at him. She would have flown off the handle and yelled at him—how dare he interfere in her life? He had no business telling her what she could or couldn't do...but not tonight. She didn't scream at him or swear and tear him apart. He'd put more effort into being around Gran this past week than he had in years. She didn't trust it, but she couldn't leave Gran here alone. She needed him here.

"What do you know about Dominic Sloan?" she asked.

"Enough to know you can't get caught up in anything that man touches."

"Why doesn't anyone else see it?"

"People see what they want to see." Gabe shrugged. "He's a wealthy man who's made a lot of people very rich. Do you think they give a shit about how the money landed in their laps? I don't know what he's into but stay away from him."

If he only knew how deep she already was with Dominic. She had to find Iris and put an end to that man before it went too far and someone else died.

"Gabe, I'm not feeling so well. Would it be awful if I went home?"

"Go. I'll stay. Can you come back in the morning?"

She couldn't make any promises, but she didn't say that to him.

"I'll be here," she said instead.

Drew patted a sleeping Gran's hand before walking out of the room.

Her phone buzzed; it was the fifth message Claudia had sent in the past hour, always asking the same thing: when she'd be at Neptune Point, or more specifically— the party at Haven.

Drew stared at the screen. Claudia's sudden interest confused her.

She left the hospital and headed for Neptune Point. She tapped the steering wheel and blasted hot air to clear frost from the window. She'd go to Haven first to find out what Claudia wanted with her, but she wasn't going home until she walked the underground tunnel. Something was in there; there was no other reason why Iris and Enid would be down there.

She knew that Nico and Piper would join her if she asked. After the fire tonight it was assumed no one was going. But this was something she had to do alone. She couldn't put them at risk.

Her phone buzzed again, but the road was so desolate she didn't dare pull over to look. She kept driving instead. It was probably Claudia again.

This time the phone rang, echoing through the Bluetooth in the car, and she jumped.

She hit the answer button and Nico's voice filled the car.

"I think someone messed with the brake line. There are holes poked through it. I'd get it if it was all rusted or something, but someone did this. I heard about the fire tonight... Dominic's not letting up."

"Yeah." She wasn't surprised; the black sedan had been at her house the night before she crashed in the ditch. It was too coincidental. Dominic made it clear that he'd do anything to stop her. He was a master of intimidation, but she wouldn't back down. Couldn't back down.

"Where are you? Are you driving?" Nico asked.

She didn't want him to know she was going to meet up with Claudia after all. He'd want to come, and she needed to do this alone.

"Drew? Are you still there?" His voice shook.

"I'm still here. I'm on my way home from the hospital."

"How is she?" he said.

"She's alright. I don't know much other than that. Gabe is staying with her tonight."

"Do you want me to come over?" he asked.

"No, I'm tired. I'm just going to take a shower and go to bed." It was all a lie, but she had to protect him by keeping him away.

"I'll talk to you tomorrow," he said.

"Bye, Nico," she said before clicking the end button.

She made it to Neptune Point, leaving the main road for an off-road parking area just like she'd done many times before. Only this time was different. Everything had changed. Her life was in danger all the time now, and she was the only one who could fix it. She refused to let Dominic win.

Passing by a bunch of cars, she parked at the entrance to the clearing.

Haven.

It was an ironic name for a place that didn't feel safe. Not anymore. Music thumped from speakers and a fire blazed into the night sky. Those same flames offering warmth in one place could cause unbelievable destruction in another. The angry orange matched her insides. How could he destroy Gran's shop? A bakery of all things? He was sending a message to her—she couldn't let anyone else pay a price for her involvement in this.

Claudia wasn't difficult to spot. Her blond head tilted back as she laughed among a group of people gathered around her. Piper was wrong; her entourage was alive and well, following her around like a bunch of lost puppies.

She marched right up to her. "Sorry, I didn't get here sooner. I had a situation to deal with."

"What situation?"

"My grandmother's bakery caught fire. I assumed you knew."

Claudia's forehead creased. "How would I know? I've been here all evening."

"Oh, I don't know... Doesn't your family know everything?" Drew couldn't control herself. She almost started yelling at her. All the frustration she had towards Claudia's father was about to explode.

People were staring with tongues wagging like they expected a fight to break out between them.

Claudia rolled her eyes and grabbed Drew's arm, pulling her off to the side. "What's wrong with you? You look crazy!"

"Maybe because I am! You don't know me. Why have you been messaging me all night? Why the hell do you care whether I'm here or not?"

"Well, you came, didn't you? Maybe you're the one who cares more than you think."

"Christ! What's your deal? You walk around like you are daddy's princess—do you even know what kind of man he is?"

"How dare you say such a thing! I thought we could be friends for once, you know? That's why I messaged you. I've never lost anyone before, and I felt bad for being such a bitch to you about that stupid bag."

Drew inhaled the cold air into her lungs. It mixed with smoke from the fire and tasted like cedar. She coughed and cleared her throat. She had to calm down or she was going to ruin everything.

"I've had a really long day. I shouldn't have come here." Drew stepped to the side, ready to leave. A few people gawking at her by the fire looked away.

Claudia reached for her arm. "Don't leave. I'm bad at this—"

"Being nice stuff?"

"I was going to say, making friends stuff." Claudia laughed awkwardly.

"Oh, please," Drew said. "Look around. You're the popular girl surrounded by friends!" "They don't care about me. They only want what I can do for them. Something you can't

understand."

"Okay. I'm leaving." She already had enough of Claudia's 'poor me' story.

"That's not what I meant," Claudia said. "See? I suck at this."

"Just say it then! What do you want from me? What's the real reason you wanted me here?"

"I don't know. You were raised by your grandmother, without parents. I thought maybe I could talk to you about something."

"You're right, I come from a broken home. It's no wonder I can't understand anything you're going through." She imitated Claudia's tone. "You take every opportunity to throw your social status in my face. One minute you're yelling at me for being obsessive over your father, and the next you want to have a heart-to-heart. I don't get you at all."

"You can't understand because you're not like them. And your home situation is precisely why I want to talk to you. You don't care about image or what people think."

"You're right," Drew said again, "I don't. But I also don't enjoy listening to gossip you spread about me either."

Claudia sat on a fallen tree trunk. "I don't have anyone else to talk to. Not about this."

She looked pitiful. Or maybe it was just the light of the fire, the shadows cast. Drew plopped down beside her, sighing.

As if on cue, the enormous owl from before flew by and perched on a branch above her head. She scanned the forest expecting—hoping—to see Enid. The untamed slapping of river water swished beyond the tree line, but nothing happened. No Enid. Nothing.

Coming here was a waste of time. She should've gone back to the shipyard to dig through those documents or up the hill back to Aurora. Instead, she was sitting here feeling sorry for Claudia of all people.

Drew sighed and slumped. "Alright. What is it you want to talk about?"

"My father had an affair, and I don't know what to do."

Drew froze. She hadn't expected that. She didn't think Claudia had known— and if she did, she'd never dreamed for a second she'd tell her.

How much *did* she know?

"I was mad at him," Claudia said. "He's always so secretive about everything and all he cares about is what college I attend to make *him* look good. He did the same thing to my brother, and he's miserable. A few nights ago, I broke into his office."

"Which office?"

"His," Claudia said, confused. "The one in our house."

"What—what did you find?"

"Letters. *Love* letters. There's a stack of them from some woman named Iris." Just hearing the name made Drew's spine go cold.

"Do you think I should ask him about it?" Claudia asked, oblivious to Drew's reaction. "My mother will be devastated. How could he do this to her? She'll leave him, you know. How would *that* look for his image?"

Letters from Iris. This could be the lead she'd been looking for! She suppressed her excitement. Claudia would be all over her if it slipped through. She had to be careful with what she said next to not scare Claudia into shutting down.

"What makes you so sure they weren't written before he met your mom?"

"Because they're dated the year before I was born," Claudia said.

"Can I see them?"

Claudia narrowed her gaze. "Why?"

Drew narrowed her own eyes. "Because it's important."

"Do you know who she is?"

Drew hesitated. She had to pick her words carefully. Claudia's moment of sharing could change in a snap. She needed to see those letters. "No. But I bet I can help you find out."

"Or… I could just confront him—"

"No! No, don't do that." That was the last thing Drew needed. "Imagine the pain this will cause your family. Don't jump in until you know for sure."

Claudia stared at the fire. "I think he knows I read them. When I went back to find them, they were gone. He must've moved them. I've looked everywhere."

If Dominic knew his daughter found out about his affair with Iris, he might destroy the letters.

"He never mentioned them or asked what you found out?" Drew said.

Claudia brushed dirt from her boots. "Never said a word." She looked at Drew. "In one of the letters, the woman said she was pregnant, and the baby was his. I'd say that's as sure as it gets. They had an affair, Drew."

Shane.

"Was there anything else about the baby?" Drew said.

"No, but I lost the chance to read through them all. I could have a half-brother or sister out there somewhere. Do you know how wild that is? How could he keep this from us?"

She knew more than Claudia realized. It was obvious that he kept a lot from his family. "Where do you think he took them? The letters."

"Who knows," Claudia said. "He had a box of keys in his office, but I don't know what they're all for. Why? Do you think you could find out who this Iris woman is?"

The keys to the safe had to be inside that box!

Drew glanced at the fire. Someone was adding wood and the flames rose higher into the night sky. "I need to see those letters. I'll find Iris."

If Claudia only knew the full story. She'd find out eventually if Drew had anything to do with it.

"Shit. You sound pretty invested for someone who knows nothing about this." Claudia quipped. "What makes you so sure you can find this woman…*mistress,* we'll call her."

"I guess you're just going to have to trust me."

Claudia smirked. "That's a tough one for me. It never ends well when you put too much of that in anyone."

"Tell me about it," Drew muttered under her breath and looked away, but Claudia heard.

"This stays between us. Promise me you won't tell anyone?"

Drew made an 'x' over her heart. "Cross my heart."

"I mean it. Not Piper, or Nico. No one."

"Okay, I get it. Not a soul."

Claudia tucked her blond hair behind her ears. It took on an orange hue from the light of the fire. If Drew eased her way into Claudia's home, she could get her hands on the box of keys. One of them *had* to be to the safe in the warehouse.

"We could talk about this more tomorrow," Drew said, "I could come over and help you look for the letters." She was trying to sound nonchalant.

"My parents have a benefit dinner tomorrow. They'll be gone all evening, so that's not a bad idea. I just want to be clear. I only want to talk to the woman. Find out who the kid is, you know?"

"Sure. Of course." Drew smiled but was sure it looked forced as hell. Claudia must've bought it because she dropped it.

"Are you sticking around for a while?" Claudia said.

There was still time to visit the house by Aurora, but Claudia didn't have to know that. "I better go home. Look, I'm sorry about your father. But no matter what happens, you'll be okay."

Claudia bounced off the log and her usual fake smile reappeared. "I hope so. It's not like someone's dying, right?"

If Claudia knew the truth, she wouldn't be making jokes about death. Drew stood and shook her sleeping leg awake. The blood rushed to her foot as the feeling returned. She'd been ignoring weird symptoms in her body since the accident. Once this was over, she'd be able to rest and get better.

Claudia walked beside her until they reached the fire pit. When she saw her friends, her face transformed in an instant. The person—the one with real issues that she'd revealed to Drew so briefly was gone. In its place was a ceramic doll of pure perfection.

"Bye, Drew. See you tomorrow," she said, and for a second, Drew thought she caught sight of the girl who just shared a fragile part of herself. But she was gone.

And it was time for Drew to go too.

Twenty-Two

Drew arrived at the keeper's house. She pulled off the dirt road and got out, grabbing a flashlight from her bag. The lighthouse beacon rotated in a constant rhythm. The wind howled off the ocean and she shivered. It was freezing and no amount of layers would keep the cold from soaking into her bones. She shone her light toward the rocky shore, the beam illuminating ocean water splashing over huge boulders. The lighthouse beacon hit her own light with each rotation. She aimed it at the forest border, checking her surroundings. Branches extended off rows of tree trunks and swayed in the harsh wind. She expected Dominic or one of his men to charge at her, but the property was deserted. No cars around, and not a soul to be seen—alive or dead.

She walked up the front porch and touched the front door riddled with bullet holes. This time it opened, inviting her inside. She stepped through and closed the door, scoping out the darkness with the flashlight.

Drew's shallow breaths puffed in front of her as it mixed with the cold. She could do this, she *had* to do this. Marching into the kitchen, she yanked on the door to the basement and descended into the abyss.

The door to the underground tunnel lay on the floor, still off its hinges from her last adventure. She took the pocket watch out and eyed the map. If she assumed it was a map of Aurora and followed the tunnel, it should take her along the river. It wouldn't be a long walk on the outside, twenty minutes at most. At the end of the map was a break in the line, which *had* to be an exit. She'd exit back around Haven. People would be around until at least midnight; they'd hear her scream if something happened.

What am I thinking?

Maybe all this was crazy. She was never going to find Iris's body! And what if her never-ending headache caused her to pass out and she collapsed? No one would ever find her!

But if she turned back, nothing was going to change either. There was no other choice. Find Iris, or he wins.

Nothing is going to happen. I'll be fine.

She said it over and over again as she ventured into the musty cavern. Stale air choked her, and she had to fight the desire to run back. She kept going forward, leaving the little door to the basement behind. It was getting hard to breathe and dizziness hit, forcing her to crouch with her hands on her legs.

Strands of her hair moved, tickling her cheek. She spun around but no one was there. A breeze touched her face. Where was it coming from? She held the flashlight up and searched the wall, moving closer to it. The draft intensified and she ran her fingers along the low ceiling through thick moss until they stuck through a gap in the stones.

She breathed deep. Stepping back, she aimed the light ahead. There were openings for air every ten feet or so. At least she wouldn't suffocate. She picked up her pace through the underground catacomb.

At first, all she heard was the padding of her own feet in the dirt, her short breaths. But there was something else, something that sounded like rushing water. A steady hiss. Drew stopped and looked over her shoulder, checking to see if the tunnel had flooded. It wouldn't matter how good a swimmer she was if the dungeon filled with water and there was no way out!

She shone the light over her head. The top of the tunnel was dry, just dead earth and roots and slatted wood. No water dripped through the vented gaps. She aimed the light on the watch again, squinting at the map. She had to have reached the river.

Drew shone the flashlight back—back to safety, back to the surface, out of this tunnel. But no answers lay in that direction, only questions. She had to keep going. No matter what.

The mud floor ended abruptly at a short staircase— a staircase that went down, going *deeper into the ground.* The stairs were made of stones, held together with mud, long dried, and crumbling mortar. Damp, musty earth was all she could smell. She ducked and held the light with trembling hands.

A voice whispered in her ear, "You're close."

Drew jumped—high enough and hard enough to hit her head on the rock ceiling.

"Drew!" Enid charged up the stone steps, her wide eyes shining in the light of Drew's flashlight. "I've been trying to find you. I'm stuck in here!"

Drew reached for her. She wanted to pull her into a hug, but her hands went right through her—something Enid noted with a grim smile.

Humming echoed below—the lullaby. "Did you hear that?"

Enid bowed her head. "She's here. She wants you to find her."

Drew tensed. She knew exactly who Enid meant. Iris. A discovery that could set her free, and one that horrified her at the same time.

"You found her," she said to Enid.

Enid swirled around in her ghostly form. "Follow me."

Drew followed her down the stone stairs, the passageway narrowing as it extended into darkness. The dream that had been haunting her for months came to life before her eyes.

Enid's figure glowed, casting light over the green and gray-streaked rock walls. The smell grew more nauseating with every step—if dampness had an aroma, this had to be it. It seeped through her clothes and her skin crawled.

Enid guided her around a sharp left turn. The walls narrowed. Or were they closing in? Drew couldn't tell anymore. She put her hands out on each side as if to keep them from crushing her. She reached above to convince herself that the ceiling wasn't about to collapse. She tried to take a deep breath, but all that did was make her cough. Her chest tightened like a snake was wrapped around her. She ran her fingers along the stone, searching for the air vents, but there were none to be found.

Just when she thought she was going to lose it, Enid stopped moving. With her back to Drew, she turned her head and pointed beside her. Drew moved closer, terrified of what Enid wanted her to see. Drew held up the flashlight slowly, almost dropping it because her hand was shaking so much. Using both hands, she aimed it where Enid pointed. There was a gap in the wall where a chamber had been hollowed out in the stone.

Was this it? Was this the moment she discovered where Shane's mother had been all this time? Hidden here in the damp underground, rotting away. Gruesome images flashed in her mind of decomposing bodies consumed by bugs. Maggots.

She was going to be sick. She closed her eyes and placed her hand on the cold, stone wall.

"I can't do it, Enid."

"You have to! Or she'll never be free, and that man will never be caught!" Enid stood in front of her. "I'll stay with you." She tilted her head back to the chamber entrance. "And so will he."

Drew looked around but didn't see anyone. Had Enid fooled her, luring her down here for something sinister?

"Who is *he*?"

"Go inside," Enid said. "He's not going to hurt you."

"No. I won't go in there. Not until you tell me who he is!"

"Jack can show you what I can't. Nothing's going to happen to you. Trust me."

Trust.

Her head pounded and despite the cold, underneath her jacket and sweater, her shirt was soaking up sweat as it trickled down her back.

She shook her head. She couldn't do it.

"If Iris is in there, I'll just call the police and tell them where she is," Drew said.

"Iris needs you to be the one to find her. You already know that."

Drew didn't want to be the person designated to solve ghosts' problems. But here she was, having to do just that because she cared too much to walk away, and the line had been crossed. Her own life was at stake.

With either blind faith or stupidity, and a bounding pulse from her neck to her temples, she held the light like a lifeline and stepped into the tomb. She met Jack Morana face-to-face.

As she held her stance, deep creases spread across his forehead and around his eyes as human features took shape. He bowed his head and covered his face. His hands transformed and were covered with skin all the way down to his fingertips. When he lifted his head, he looked heartbroken as he pointed to the floor in the corner.

It didn't seem as if the old man was going to kill her.

"Is Iris in there?"

He reached his hands up to her face and she flinched, backing up.

"Trust him. He's going to show you." Enid's voice came from outside of the chamber, sounding distant.

"Show me what?"

His hands moved closer to her face, and she pressed herself against the wall. He held eye contact with her, and a rainbow of colors flashed between them. His cold hands covered her cheeks like ice blocks. Rooted to where she stood, her muscles stiffened. What if she was wrong to trust him and he was going to suck out her soul!

"Close your eyes." His voice was a hoarse whisper.

She pulled away from his grip. Images rolled through her mind like an old projector without sound. A young Jack Morana stood alone in front of Aurora and a woman with a baby in her arms and tears in her eyes waved before climbing into a station wagon. As she drove away, the silent film in Drew's mind changed. Enid and Blythe stood on the rocky shore laughing as they helped Ezra with a fishing pole. They looked so happy.

The moving pictures shifted again, but this time they were darker, ominous. Dominic at the helm in the cabin of a small boat, Enid helping Ezra reel in a fish. The look on Dominic's face was like the one in the photograph. Soulless, foreboding. Like a scene in a movie, the image faded to black and when the picture returned, they were in the middle of a terrible storm. Ezra fell into the water and desperate to save him, Enid jumped in after him. She slipped out of her lifejacket and disappeared beneath the waves. Drew screamed through sobs as she gripped the old man's hands.

"I don't want to see anymore!"

"Please," he whispered. "Wait."

The image vanished, and she was transported to the living room of the keeper's house. Only now...it was brighter. Summertime. A woman was yelling but no sound came out. She appeared furious as she shook her fist in the air. But it wasn't just any woman.

Iris.

Dominic towered over Iris, raising his arm. His nostrils flared and he bared his teeth like a barbaric animal. He wiped his mouth with a gun-wielding hand and aimed it at her. Iris picked up a broken spindle from the floor and hit him across the head with it. Stunned, he reached up and touched his bloody face before grabbing the sleeves of her dress. She struck him and kicked him, but it was no use. A venomous sneer spread across his face. He pulled the trigger and she fell to the floor. Crimson soaked her dress as the blood oozed from the lethal wound.

Blackness flashed with a soundless picture change of a projector. This time Drew stood by the Coda River at Neptune Point. Shane stumbled up from the ground, blood trickling down the side of his face. Dominic lifted his hand to strike him as Shane raised both hands in surrender. His lips moved soundlessly. Dominic shoved him toward a black sedan and held the door open. Shane yanked his arm away and climbed in.

Jack Morana released her, and his supernatural hold broke. Shrill ringing sounded in her ears and her face prickled like a rash. The scenes in her mind had ended, but she had no control over the extreme anguish that remained. She collapsed to the ground, sobbing. She wept for Enid and Ezra. For Iris.

And for Shane.

He hadn't left her of his own free will as Dominic told her. She knew the truth now; he'd been forced to leave by a man who was his father by blood only.

The flashlight rolled out of her hand. The light sputtered, turning off and back on again as it landed in the back corner. It illuminated a crevice underneath a boulder that appeared out of place.

Enid was right. She had to be the one to find Iris.

She got up off the floor and with trembling hands picked up the flashlight.

Jack Morana was gone. She was alone.

Sticking her hands on either side of the misshapen rock, she heaved and pulled. It moved a couple of inches, offering a better grip. With one final shove, it gave way. A sickening stench of decay escaped in the air, and she turned away with a jerk.

Death. It smelled of *death*.

She dropped to her knees and aimed the light inside.

It was a tomb.

The blood-stained dress was torn and covered in mud—entangled in bones. The flesh was gone, decomposed, or gnawed away by the dead bugs splattered around it. Bits of hair formed a halo around the skull and its hollowed eye sockets stared upward. Drew dropped to the ground, shivering. Her stomach tightened and churned. Saliva filled her mouth and she only turned just in time to throw up. Bile burned her throat. She couldn't understand how Dominic could kill his child's mother.

"I'm so sorry, Iris," she whispered into the void.

A hand touched her back, and she lifted her head. Iris hovered over her. Her ghostly figure solidified into its once-human form. Blood appeared over her dress, spreading out, a deep crimson wash, blackening.

Drew's throat constricted. "I don't know what to do."

"Yes, you do. You know exactly what to do." Iris brushed the hair from Drew's face and cupped her cheeks in her hands. "Shane is coming home. Dominic must be caught before he arrives. You're the only one who can help." She sailed away leaning her head inside the tomb. "There are bullets here. Bloody. His gun is locked in the safe."

"I don't have a key—"

"No, but she does."

"She?"

Iris stared back at her meaningfully. She couldn't possibly mean Enid. But if not her, then—

"Claudia!"

A crashing, like rocks tumbling, sounded from back in the tunnel. Someone else was out there!

Iris shifted and blurred. "Go! Before it's too late." A draft whistled through the chamber and Iris blanched into a cloud before vanishing.

Drew climbed out of the chamber back into the tunnel. Enid materialized in front of her, and she jumped.

"I know the way out."

Drew stopped and swung the light between each end of the tunnel. A crash thundered from behind her. She couldn't go back. Water rushed above, getting louder as she walked with Enid through the tunnel. A stream trickled over the moss-covered walls.

"I don't see an end to this." Drew stopped and opened the pocket watch to examine the map. If this was a dead end, she would be trapped. If the half-circle at the end wasn't an exit...

"Where did you get that?" Enid asked, staring at the watch.

"Do you know who it belongs to?"

"It was my grandfather's." Enid reached out and tried to touch it, but her fingers went right through the watch and Drew's palm. She kicked at a rock on the ground in anger, but her foot also went right through it. "I hate this! Why can't I do anything? Where did you find it?"

"It was in Shane's bag...or it was supposed to be. I found it in my car after the accident."

Enid stared at the watch. "Jack Morana is my grandfather. Why are we all here together?" She lifted her head and faced Drew. "Will Ezra and I be stuck here forever?"

"No, you won't." Loud thuds echoed from somewhere in the distance behind her. "I'll help you, but I can only do that if I get the hell out of here!"

"Follow me." Enid floated toward the end of the tunnel and Drew ran after her.

Enid stopped as the tunnel narrowed before abruptly turning into a dead-end.

"You have to go up. It'll take you by the river and you'll be free. But please, Drew, don't forget us!" Enid cried as she swirled into an explosion of mist and disappeared.

Twenty-Three

The river's current coursed above her like a freight train. Drew aimed the dimming flashlight up to reveal a trap door covering a round hole. She had to escape and call Detective Porter. Iris's body must have evidence against Dominic. First, she had to get out of this dungeon.

But how?

Pushing her fingers through the moss-covered walls, she searched for steps, a ledge, *anything* she could use to boost herself to the top. Something crawled over her hand. She jerked it back and swatted at a spider with freakishly long legs. Cringing, she stuck her hands through the damp moss on the other side.

Slats of wood formed a ladder leading up. She jammed the flashlight under her chin and climbed to the top. She pushed on the wooden slab lifting it only a crack. Air flowed down and she inhaled like it was her first breath.

The flashlight slipped and she reached to grasp it but missed. She caught her foot between the ladder and the stone wall. Pain shot through her ankle, and she winced. Just another bruise that her body was going to have to deal with. She twisted it free and pulled herself up. Fueled by adrenaline, she stood as tall as she could, using her shoulders to move the wooden door open.

"Come on!" she grunted.

The weight shifted and she thrust the door to the side, allowing just enough space to climb out. Exhausted, she flopped to the ground. Her ankle throbbed with its own pulse as it swelled inside her boot. Turning on her belly, she hoisted herself up.

Rocks jutted up through rushing white water along the river's edge. Downstream, a fire glowed through the trees casting long shadows. She wasn't far from Haven; there were still people there who could help her. But there was one huge problem.

She was on the wrong side of the river.

Digging in her pocket for the light from her phone, she scanned for a crossing point. A pair of eyes glowed at her from the dense forest only a few feet away, and she stopped. Were there wolves in this area? If it was growling, she couldn't hear it over the sound of the river. Even if her ankle wasn't slowing her down, she had nowhere to run.

She was easy prey out here.

Picking up a stick, she held it in front of her like a sword. As she moved past the reflecting eyes, a branch snapped under her feet. The deer stood to attention with its ears flicking before it darted through the trees with expert precision.

Drew let out a breath. It was a deer. Just a deer.

The relief was short-lived. She wasn't going back in the tunnel. That left one option. She had to cross the raging water that could pull her under, and no one would hear it happening.

She'd faced the ocean many times and made out fine. She could do this. Limping to the edge, she stepped in. Frigid water spilled around her legs up to her knees.

She took deep breaths. This was going to be cold, hypothermia cold, so she'd have to be quick. She waded deeper. Torrents of water flood around her, trying to sweep her away and stealing any heat she had left. Her feet no longer touched the bottom, and goosebumps covered every inch of her. She forced her numb arms to propel her across as fast as she could go.

The undertow gripped her, submerging her underwater. Bobbing back up quickly, she coughed up water and regained control over her flailing arms. Her waterlogged jacket weighed her down, but she pushed through the current. Trees lined the other side, close enough to the edge that she could almost touch them... She reached for a low-hanging branch but missed.

She was so close to the other side, but the current was too powerful. She still couldn't touch the bottom and the rushing water twisted her around, tugging her under again. Her arms weakened, numb with cold.

The next time she came up, she could hear something—music! And laughter! The fire was getting closer.

She did the only thing she could: she screamed. Someone—*anyone*—had to hear.

"Help!" she hollered again and again until she was hoarse. As the current carried her along, her attention snagged on a broken bough hovering over the water.

This was the one! She had to grab it—failure wasn't an option.

Lunging out of the water with all her energy, she grabbed the wet branch with both hands and clung to it with every ounce of strength. Water rushed around her, and she fought to hold on.

"Who's out there?" a voice called.

"Please, help!"

Branches snapped under footsteps. The chatter got louder and with it came lights shining over the water until a beam covered her face, blinding her.

"Drew? Drew, is that you?"

She'd know Claudia's high-pitched shriek anywhere. Only this time, Drew was grateful to hear it. Her hands slipped and she wrapped her arm around the branch for a better grip.

"Do you have rope or something?"

Claudia raced to the edge surrounded by her friends but the spotlight on Drew kept them in the shadows. They lined up linking arms with Claudia as she waded in the water holding out a long tree branch. "Can you grab it?"

Drew stretched her arm out, but her fingers were a bit shy of reaching it.

"I can't reach!"

Claudia plunged deeper extending the branch closer, her hair floating in the water as it rose higher on her chest. "Try now!"

With the light on both of them, she locked eyes with Claudia. "What if it breaks?"

"It won't. We're all holding it. We'll pull you in."

Drew looked past Claudia at the row of shadows. The light illuminated someone holding Claudia by the jacket.

"You've got to trust me, Drew!"

Drew reached out her frozen hand and grabbed the branch, still hanging onto the dangling bough with the other.

"Let go! Now!" Claudia screamed over the rushing water.

If she was going to get out of this, she had to let go. She slid her hand off the bough and gripped the branch with both hands. Her head dipped underwater, popping right back us as she was tugged to shore. She kicked her feet until they touched the bottom, and she could stand.

Claudia grabbed her by the arm and pulled. Two guys she knew from school swept in on each side and wrapped their arms around her. They helped her walk up the mound of dirt and snow through the trees to safety. She didn't want to think about what people would be saying about her now, but deep down she didn't care anymore. She'd found Iris.

Dripping wet and shivering, she flopped to the ground in front of the fire. Claudia plopped down beside her trembling. Her wet hair stuck to her head and shoulders.

Someone wrapped a blanket around her. A sharp ringing drowned out the voices surrounding her. A huge owl flew over her, landing on the embankment by the river and settling beside Jack Morana. He stood watching her, then nodded and tipped his hat before disappearing into the forest. Every time she was in trouble, he'd made an appearance. But not once had he tried to help.

Unless he was incapable of helping.

As Jack vanished, so did the high-pitch sound. It just stopped, breaking her trance. People were asking questions, but she didn't answer. She had no time to explain how she wound up almost drowning in the Coda River. She had to get the police to Iris before someone else beat her to it.

Her phone was gone. Probably at the bottom of the river.

"I need your phone."

Claudia held hers out. "There's no service," she said through chattering teeth. "What happened to you? I thought you were going home."

Drew stood up, her legs shaking as the blanket fell to the ground. Her keys! She unzipped her jacket pocket and grasped them. "I have to get out of here."

Claudia got up and followed her as she limped away from the fire. Putting any pressure on her ankle hurt like hell.

"I'm coming with you," Claudia said and ran after her. "*Wait!* What in the hell are you hiding!"

Drew stopped and spun around. Her shivering body mirrored Claudia's. "I found bones. A body—A dead person!" She couldn't string a cohesive sentence together. "I'm calling the police!"

"You found a *dead body*? Where?"

"Under the old house. By the lighthouse. Claudia,

I've got to go. Can I have your phone for a minute?"

"I'm not giving you my phone!"

"Fine." She traipsed off toward the clearing through the trees. Claudia's friends caught up, fawning all over her. A few passed Drew and asked if she was okay. These were people she'd known for years, and they'd never spoken to her before. Maybe they weren't all assholes after all.

Drew rounded the turn in the path to the parking area with Claudia hot on her heels. She was more than surprised to find Nico waiting there holding blankets.

"How did you know I was here?"

"Piper got a message that you almost drowned in the river," he said.

"There's no service here."

Claudia held up her phone. "There is from the parking lot. Still need it?"

"You're both going to freeze to death if you don't get warm." Nico handed a blanket to Claudia and wrapped another one around Drew. He held her and rubbed her arms creating heat. Her clothes were drenched through to her skin, but her nerves had deadened to it at this point. She took the phone from Claudia and dialed 9-1-1.

Piper sprinted from a bright red SUV. "My phone was blowing up! Is it true? Did Claudia save you? For real?"

"She was about to be dragged out to sea. I heard her screams, and I stepped in. I didn't do it alone. Why is that so shocking?" Claudia asked.

Drew described the location to a man on the other

end of the phone. Piper looked serious as she listened to the one-sided conversation.

"Yes. A *body*. Please, hurry!" Drew explained as fast as she could. What was so damn hard to understand? Did this guy think she was joking?

Headlights turned on over the hill. A black sedan was parked almost out of sight. She knew it! Someone was in the tunnel behind her. What if they moved Iris?

She hung up the call, nearly throwing the phone back to Claudia. "Where's your car?"

Piper dangled keys in front of Drew. "We can take mine. Where are we going?"

"Back to the house."

"You went back in that tunnel, didn't you? Oh my God—was she in there?" Piper whispered, turning her back to the spectators.

"Are you driving, or am I?"

Piper clutched the keys in her palm. "Let's go."

Drew followed her to the SUV. Claudia grabbed her by the arm. "I'm coming with you!"

Nico opened the door and Drew boosted herself in beside Piper before he hopped in the back with Claudia.

"No way your parents handed you the keys to their Mercedes. Did you steal it?" Claudia said.

"Not exactly. I'm sure they won't even notice it's gone." Piper blasted the heat. The icicles that were Drew's hair melted. Her wet clothes clung to her, and she shivered uncontrollably.

"I'm so cold it hurts," she said.

Piper looked over at her. "Drew, you've got to get warm. Get out of those clothes. Nico hand over the blankets."

She couldn't get naked right here in front of everyone!

"Would anyone mind if I tore off *my* wet clothes? I'm freezing too," Claudia whined, but no one said a word. Not even Piper.

Claudia sighed. "Tough crowd."

Drew reached back for blankets from Nico as Claudia started to undress.

"What?" Claudia said. "I don't care what you think. Piper's right. We've got to get out of these wet clothes. It's that or freeze to death. No thank you."

Claudia sat in her bra and leggings and wrapped a blanket around herself moving closer to the middle seat beside Nico.

Piper had the heat pumping, but it wasn't helping. Drew took her coat off, then her sweater.

"Here." Nico handed her his sweatshirt. "Take it."

She pulled off her t-shirt and yanked his sweater over her head, hiding as she dressed. It was still warm from his body heat and the relief was immediate. But as numb as her legs were, Drew couldn't bring herself to take her pants off.

"Okay, Drew. How did you end up in the river? And where's this body? Was it disgusting?" Claudia asked rapid-fire questions.

Piper swerved around the corner and came to a halt behind Drew's hatchback. She snapped around to face Claudia. "Shut up. Shut up! You have no idea—"

"Piper, don't."

The house came into view over the hill. Ignoring

the pain in her ankle, Drew got out of the car and raced over the bank toward the front porch. She gripped the broken railing out of breath. Claudia charged after her holding together an oversized coat over bare skin as she ran.

"Wait! What are you doing? Why won't you talk to me!" Claudia screamed as she approached her.

Drew caught her breath and faced her. "The woman your father had an affair with—she was murdered. She was murdered *here*! I found her remains tonight."

Claudia gaped. "The woman in the letters? Iris*?* You said you didn't know her! Did you lie to me?"

"No! No, of course not! I don't know her—not in the way you think," Drew said.

"Right. Because you know so much about how I think. You talk around me like I'm stupid, whispering to Piper and Nico. But where were they tonight? If it weren't for me, you'd be the body swept away here, but not once did you say thank you!" Claudia wiped her eyes and tucked wet hair behind her ears and yanked the hood up. "How do you know it's the same woman? How do you know she was killed? How the hell do you know anything?"

"I saw it. *All* of it."

Claudia folded her arms across her chest, hugging herself. "You're seriously crazy. You know that?"

Drew glared back at her. Claudia had no idea her whole world was about to fall apart, and Drew would be one of the few people who would be able to help her pick up the pieces. She swung the front door of the house open and turned to Claudia.

"I am not crazy," she said. "You're right. Maybe I would've been carried out to sea tonight if it hadn't been for you. So, yes, thank you." Sirens sounded close, approaching. "Wait here for the police. Tell them I'm inside."

Drew hurried inside the house and down the rickety steps to the basement. The tunnel door was propped back in place under the table hiding the entrance. She pushed it aside as boots thudded above her head, getting louder as they thundered down the steps.

"Put your hands on your head!" a man's stern voice ordered.

Drew froze. *Not now.*

No one would believe her if Iris's body was gone.

"Turn around!" the man said.

Trembling, Drew shifted to face him. Officers wearing full armor with guns drawn stood behind Detective Porter.

"You can drop your hands," she said. "Drew, what are you doing here?"

Drew pointed to the hole in the wall. "I found her. Iris Bishop. I can show you."

At least she hoped she could. If whoever was just here had moved Iris's body, the evidence would be gone. And if the evidence was gone, it would be all over, and he'd win.

Detective Porter looked back and gestured to the team of police. She walked to the entrance and shone a high-powered light inside. "In there?"

She let Drew lead them to Iris. She reached the chamber and climbed inside, breathing deeply as she pointed to the nook in the wall.

The tomb.

Please still be there.

"Don't worry; I didn't let him inside." A hushed whisper came from Iris whirling beside her.

Detective Porter leaned down. She illuminated the space inside and bowed her head. "Secure the scene and get forensics down here."

Iris's transparent silhouette shimmered. Bit by bit the blood evaporated off her dress and arms. She smiled at Drew and disappeared.

Detective Porter led her to a police car with another officer and asked her about the events of the evening.

"You need to investigate Dominic Sloan," she begged as she sat in the passenger seat.

A skeptical look crossed the detective's face. "What does he have to do with this? I don't understand."

"Please, listen to me. He kidnapped me. Brought me to his warehouse. Held a gun to my head and told me if I said anything to anyone, he was going to kill me! Kill my family! He set that fire at the bakery tonight. I know he did!"

"Dominic Sloan? Are you sure you've got the right person?" Detective Porter started the car and turned up the heat.

"You don't believe me. You think I'd make this shit up?" Drew laughed, but she didn't find it funny at all. "I don't care about his charities or benefits...he's a murderer! I wouldn't make this up. I'm not crazy! You're going to see it too once you run whatever forensic stuff that you do on Iris's body. He killed her. And he wants me dead too!"

Detective Porter wrote in a notepad. She looked at Drew with a confused expression. "I'll bring him in and talk to him."

"Right. *Talk* to him. You think he's going to admit any of this? You need to investigate him! Go to the warehouse. You'll find all the evidence you need!"

"It's not that simple. Look, you must be exhausted and near hypothermic. I'll have someone drive you home—"

"No. I don't need anyone to do anything for me. I can get myself home." She opened the car door and the frigid air soaked into her bones sending her into a shivering fit all over again. She leaned down to look Detective Porter in the eyes. "I'm telling the truth. You'll see."

Slamming the door, Drew walked away. She had divulged what happened the night at the warehouse. She'd asked—*begged* Detective Porter to investigate Dominic Sloan, but the skeptical look on the woman's face wasn't promising.

None of it went as she planned. She thought Dominic Sloan would be brought in, questioned, and put behind bars. All they'd need was a body. But she couldn't have been more wrong. If the police didn't think she was telling the truth, what if the evidence around the body failed her as well? She'd have to find a key to the safe and retrieve those files from the warehouse.

She trudged up the hill to her car. Claudia glared at her before climbing into a car with her friends and driving away. Piper and Nico stood near her hatchback. A stabbing headache made her feel sick to her stomach, and her legs were weak. She didn't trust herself to drive home alone. She grabbed her jacket from Piper's SUV and dug for her keys.

"Nico, can you drive my car? I want to go home."

"Sure."

Piper hugged her tight. "You should've called. We had a deal, remember? We're in this together."

"I know," Drew said, but she had nothing else to say. She made a promise she couldn't keep.

Piper got in the big SUV and waved before pulling away. Spinning tires on mud and snow squealed as the rest of the cars sped away. The party was over.

She climbed in her silver hatchback beside Nico. She stared out the window in silence as he drove home. She couldn't let Dominic get away with this! Why weren't police swarming his house? It all made her so damn angry.

Nico pulled into his driveway. "Are you okay to drive from here?"

"Yeah. Thank you." They got out of the car, and she sat in the driver's seat. He held the door open and turned to her.

"You're so quiet. Do you want to talk about what happened back there?"

The knowledge that Shane didn't cast her aside like she'd thought weighed on her, but she couldn't bring herself to tell him. She wasn't sure what it meant for her and Nico.

"I'm just exhausted. I don't even know what to say," she said.

He tapped his fingers on the door frame. "I can imagine. How about I call you tomorrow."

"My phone is gone. In the river."

"Right." Nico winced. "I'll call the house instead. And when your grandmother's car is ready, I'll drive it over and check on you. Is she home from the hospital?"

"She was supposed to be discharged. I think Gabe took her home." Drew covered her face. "Isn't that awful? I'm a horrible person. I have no idea how she is right now."

"You're not horrible. You did what you had to do." He bent down and kissed her forehead, holding her close. The profound connection still hung between them. It had been easier to brush lingering feelings for Shane aside before knowing what she did now. She was in limbo being pulled in both directions.

"I want to give you something. Wait here." He got out of the car and ran up to the huge garage. A light came on inside and turned off as he dashed back to her car.

"Here." He handed her a folder.

She took the thick folder. "What's this?"

"Dad's records. Transactions of money from Sloan Industries for work that was never done. But I don't know if it's proof enough. Dominic could just say we did the work he'd asked for. He's using the garage to launder money. It comes in and goes back out. It's all there, but he'll probably just say he's doing legit business with my dad."

"I don't know what to say. What if Dominic finds out and comes after your dad—"

"I won't let that happen. Take it. I'll try to find more. Everything is going to work out, it has to. He's going to get caught. Go home, dry off, and get some sleep. If you need me, call from the house and I'll be there."

She left Nico and drove the few minutes up the road to her home. The house was dark when she arrived.

"Gran? Gabe?" she yelled as she entered the house, but it was empty. The harsh ring of the landline cut through the silence. She dashed to the kitchen to answer it.

"Hello?"

"Finally! Where have you been?" It was her father and he sounded irritated.

"Where's Gran?" she asked.

"We're still here."

"In the hospital? I thought she'd be home by now. What's wrong?"

"I've been trying to call you for hours—"

"My phone died. *What's wrong?*"

"She had a heart attack," Gabe said.

"What? How! The fire?"

"They're not sure—"

"I'm on my way." Drew turned around, ready to run to her car.

"She's stable, Drew," Gabe said. "I'll stay with her

tonight. We're no good to her if we're both burned out. Come in the morning like we said."

"I need to be there with her—"

"Let me do this. Look. I promise I'll call the house if anything changes. Sleep, and come tomorrow. Okay?"

"Yeah. I guess."

He gave her Gran's new room details and hung up. She was inside a warm house, but the chills started all over again.

She dragged herself upstairs and showered using water as hot as she could stand it. She got dressed and peeked through her bedroom curtains searching for the black sedan. The road was deserted.

All this was the fault of one man.

Dominic Sloan.

For the first time ever in her life, she wanted another human being dead.

Twenty-Four

Drew spent the next day in the hospital at Gran's bedside. She'd planned to visit Claudia at home and read those letters, maybe find a key to the safe. But she couldn't leave Gran until Gabe came back. Not like this.

IV fluid dripped into Gran's frail arm. Oxygen tubes were stuck in her nose, and her skin looked a sickly gray. She turned her head to face Drew.

"Did you see the bakery? We lost everything." Tears trickled over Gran's wrinkled cheeks.

Her throat choked up. "Don't worry about the shop. Just get better. We'll take care of the rest."

Drew held her hand. It was as cold as Jack Morana's when he'd touched her face.

"Where's your dad?" Gran's voice was barely a whisper.

Drew cringed. She hadn't called Gabe 'dad' in forever, but she wasn't about to argue with Gran. None of that mattered now. She was on the cusp of adulthood, and it was too late for him to be a dad!

"Gabe is gone to do…whatever it is he does. He'll be back."

Gran coughed, gasping for a second before she closed her eyes. Drew sat upright with her hand on the call bell. Gran had always been the one constant in her life. She couldn't die. Her chest rose and fell in a gentle pattern. Drew relaxed her hand on the call bell and collapsed back in the chair.

The clock on the wall ticked in pace with the intermittent buzzes of the IV machine. It was late into the afternoon and Gabe still hadn't returned.

Out of habit, she reached in her pocket for a phone that wasn't there. She'd dropped off Nico's documents at the police station on her way to the hospital and called Detective Porter on a courtesy hospital phone at least five times before she answered. She was bringing him in for questioning, but the information was vague and didn't necessarily prove fraud. She didn't have enough evidence to arrest Dominic.

Not yet.

But for now, it was Drew's word against his. The forensic report from the body could take days, maybe longer and she didn't have that kind of time. He was a time bomb about to explode and she was the target.

Dr. Wymond strolled in with a chart in her hands. Drew hadn't expected to see her. The scar across her cheek stood out more than ever. There was no doubt she was Enid's twin sister.

Drew wanted to jump in and ask questions about her family, but she hesitated. How would Dr. Wymond react when she told her about Enid and Ezra? She wasn't sure how to say it. She eyed her backpack. The album was inside; maybe she could show the doctor the photos to open up the conversation.

"Hello," Dr. Wymond said "Drew, right?"

"Yes. How is she?"

Dr. Wymond looked from the chart to Gran. "Stable. But as I mentioned to your father, plan for surgery in the next few days. I'm hopeful she'll be able to make a full recovery, but we'll have to monitor her closely."

"Did the fire cause it?"

"It could have triggered something, but from what I've gathered, this has been building for some time."

The doctor turned to leave. Drew couldn't let this opportunity pass her by.

"Wait. Doctor Wymond?"

"Yes?"

"I…Can I talk to you?"

"Of course." She smiled at Drew. "Do you have questions about your grandmother?"

"No. Not that. Your family."

"You mean Cole? What about him?"

"Not Cole. Your *other* family. The Morana's"

Dr. Wymond stiffened. "I don't know what you're talking about."

Of course, she did. She looked nervous—and for good reason. Drew wondered what was going through her head. She looked scared. Maybe she knew more than Drew realized. But why did she keep this part of her past so hidden?

"This isn't going to make sense, it barely makes sense to me, but I've been talking to your sister, Enid. Ezra too."

Dr. Wymond's reaction was what Drew expected. Her mouth gaped open, and she stood scrutinizing Drew, probably wondering if she was being cruel or crazy. "That—that's impossible. They're dead."

"I know." Drew squirmed. This next part was never going to be easy. "That's—that's why I can see them."

Dr. Wymond leaned against the wall and put the chart on a table. "You're making this up. Why would you do that?"

"I promise you I'm not. I don't want to hurt you, but I'm telling you the truth. I see them. Enid especially. She has a scar just like yours." She pulled the album out of her bag. "And I found this."

Dr. Wymond took the album and flipped it open, covering her mouth with her free hand. "Where did you get this?"

"In the house at Neptune Point. It was in the attic."

"This is how you know?"

"This confirmed what I was seeing. It started with Enid—no, that's wrong. It all started with Jack."

Dr. Wymond's face turned from shock to a blank stare. "My grandfather? What...how?"

"Like I said, I see them. He scared me at first, but now I know he doesn't want to hurt me. He wanted to warn me."

Dr. Wymond snapped the book shut and closed the door. Gran stirred but remained asleep. "That's a part of my life I keep buried. No one knows. No one! I like it that way. Do you understand?"

"Then why come back here?"

"This is my home," Dr. Wymond said. "I grew up in this town. I was tired of being afraid. My husband found work here and we returned to raise our son. I'm still not understanding how you know all this."

"I told you. I *see* them, I *talk* to them. But what I can't figure out is Dominic Sloan. He's in those pictures, but his name is Ben. Ben Morana. Is he your older brother? When did he change his name? Why?" Drew lowered her voice. "Did he kill Enid and Ezra on that boat?"

Dr. Wymond reached for the arm of a chair and pulled it close to sit down, not taking her eyes off Drew. "I...I don't know. We never really knew what happened, but he was devastated. He was always so different. Eccentric but not in a good way. We'd find dead seagulls all around the property. I saw him do it once—kill one. I never breathed a word. I was afraid of him. My mother disowned him after they died, and he ran away from home. She killed herself a month later. Couldn't live with herself." She wiped her eyes. "That man is no brother of mine. We are nothing to each other. Do you hear me? Nothing!"

Drew reached into her pocket and handed her the watch. She shared her encounters with Dominic, telling her everything, about Iris, and even Shane. The time for keeping secrets was over.

Dr. Wymond examined the watch. "This was my grandfather's. I always wondered what happened to it. I lived in that house caring for my father until cancer took him a year later. After he died, I sold the house and left Neptune Point for med school. I never looked back.

I swore I'd never return to that place. And I haven't."

"Have you talked to Dominic—*Ben* since you've been back?"

"Once. About a year ago I saw him on the news. I couldn't believe it. I had no idea Ben lived here! He looked so different. Older. He'd become this prestigious man—*Dominic Sloan*. I went to see him. I don't know why. I felt like I needed to hear his side of things." Dr. Wymond paused, a faraway look in her eyes. "But he looked me in the eye and told me I had the wrong person. He was so cold. Soulless. We've had no contact since."

Gran's IV beeped and Dr. Wymond pressed a button. She fixed Gran's blankets and touched her face.

"I can't talk about this anymore. Especially not here. I don't know what to think right now. You claim to talk to my dead brother and sister. It's incomprehensible." She took a pen out of her pocket and wrote a number on a piece of paper. "This is my personal number. We can talk more later. I ask that you leave my son out of this. Dominic Sloan has a reputation, but I know the real man behind the façade and what he's capable of. I can't get involved with this. Neither should you."

"I already am," Drew said and took the piece of paper.

The door opened and Gabe walked in holding coffee and a brown paper bag. He eyed the doctor and Gran.

"Is everything okay?" He rushed to Gran's side.

Dr. Wymond switched back on and she talked

about the surgery to him, reassuring him that everything was being done to help Gran. When she finished answering his questions, she nodded to Drew before leaving the room.

Drew gathered her jacket and keys.

"You're leaving?"

"I have work." It was a lie, but what else was she supposed to say? This was the only way to leave Gran's side without receiving a guilt-ridden glare.

"I brought you a sandwich."

"You didn't have to do that."

"I wanted to." Gabe took a paper-wrapped sandwich from the bag and handed it to her. She hesitated, wondering if his kindness would be short-lived. It was uncomfortable, unfamiliar. How many chances could you give someone? She took the food from him.

"Thank you."

"You're welcome. Thanks for sitting with her."

"She's like a mother to me, of course I'm going to sit with her! She's all I have." She leaned down and kissed Gran's forehead.

"You've got me. I don't know how long you plan on punishing me for being a shitty father, but I'm here now. I'm trying, Drew." Gabe looked sad as he spoke. "You keep saying it's too late, but I'm not giving up. I love you. That's not gonna change."

Why was he acting like this? She didn't recognize this person and he was making it hard to be angry at him.

She held her ground. "I should go." She headed for

the door and turned back. "I don't have a phone right now, but I'll check in later."

***

Drew drove to Claudia's house. A large, decorative wreath was suspended over the door and clear lights were strewn across the roof in classic fashion. She parked at the end of the driveway; there was only one other car, but the garage could hold two, maybe three, vehicles so anyone could be home. She didn't have a plan other than *get inside*. She hadn't spoken to Claudia since the night before and wasn't sure whether she'd be welcome here or not.

She walked up to the huge front porch unsure of how she was going to handle this. If Dominic came to the door, she could either bolt back to the car or ask for Claudia like nothing happened. Iron fencing surrounded the back yard and cameras hung on every corner of the elaborate home. It must be under constant surveillance. She peered through the window but saw nothing through closed drapes, although lights were on inside.

She pressed the doorbell and a melodic song chimed. She waited. Maybe no one was home. If she stayed below the cameras, she could try and break a window.

The door opened and she jumped back. Claudia stood with her arms crossed. Her pink lips matched her sweater. Her eyes were puffy. "It's not a good time. I'm heading out."

Drew tried to peer around Claudia to see inside. "Are you alone? I want to talk to you."

Claudia closed the door just enough to block Drew's view. "My parents are at some charity event, so yes, I'm alone. What does it matter? Those letters I told you about are gone. I don't know what he did with them, but they're not here. I'm not letting you come in."

"But I thought—"

"It doesn't matter anymore. You lied to me," Claudia said.

"No, I didn't!"

"You told me you didn't know that woman, but you knew enough to look for her dead body! I think you should leave."

Claudia started to close the door and Drew stepped closer. "There's more to it, Claudia."

"Really. Like what? Last night was chaos! My father is so mad."

"He knows?" Panic rose in Drew's chest at the thought of what Dominic would do next.

"Of course he knows, he owns the property, remember?"

"Your father has keys in this house. You said so yourself. I think they're for a safe in his warehouse. Let me come in."

"Why should I? So, you can prove some sick theory that the dead woman you found is the same one my father had an affair with? I made a mistake. I never should've told you." Claudia pulled her jacket on and zipped it. "You need to go."

"Claudia. I'm trying to help you."

"No, you aren't. You're here to help yourself."

Drew's stomach tightened. Was Claudia right? Was she only trying to help herself? She peered over Claudia's shoulder. Two staircases wound in either direction with a sparkling chandelier in the center. It looked like a ballroom. If Dominic went to jail, would Claudia's family lose everything? Drew didn't want that to happen. She didn't want to destroy lives. But she couldn't let him destroy hers either.

"Just give me ten minutes. Please."

Claudia stepped outside and closed the door. "I have plans." She pressed a button on her keychain and headlights lit up. "Goodbye, Drew. I think it's best if you stay away." She got in her car and drove away, not waiting for Drew to leave the step.

Drew scanned the house. It was quiet and appeared empty. The cameras didn't move or follow her. She hadn't seen Claudia lock the door.

Reaching for the door handle, she pressed on the metal latch. It opened.

Had Claudia forgotten? Or—maybe she left it open for her.

Drew pushed the door she stepped inside.

Removing her boots, she tiptoed across the entryway and up the stairs. She walked along a hallway overlooking a grand living room filled with white furniture. It was beautiful. Untouched. It did a good job at covering the darkness that lived here. A corner room was decorated with a huge mahogany desk and chair and floor-to-ceiling shelves. This had to be Dominic's office.

333

Drew walked in and set to work pulling drawers open. The bottom one was locked. Where would he hide keys? Claudia knew where those keys were; she'd mentioned a box full of keys in his office…they had to be here somewhere!

The room was uncluttered. Nothing lingered over the desk except a marble canister with a few pens and a letter opener. Books lined the shelves by category. There were books on finance, real estate, the stock market—but one didn't fit the filing system in place. She pulled a dictionary off the shelf expecting it to be heavy, but it wasn't at all. Something jingled inside. She opened it revealing a secret compartment with a set of keys.

She rummaged through and tried each one in the bottom desk drawer. The faint rumble of an engine sounded outside, and she peeked through the blinds on the window. The black sedan slowed down passing the house.

She'd been followed!

Fumbling with the keys, she tried each one in the locked drawer until it opened. Stacks of money wrapped in bunches lined inside, but there were no letters anywhere. The car passed by again. She had to get out of there.

She locked the drawer and stuffed the keys in her jacket. Placing the book with care on the shelf, she left the room and crept down the stairs. Shoving her feet back in her boots she stepped outside, closed the door, and dashed to her car. As she backed out, she slammed on the brakes as the black car passed by, circling her like a shark with its prey. It pulled into the driveway, but she sped away. She knew who was in that car, and she refused to let them catch her. Someone was always watching.

He knows.

She clutched the keys in her pocket. One of them had to open the safe—this would be her only chance. As soon as he found out the keys were missing, he would come for her. She had to get to the shipyard before he did.

Twenty-Five

Drew hurried to the port, swerving down dark alleys that she knew like the back of her hand. She grew up here, spending more time at the bakery than she did home at times. She pulled into an alcove and turned her headlights off as the sedan passed the alley. She ditched them!

She took the opposite route to the shipyard and parked behind an adjacent building to the warehouse. She stepped out and put her backpack on her shoulders. A large boat was docked close by. That hadn't been there before.

Dusk turned to darkness. She was wasting precious time. Cutting across the pavement, she snuck along the side of the building to the back entrance. She picked up a stick and angled the camera away from the door. She turned the knob, but it was locked.

"Need help?"

She spun around. Enid stood behind her. "How did you know I was here?"

Enid shrugged impishly. "I appear where I'm needed, and it seems I *am* needed."

Drew couldn't argue with that. She set to trying the

keys again. "None of them work. I need to get inside!"

Enid grinned. "So, let's go inside." Just like that, she walked through the wall.

"Enid!"

The doorknob jiggled and stopped. Enid emerged back through the wall. "Try it now."

Drew turned the knob and this time it opened. "How—how'd you do that?"

"I've been practicing. It takes a lot of focus and sheer will. Sometimes it works and other times I can't do anything no matter how hard I try. Do you have any idea how frustrating that is?"

Drew focused on one thing. She ran past her up the stairs and found the door to the office locked. She turned to Enid. "Can you do that again?"

"I can try." Enid slid through the door, taking human form on the other side. The door clicked and Drew opened it. She turned the light on and took the painting down exposing the lockbox in the wall. There were two places for keys and a number pad.

Drew plopped her backpack on the floor and set to work fidgeting with the keys. One of them fit. But only one. Where was the other key? She stood with her hands on her hips looking around the room. The cabinet in the corner had a padlock. The smallest key on the ring opened it. She grabbed the files and shoved them in her backpack. She searched the other drawers.

"What about the desk?" Enid said from behind it.

The desk. The stools. The room. Without warning, it all triggered flashbacks from the last time she was stuck in here with Dominic. The threats echoed in her mind. She could almost feel the gun at her back and the slap to her face. She'd been running on adrenaline, and it all crashed leaving her with an overwhelming feeling of dread.

"I'm going to get myself killed. What am I doing?" Drew covered her face with her hands.

"You're helping Iris and Shane. You're freeing everyone from that horrible man! You are brave and strong, and you're not alone."

"I'm not any of those things, Enid."

"But you are!" Enid said.

Drew went behind the desk and stuck each key into the locks on the desk. "Nothing's working! I can't do this."

Enid shifted back into a translucent figure and leaned her head through the top of the desk. "It's in there. I see it."

"Can you get it?"

"No, but you can."

Drew needed something heavy. Something able to smash wood. She ran down the stairs and searched for something that could break into the desk. She found an axe mounted to the wall by the fire extinguisher, illuminated by the glow of the exit sign. She took it into the office and swung into the wooden desk. The axe got stuck. She pried it free and swung again, this time splintering the wood. One more swing and the wood cracked open. A key was the only thing inside, and it was worth more than gold.

She held her breath and jammed it in the other lock, turning them both together.

The lock box opened. With shaking hands, she reached inside and pulled out the letters and a cell phone. When she powered the phone on, a family picture of Iris, Paxton, and Shane popped up. She couldn't move past that screen without a password.

"This was Iris's phone! He had her phone!"

A look of pure joy spread across Enid's face. "You did it!"

Drew grinned, but the victory was short-lived, as she saw Enid's face fall. "What is it?"

Enid shook her head. "I think—I think you better leave. You've got to get out of here!" She got more frantic. "Someone's coming, Drew! I can feel it. I'm being pulled away again. I'm so sorry!"

Drew stuffed the envelopes in her backpack and threw it on her back. Clutching the phone, she bolted down the steps, but the sound of a car door slam outside made her stop. Her pulse quickened in her ears and her nerves pricked all over her skin. Her fingers gripped Iris's phone so tight they went numb. It was her lifeline for help. She darted between storage barrels and found a door. She pulled it open to find a shelf of cleaning supplies and a mop. She stepped inside and shut the door. The only sound inside were her shallow breaths.

The groan of a door opening and shutting with a bang echoed through the building. Footsteps scuffed along the cement floor before clanging up metal stairs. Drew could only assume they were going to the office. The mess she'd left behind was a dead giveaway, but she thought she had enough time to get out and take what she'd found to the police.

Smashing glass sounded. More footsteps slammed down the stairs.

"Drew? I know you're in here. It's just a matter of time before I find you." A crash echoed. "Come on out! I just want to talk to you."

She knew that voice. Too well. It was Dominic.

Drew held her breath and stilled. If he left, she could escape. It was the only way she was getting out of this mess alive.

The voice sounded closer. "You saw it, didn't you? The boat. I assume Shane disobeyed me and came back. Where is my son?" More smashing rang through the warehouse. She tucked into the corner of the closet. It was too dark to see. She held the phone in her hand. If she called 9-1-1, he'd hear and start shooting. But if she didn't call for help and he found her… She didn't want to think about it.

She waited, listening.

His footsteps resonated further away, and the door opened again, slamming closed.

Silence.

He was gone. But he'd be back, with more of his goons in tow. She had to get out! She opened the door a crack and peered out. The light from the office illuminated the path to the exit. She listened for the car to start, but it was quiet. He was waiting. She scanned the huge room. A red exit sign at the other end lit up. She could run along the wall, concealed by darkness. If she escaped out the other side of the building, she could call for help and run.

She slid out of the closet and started for the door.

She couldn't see her hand in front of her face. She ran her hands along the wall navigating her way toward the door, toward freedom. She pressed the metal bar as slowly as she could to not make a sound. The door pulled open from the other side.

Dominic stood in front of her, staring at her with wild eyes.

"You trashed my office and stole from me. You're about to find out what happens to people who don't respect me."

He shoved her back inside and she fell to the floor. The door shut behind him and he hovered over her. She crawled backwards along the floor with the phone in her hand. He grabbed her by the hair and pulled her up. She screamed and he cuffed her across the face.

He was going to kill her. Just like he killed Shane's mother.

"Where is he?" he fumed. "You're the first person he'd run to!"

Her throat dried and tears stung her eyes. Hard metal was pressed against her chest. "I don't know where he is!" she whimpered.

He dragged her to the stairs and shoved her down, aiming the gun at her head. She held the phone under her leg, desperate to hide it from him. As soon as he took that from her, she was dead.

"What were you doing inside that old house? There were police everywhere. What the fuck did you dig up?" He crouched in front of her and grabbed her chin. "You saw her, didn't you?"

"Who?" Tears blurred her vision before coursing

down her face.

"You know exactly who I'm talking about, don't make me say it! You have no idea who you're dealing with. How many fires do I have to set before you get it? You think you've got no family now? Just wait. Your life will be a living hell."

"You killed her! Your son's mother." Her words shook through hyperventilating breaths.

"How dare you accuse me!" As he moved from his crouching position to stand, he tripped, falling back against a wheeled cart. It moved with his weight, and he landed on the floor. She leapt from the stair and made a break for the door.

As she ran, she pressed the emergency button and the phone dialed 9-1-1. A voice came over the phone asking for her emergency. She yelled for help as Dominic hoisted himself off the floor, tearing after her. She burst outside and sucked frigid night air into her lungs. He grabbed her, heaving her back inside.

She screamed until her throat was raw.

The phone slipped from her hand, landing on the snow-covered pavement before the door closed, trapping her inside with him. He pushed her to the floor and held the gun to her head.

"I thought we had an agreement, but this? This isn't going to work for me."

"Please don't do this! I'll back off, okay? Is that what you want?"

"No more talking." He raised his hand and brought it down to strike her.

He hit the pavement as she curled to the side,

avoiding him. She heard him swear in anger before a blast reverberated through the warehouse. Stabbing agony exploded in her leg and hot liquid gushed, soaking through her jeans. Ringing sounded in her ears, drowning out her own cries. She shook all over, grabbing at the railing of the stairs and pulling herself up. Blood streamed down her leg, and she felt light-headed.

If she didn't do something, she was as good as dead.

Dominic raised his hand and aimed the gun at her again.

"Haven't you had enough?"

Her lungs were on fire, she couldn't speak through the pain.

He laughed. "I told you. I protect what's mine."

"Like you did with Enid and Ezra?" she gasped. "Were they in your way too?"

"That wasn't what happened! I didn't do anything wrong!" He sounded crazy and his eyes were wild as he moved closer to her, raising the gun.

The door swung open.

"Dad?" Claudia stood at the entrance, her eyes wide with shock. "What are you doing?" She ran toward them.

Dominic lowered the gun. "Get out of here, Claudia. This isn't for your eyes."

"What?" Claudia walked to her father. She looked Drew up and down. "She's bleeding! What did you do? Did you shoot her? My god, Dad! She was right all along, wasn't she?"

"Honey, please leave," he seethed through his teeth. He stepped closer to her.

"Don't come near me!" Claudia had her hands up. Despite her words, she moved in between Dominic and Drew, facing her father with her back to Drew. Protecting her. "I'm calling the police." She lifted her phone up and he smacked it from her hands.

"I don't want to do this. You leave me no choice. Move away from her."

"Or what? You're going to shoot me?" Claudia laughed hysterically. "I'm your daughter! You're insane!"

Drew thought she might pass out. She had to tell Claudia everything in case she never woke up.

"He murdered Iris," Drew said hoarsely. "The woman in the letters had a baby. It's Shane."

Dominic wiped sweat off his forehead. His suit jacket was ripped. He looked like a killer in every sense of the imagination. He raised the gun and lunged, shoving Claudia aside and knocking Drew to the floor. She flopped to her back, writhing in pain. The ringing sounded in her ears again as a sharp pain cut through the side of her head. Dominic stood over her, panting, aiming the gun at her face.

Claudia whacked him across the back with what looked like a metal pipe. He dropped the gun and fell to the floor, yelling.

"Drew!" Claudia screamed and ran to her side.

Sirens wailed outside getting louder. Dominic looked at the door the same time Drew did.

Help was coming.

Drew gathered all her strength and dove for the gun at his feet, grabbing it up. It was heavy in her hands. She'd never shot a gun before, or even held one, let alone thought about *shooting* someone with one.

Dominic smirked. "What are you going to do with that?"

Drew swallowed and pulled the hammer back. Just like she'd seen in the movies, hundreds of times. "I'm going to shoot you if you come once step closer!" Her hands trembled. "Stay back! I'll do it."

She wanted him dead. She never wanted to see his face again. But taking a life scared the hell out of her.

Where were the damn police?

Dominic held the pipe up in his hands. It was a crowbar. Claudia crouched behind her, crying. "Daddy, please don't do this!"

He charged at Drew and swung the heavy metal toward her face.

She pulled the trigger.

A menacing blast reverberated through the warehouse, and he hit the floor hollering like a wounded animal.

Claudia screeched and started wailing.

A glow ignited around her. Enid crouched beside her. She didn't look real—her features were fuzzy and delicate. She didn't speak, only hovered over her as if waiting. Drew melted to the floor.

So, this was it, she was dying. Bleeding to death. Would she walk through some door to the other side and roam Atlas Cliffs with Enid? She thought of Gran having to live alone without her. She'd never see Piper again. Or Nico. She could feel the life draining from her body like a popped balloon.

Sirens blared and car doors slammed outside. The warehouse door across from the stair burst open and police charged inside.

She strained to see through her blurry eyesight. Claudia was crying, holding her hand. Someone was applying pressure on her leg. Her eyes landed on tousled hair. Blood was splattered across their jacket. Breaths heaved out in a cloud among the cold.

"Who are you?" She coughed. Pain seared through her leg.

"Don't move. I've got to stop the bleeding." The voice was shaky, but familiar. "I should never have left."

"Shane?"

His hands tightened as he pressed down on her thigh. He lifted his head, and the light caught his face. Using her elbows, she propped herself up. She saw little stars cascade around her.

She was going to pass out.

Flopping back down, she took her hand from Claudia and reached out to touch his face. She closed her eyes to clear the tears. His bloodied hand reached up and covered her own.

"I—I'm just so sorry. I can't believe he did this to you. He promised he would leave you alone!"

She grabbed his jacket pulling herself up toward him. She hugged him with one arm before letting go and sinking back to the floor.

"If I let go the bleeding won't stop." His voice

cracked. "You're in this mess because of me. All I want is to hold you, Drew." He stared at her with unblinking, terrified eyes.

Police yelled out as medics arrived with a stretcher. Her focus faltered as Shane was pulled away.

Cold fluid dripped into her arm following the sharp puncture of a needle. The hammering in her head dulled to an incessant tap. She faded in and out until someone's warm hands covered her own.

When she opened her eyes, she was sitting on the rocky shore at Neptune Point in front of Aurora. The sun was shining, and the water was calmer than normal. Iris sat beside her in a clean dress, her hair dancing in the tender breeze. Her face looked angelic. She emitted peace.

"Thank you, Drew."

"You're welcome."

"Tell them I'm okay, will you?" Iris said. "Tell them I'll love them forever."

"I will."

She stood and cupped Drew's face with her hands. "You're going to be okay."

She whirled around and disappeared.

She knew it would be the last time she'd see Iris.

Twenty-Six

Three days in the hospital. That's how long they'd kept her there. Three days for a gunshot wound, but finally, Drew was being released. Gran's surgery had been the day before and she was recovering down the hallway. Drew had been using a wheelchair to visit often.

She'd had enough of the hospital to last a lifetime. She put her hair in a ponytail and pulled a pair of loose sweatpants over her bandaged leg.

Everyone kept telling her how lucky she was. She didn't feel lucky.

She'd been rushed into surgery to repair what the doctor called 'vascular injury'. He wore a bowtie and a blazer under his lab coat and explained using facts devoid of emotion. All that mattered was she was getting out of there.

Dominic Sloan survived. It took eight hours of surgery, but the asshole was alive. She didn't know how to feel about that; she'd wanted him dead, out of her life forever, but it would have been at the cost of taking a life. As much as she thought killing him would be a victory, she didn't know how she'd have lived with blood on her hands. A life rotting in prison, especially for a man like Dominic Sloan, was a painful enough punishment.

The docked boat turned out to be the *Light of Aurora*, the boat Shane returned home on. She hadn't seen him since the warehouse and didn't understand why he wouldn't come to see her. Whether he meant to or not, he was hurting her all over again. The whole thing had been surreal, like a dream she couldn't wake from.

Piper visited daily. So did Nico. He hadn't left her side. He also didn't ask about Shane—maybe he didn't want to know; not like she even knew what to tell him. They'd have to talk about it though. Eventually.

Enid disappeared once paramedics took Drew from the warehouse, and she hadn't seen her since. She wondered where she and Ezra were now. She had to see them again; she couldn't forget that she'd given her word to help Enid.

A rap at the door startled her thoughts.

"Can I come in?" Detective Valerie Porter opened the door a crack.

"Yeah," Drew said. "Where's Shane? I've been trying to get hold of him. No one seems to know anything."

"Last I heard, he's home with his dad."

"Have you talked to him? How is he?"

Detective Porter pulled up a chair. "May I?"

"Sure."

"As for Shane, I could get a message to him, but I think you'll have to talk to him yourself. I can't speak for him or his dad." She leaned forward in the chair.

"The reason I stopped by was to see how you're doing but to also apologize. I take full responsibility for letting you down. You tried to warn me about Dominic Sloan, and I should've acted on it more forcefully than I did."

"Just make sure he never gets out. Never."

"Mr. Bishop gave his permission so I can talk to you about his late wife. I can't share all the details, but we received the forensic report for Mrs. Bishop—Iris. With the evidence we have from the report, her phone, and documents found at the scene, we have more than enough evidence to make an airtight case against him. He's been charged with murder, attempted murder, assault, not to mention the fraud and weapons charges against him. I vow to do everything I can to make sure he never sees the light of day. Drew, what I'm trying to say, and I'm not doing a good job of it, is thank you. You're a brave young woman to have experienced and survived what he put you through."

Drew didn't feel brave at all. She felt sad. Despite Iris finding her peace, she was left emptier than what she'd imagined this moment to be.

Gabe stepped into the room holding a Styrofoam cup with steam rising off the top. The lines between his brows were deeper and new stubble grew beyond his bearded face. His hair hung in a mess around his jawline. He looked like hell.

Detective Porter excused herself with a promise of getting a message to Shane. Drew had to see him, talk to him, even if he didn't want to.

"How's Gran?" she asked.

"Better. She's up and moving. They'll discharge her soon, so she's making a list of stuff around the house that needs to get done. I'd say she's coming around. I'm here to take you home if that's okay. I let your friends know. They'll stop by the house later."

Being alone in a car with Gabe. How would that conversation go? All that mattered was getting home. She bent down for her boots and winced. He set his coffee down and crouched in front of her.

"Here." He put one boot on, and then the other. "Better?"

She remembered falling off her bike and skinning her knee when she was a kid. Gabe was so caring as he put a bandage on it and kissed it better as any good parent would. It was a time of innocence before he left her jaded and hurt. It changed her perspective on relationships and trust. It changed her perspective on everything! She was damaged. But maybe it wasn't entirely his fault. Maybe she allowed it to happen too. She didn't know how she could repair that.

He stood up with tears in his eyes. "If I lost you, I don't know what I'd do. What's it going to take for you to forgive me? I don't know what to do, but if you tell me what you need from me, I'll do it. I'll do anything to get my daughter back. *Anything*."

"I can't do this," Drew said. "Not now. I don't have it in me." For the first time in a long time, she saw with new eyes how broken he was. She could step away from her feelings and witness his genuine desperation to right his wrongs. He was her father and all he wanted was her love. She thought of Claudia and how different her life must be now without a father. And Shane dealing with the loss of his mother.

It was going to take time to build trust with Gabe. She might not be able to forget that he'd left her, but she had to find a way to forgive him. She needed to let him know that if he wasn't giving up on her, she'd grant him the same in return.

"I need to talk to Shane. If you want to do something, get me out of here and help me contact him. Can you do that…Dad?"

His head snapped up from his hands, stunned. "I can do that." He helped her stand and put her jacket on. She sat in a wheelchair, and he rolled her out of the hospital to the truck.

"Where's his house?"

"Really?" She couldn't help but be suspicious.

"Really."

She directed him to Shane's house, and when they got there, he pulled up the driveway and helped her to the front door. She rang the bell. Her father walked back to the truck leaving her alone.

Shane opened the door. "Drew?"

"Can I come in?"

Shane nodded quickly. "Of course!"

Seeing him standing in front of her and hearing his voice brought her back in time. Back to that happy place when the two of them were intertwined in each other. But it was just a memory. He'd made his choice the day he let Dominic Sloan force him away from Atlas Cliffs. Too much had happened in the time he'd been gone. *Nico* had happened. She was attracted to him, and it went beyond his crooked smile, the way he ran a hand through his hair when he was stressed, and the confident way he carried himself. She cared about him. He was one of her best friends, he was a constant in her life. He was *home*.

She couldn't go back, but she didn't know how she was going to let Shane go.

He wrapped his arm around her waist and helped her to the sofa. Before he could release her, she gripped his sleeve, and he didn't let her go. She looked into his blue eyes, and the most private memories flooded back. She was in his arms again, like she had been before. But something was different; the innocence of their love was gone.

"Sit with me," she said, her voice catching. He sat beside her, and she held on to him. She couldn't let go. How could she ever let go?

He gave in and wrapped his arms around her, his body relaxing against hers. She buried her face into his neck trying to smother the ache in her chest.

"I missed you so much. I'm so sorry I hurt you. You must be mad as hell at me."

She lifted her head, pulling back. "No. I'm not mad at you. You did what you thought you had to do. You broke my heart though, Shane, I can't lie about that. But mad? No, that's not what I'm feeling anymore."

He broke away and leaned his elbows on his knees. "He killed my mom. He ruined my life, my dad's life. I found out who he was. I found my mom's phone. She'd gone to meet him at that old house and that was the last message between them... Her last message." He turned to face her and wiped his eyes.

"Drew, I drove out there to find her—God, I don't even know what I was looking for—and the bastard followed me. He beat me and held a gun to my head. Said he was going to kill dad. You. Your family. He knew everything about me. Said he would keep me alive because I was *his son*. All I had to do was follow his orders to keep everyone safe. Ditch the car, play dead. Never come back. I did what he wanted for months, but out of nowhere he started calling me and threatening to hurt you if I talked. I didn't get it! I hadn't said anything! I knew I had to come back. I heard his people talking on the boat; they were coming to Atlas Cliffs. They forced me off the boat, but I snuck back on before it left port. They had no idea. I had to come home to you."

She watched him as he shifted his gaze to his hands. She didn't say a word and he continued.

"We were on deck and heard shots fired. When I saw you bleeding all over the floor…He almost killed you! That disgusting piece of shit is my *father*. I can't even look at myself in the mirror. I couldn't bring myself to come see you at the hospital."

"I know what he is, and you're not him." She didn't know what else to say. Her insides hurt.

"I heard he has an older son in university who he doesn't see much. And Claudia Sloan is my *sister*? I remember her as the bitchy, popular girl in school."

She thought of Claudia. The real Claudia, the one hidden underneath the whole mean-girl-thing she had going on. "I don't know his oldest son, but Claudia is a good person, Shane. So are you."

"I'm surprised you came. I didn't think you'd want anything to do with me."

"When you disappeared...I was shattered. But I didn't believe you were dead. I couldn't *see* you, ya know?"

He sat nodding slowly. "Did you see her? Mom?"

"That's how I knew where to find her."

"Is she still with you somehow?" His voice cracked and a look of profound sadness filled his blue eyes.

She reached for his hand, and he linked his fingers through hers. She told him about his mom's goodbye, that she loved them both. He covered his face with his hands and cried. He held Drew like his life depended on it. She leaned back and reached in her jacket pocket.

"Here. She'd given it to you, and I wanted you to have it back." She held out the pocket watch. "It belongs in your family. It was your great-grandfather's. I think Iris took it from Dominic, so you'd have a piece of where you came from."

He stared at it. "I can't...what about that woman? Blythe. She should keep it."

"She told me to give it to you." Drew handed it to him. "It's okay, really."

He took it from her and closed his fingers around it. "Thank you." He hung his head. "I read stuff on my mom's phone. She wanted me to know where I came from. She'd taken that watch and hung on to it since I was a baby. He didn't know I existed. I think the guilt was too much for her. That's why she went to see him. Maybe she thought I needed to know who my real father is, I don't know. I'll never know what was going through her head. Paxton is my dad. Mom went to see that asshole, was at the wrong place at the wrong time, and found out everything. He wasn't letting her go knowing what she knew." He wiped his eyes and lifted his head. "We're having a funeral for her."

Drew grasped his hand and squeezed. "I'd like to come if that's okay."

"Of course it's okay. I love you, Drew. I love you so much. I want us to be together again. Like it used to be."

"Shane," she said, her throat tight, "I...I can't be with you. It'll never be like it was before. Everything is different now. *I'm* different."

She just got him back, but this time, she was the one leaving. It was time for her to move on from him, from this chapter in her life. If she'd questioned her decision before, it was clear the moment he answered the door. The change in him was palpable. He wasn't the person she'd known so well before, but somehow it was okay because neither was she. Not anymore.

Dominic stole everything—but she couldn't get past Shane choosing to let her believe he was dead for months. Regardless of Dominic's threats, he should've tried to contact her. While she could appreciate the mess of a situation he'd been in and forgive him for hurting her, she'd never be able to trust him again. She risked her life trying to find out what happened to him. In many ways, she'd put her love for him above herself.

She would never do that again.

"We could get to know each other again. Take it

slow. I can't lose you again," he said. He looked at her with desperate eyes. Their faces were so close they almost touched.

"You'll never lose me. I'll always love you, no matter what happens," she said through tears. "But I have to walk away, Shane."

He hugged her and she let her fingers trail through his hair. She knew once she let him go, he'd be gone. He kissed her neck and moved along her jawline until he met her lips and they kissed. It was soft, gentle.

This was the Shane she remembered. Her first everything.

Time stopped and she closed her eyes allowing herself to crash into the moment. That pain and heartache from the past year melted away. She had him in her arms one last time. She breathed him in before it all ended for good.

The Drew-and-Shane she'd held onto for so long was over.

Breaking away she rested her forehead on his chest and hung on to him.

"Why does this feel like goodbye?" he asked.

"Because it has to be."

He walked her out to the truck. As Gabe drove away, she hung her head and let it all out. It came in uncontrollable waves, and she couldn't stop it. Her father reached over and squeezed her hand.

***

Drew settled in the big chair across from the crackling

fire. It had been a week since she'd seen Shane. The gap between them grew with each passing day, but it was different than the past year. She meant it when she told him she loved him and knowing he was alive, and home calmed something inside of her.

A memorial was held for Iris and the whole town came with flowers and kind words. She talked to Shane at the service to discover he was leaving town with his father after the holidays. Paxton got a job in Boston where his brother lived. The distance was necessary. It was unspoken, but they both knew it.

The community was in shock as the news was released about Dominic. She reached out to Claudia a few times but hadn't heard back. Maybe she never would.

Nico spent a lot of time with her. He let her go through the motions without pushing her for anything. She told him about Shane—even the kiss goodbye. She had nothing to hide, not anymore. Nico accepted it all.

She shifted focus to the unfinished business hanging over her. She'd made a promise to Enid and Ezra, and she had an idea. She'd convinced Dr. Wymond to join her for a drive to Neptune Point. Maybe if she brought them together one last time, they could finally be free.

She jumped when the doorbell rang. She pushed herself off the chair to answer the door, looking through the window first.

Claudia stood on the other side wearing a fur-trimmed hat with her hands in the pockets of her puffy coat. Drew took a deep breath and opened the door, hoping she'd know the right thing to say.

"Can I come in?" Claudia asked.

"Yeah, of course." She opened the door wider and gestured for her to come in. "Can I get you anything—"

"No…I'm good. Can we sit?"

"Sure."

Drew led her to the living room where they sat beside each other on the sofa.

"How are you?" Drew regretted asking as soon as the words came out. Claudia was a mess. She could see it all over her face. "I'm sorry, that was a dumb question."

"I've been asked worse," Claudia said. She sat for another moment in silence before words rushed out of her. "My mom filed for divorce this week and she's selling the house. I just can't believe it, you know? How didn't we see it? *Ben Morana*. Did you know that's his real name? You know Piper's boyfriend, Cole? He's my cousin! I have an aunt. And Shane—he won't even take my calls. Drew, can you please ask him to call me? I only want to talk…That's it."

"We aren't together anymore. I'm not much good to you."

Claudia pulled the fuzzy hat off and placed in in her lap. "Oh, I'm sorry."

"It's okay. Really. He's alive, that's all that matters. I have to move on, you know?" She adjusted a pillow cushion under her sore leg. It was healing, slowly, and maybe with time they'd *all* heal from this mess. "Give him some time. I don't really have answers for you other than that. Maybe one day you could actually be, I don't know—"

"Family?" Claudia asked. "I don't know about that. My mom is ruined. She had no idea. None." Claudia's face reddened and her eyes glassed over. "That night when you were at my house…I left the door unlocked. My father asked me about the letters and slapped me when I brought up what I read. He had cameras everywhere. I couldn't risk taking you inside."

"I thought I lucked out when the door opened. I started all of this when I found those keys. All hell broke loose."

"You didn't start anything. He did this." Claudia looked angry, but Drew knew her anger wasn't for her. "When I left you at my house that night…I don't know what, but something inside of me felt sick. Like he was up to something bad; I just didn't realize how bad it all was. I couldn't let you do it alone, so I drove to the warehouse. I knew if you'd gotten those keys, that's where you'd be. When I walked inside and I saw he had shot you…Drew, I just feel so embarrassed. I don't want to show my face in town."

Drew hugged her, surprising them both. "If anyone can rise above this, you can. You're the strongest girl I know. Aside from Piper."

Claudia smiled and squeezed her. "God. That girl can kick my ass any day of the week, don't think I don't know it. She does drive me crazy though, no offense."

"None taken." Drew laughed.

Like everyone else, Claudia wanted to put the pieces together and she had a lot of questions. She desperately needed to know how Drew knew what she did, especially about her father and Iris. Drew told her everything. It was her truth, and she wasn't hiding it anymore.

***

Drew stood beside Dr. Wymond on the rocky shore at Neptune Point, the lighthouse towering above them. Fresh snow covered the ground and coated the abandoned house. The time had come to say goodbye to old ghosts.

Enid appeared in human form with Ezra at her side. "You came back. You brought her—how did you know?"

"Doctor Wymond, they're here," Drew said.

"Call me Blythe," she said absentmindedly, glancing around while she grasped the locket around her neck. "Where? I don't see them. Are you sure?"

Enid touched the scar on Blythe's face.

Blythe raised her own hand, touching her face in wonder. "My face... It's warm."

"She's touching your scar," Drew said.

"It's a birthmark," Enid corrected.

"Enid just corrected me," Drew said, smiling at Enid. "It's a birthmark."

Blythe smiled too. "That it is. Are they okay?"

"Tell her she's freed us," Enid said.

Ezra grasped Blythe's fingers and she looked down. "Is someone touching my hand?"

Drew smiled. "It's Ezra."

"I miss you," Blythe said, tears running down her cheeks. "I love you."

"I love you too, sis." Enid wrapped her arms around Blythe before stepping back with Ezra.

For the first time, Drew looked at her ability to see the dead as a gift instead of a curse.

Enid looked at Drew. "Thank you. I'll miss you."

"Me too. Maybe I'll see you again?"

The familiar impish smile crossed Enid's face. "Anything is possible. Bye, Drew."

Drew rubbed her arms. Goosebumps covered her skin underneath her coat. Enid was moving on too. She saved Drew in more ways than she'd ever know; she helped give Drew her life back.

Enid nodded and looked down at Ezra. They walked over the water and disappeared.

She looked up at the lighthouse. Jack Morana stood on the landing outside. He tipped his hat and turned, walking through the lighthouse wall.

Twenty-Seven

Drew sat on the porch swing using her good leg to gently push herself back and forth. A breeze wafted up over the cliffs and rustled the leaves on the big oak trees around her. She could hear the waves swishing to shore from where she sat. Gran's flowers bloomed and a bee hovered over the pink and blue flowers. Summer had arrived, and she somehow managed to graduate high school.

It had taken six months for her to stop looking over her shoulder. The physical wounds had healed leaving her with a long scar and loss of full sensation in her leg. But it was the mental wounds that were more difficult to heal. Loud noises or any black car triggered anxiety, but therapy was helping. It also helped that Dominic Sloan was in jail serving a life sentence.

Drew no longer saw herself as cursed. She stopped running from it, stopped fighting it. While she didn't see Enid, Ezra, or Iris anymore, old man Jack made an appearance sometimes, just not in her dreams. He liked to show up around the Tough Cookie as it was being rebuilt, but she found his presence comforting in an odd way; she trusted him now. Gran had given her and

Nellie full reign on the decisions for the bakery. She even quit the Casting Spoon and agreed to work there for the summer.

She'd been accepted to an art school in Boston in the fall. She planned to go but hadn't told Shane yet. She missed him, she really did, but he kept in touch. Maybe their paths would cross, but it would only be as friends. They were getting to know each other again bit by bit, like the first time, only without the awkwardness. It was uncomplicated, and she liked it that way.

In a few hours, she'd be going to her prom with Nico. She wasn't sure she'd go at all, but Piper convinced her it was better to go to prom than have regrets about not going later in life. Maybe she was right. It didn't matter to Drew either way, but her friends were excited, especially Nico, and she'd promised to go with him.

A car zoomed up the road and swerved up the driveway. Piper had finally saved up enough to buy one of her own. She hopped out and bounded toward her. Her newly purple-streaked hair bounced as she walked.

"I think you should forego Law school and become a race car driver," Drew said.

"You can make jokes, but don't think I haven't considered it!"

"Do you want me to help you get ready? What time is Nico picking you up? If you wear your hair up it won't get messy in the convertible." Piper sat beside her on the swing and played with Drew's hair, holding it up on top of her head.

"It's a school dance, not a grand ball. We should all boycott it and throw a beach bonfire across the street instead."

"After party?" Piper grinned.

Drew laughed. "I think prom will be quite enough, thank you."

Piper arched her perfectly groomed eyebrows. "Okay. I get it. I'm just happy you're coming to prom. It's tradition! A rite of passage. We'll make memories that will last forever."

"I'm going! You don't have to sell it anymore."

They sat back, moving on from prom to talking about their best memories from high school. It was sweet and nostalgic. Drew didn't know how many more summer days they'd have like this; Piper was going away to school at the end of the summer too, and she hoped they'd be able to keep their friendship strong forever.

***

Drew sat on the bench seat under the open bay window in her bedroom. The curtains danced as sea air entered the room. She stared at herself in the mirror. No more messages scrolled across its surface and looking at it didn't scare her anymore.

She'd found a pale green vintage dress at a second-hand store downtown. Its silky texture was soft on her skin, and it fit as though it was meant for her. The thin straps held the square bodice in place, while the green chiffon cascaded to the floor like air. Her red hair flowed free past her shoulders, and the only makeup she wore was mascara and lip-gloss. Her freckles emerged with the recent weeks of sun, and she made no effort to cover them up.

She felt more herself than ever before.

An engine revved up the road. She finally was getting a ride in the Mustang. It made her smile. She never dreamed of prom and graduation as others did; even when she'd been with Shane, it wasn't something they'd talked about. But here she was about to go off to prom and leave this chapter behind.

Slipping on a beaded pair of sandals that matched her dress, she held up the chiffon layers and went downstairs. Her father and Gran fussed over her with compliments and pictures despite her protests. Secretly, she loved being a family again. She stepped onto the front porch and Nico stood beaming at her, looking handsome in his light gray suit. His vest and tie matched her dress, and he handed her a unique wrist corsage of pink orchids.

"You look beautiful, Drew. I'm the luckiest guy in the world." He leaned over and kissed her. "Are you ready?"

She beamed at him. "Let's do this."

He opened the door for her, and she climbed in. They drove along the coastal road with the top down and she let her hair fly free. If she was going to do this, she may as well have fun.

The sun was setting over the harbor as they arrived at the Atlas Cliffs Marina, a fancy event center on the boardwalk. The decorations were an over the top starry-night-happily-ever-after theme. She was transported into a magical world of fairy gardens filled with flowers and sparkling lights. Inside, the lights twinkled like stars above her head. A DJ spun music from a small stage and students took selfies with their phones, hugging and laughing.

"This is something, isn't it?" She poked Nico, smiling. She was doing more of that these days.

"There literally is no place in the entire world I'd rather be right now." He put his arms around her and kissed her.

Piper strolled up, linking arms with Cole. Her dress flared out just above the knee—purple to match her hair, but with black polka dots. A lilac sash wrapped around her waist and the bodice was adorned with black and purple sequins. She radiated cool.

"You look amazing, Piper!" Drew exclaimed.

Piper released Cole and spun around. "Thank you! You look stunning! That dress is perfect on you!" She embraced Drew, fluffing her red hair as she pulled away.

Claudia sauntered over with heels so high, Drew didn't know how she could stand. Her wrist was adorned with a beautiful corsage of red roses that matched her silk dress. She exuded self-assurance. Drew smiled at her as she approached, knowing how long it had taken for Claudia to find her confidence again. No one else saw the pain and humiliation Claudia's family experienced behind closed doors.

"Isn't it fabulous?" Claudia burst with excitement.

"It really is. You did a great job decorating this

place," Drew said.

Piper rolled her eyes and Drew gave her a look. Piper didn't understand the newfound friendship between Drew and Claudia, but Drew had an insight into Claudia that no one else seemed to have, not even Claudia's gang of admirers.

Soon, Claudia's friends pulled her away to the dance floor, and Piper and Cole were caught up in each other's bubble.

Drew and Nico sat at one of the elaborate tables, talking. Conversation always flowed so easily with him. A slow song came on.

"Dance with me," he said, holding his hand out.

They held each other as they moved to the music. She loved being in Nico's arms. It was comfortable. He'd been exactly what she needed. But she didn't want to hurt him, and the deeper their relationship grew, the more it worried her. As school came to an end he started talking about the future—*their* future together.

Drew had plans to leave Atlas Cliffs. She needed to go away to school and be on her own. It was time. When she thought of her future, Nico wasn't a part of it. Not like he was now.

The song ended and they stepped outside on the patio overlooking the marina.

Nico looked at her. "There's a party at Haven after if you want to go. Only if you want to. I don't care either way."

"I really don't want to go back there, but you can go."

"I get it. We can hang out at the beach. Make a fire

or something."

"Tonight has been fun. I'm so glad I came." She held his hand. "I'm especially happy that I could come here with you, but I just want to go home after."

"Are you alright?" He looked at her leg. "Are you in pain?"

"No, I'm fine," she said.

"Drew, should I be concerned here?" Nico asked. "About you and me? You've seemed off lately."

"Nico, you know I'll be around this summer, but that's only a couple of months."

"And then you're gone. I know." He let go of her hand and leaned his elbows on the railing. He turned to her with his intense brown eyes and dark lashes. "I love you. Would that change your mind?"

She touched his face. "I love you too."

"No, like I *love* you."

She kissed him but didn't let it linger. "I love you too, Nico. But I don't want to hurt you."

"Why don't you let me worry about that? I'll come visit you at school—"

"Nico, we're young. I can't promise you an entire future. I don't even know what that looks like for me yet."

"Is this about Shane? Do you still have feelings for him?" He shook his head. "I wouldn't blame you if you did, but I've got to ask."

"No. I can honestly tell you that I don't. This isn't about him, and it isn't about you. This is about me."

"It sounds like you're breaking up with me," he said.

"That wasn't my intention," she said. "I don't know what to say—I'm just trying to be honest with you. No secrets. No surprises."

"And I appreciate it. I do." He ran a hand through his hair. "Jesus, Drew. You're breaking me here."

She hugged him as tight as she could. He deserved to know the truth about how she felt.

"I'm not giving up on us. I want you to know that." His words were muffled in her hair. She kissed his cheek and took his hand, leading him back inside.

***

At the end of the night, Nico drove her home. He opened her door, and she stepped out.

"Thank you for a night I'll never forget," he said. "I hope this isn't some weird goodbye forever thing."

"We've known each other too long for that. We have a history together now. I don't want to lose you from my life either. I just don't know what I want, and I have to figure that out. I hope we can still be friends."

"*Friends*. I can't believe I'm in the friend zone." He sighed. "You'll never lose my friendship, Drew. That won't change."

"Ditto," Drew said.

She held him and they kissed one last time before he climbed back in the car.

"Goodnight." He waved and started the car. The engine rumbled out of her driveway and down the road as he headed home.

She stood in front of her house alone, but she

wasn't ready to go inside yet. She needed time alone to think. She walked across the road to the beach lit up by the full moon and a sky full of stars. She unstrapped her sandals and sat barefoot on the beach. She wiggled her toes and ran her fingers along the soft sand. She picked up a handful and let it slip through her fingers like time through an hourglass.

Standing, she picked up her dress and walked closer to where the surf met the sand. She stepped in the water. The cold on her feet refreshed her.

Gusts of wind tossed her hair in her face, and she tucked it behind her ears.

Atlas Cliffs would always be home. She'd made peace with the wandering souls as they crossed between the thin veil of life and death.

"Drew? Is that your name?"

She whirled around. Her dripping wet dress was too heavy to follow. A boy about her age with blond hair pulled into a low ponytail and blue eyes walked towards her. His athletic build compensated for his lack of height. He wore checkered Vans and a Sublime T-shirt.

An uneasiness gripped her stomach, and she stepped back into the water. The surf battered her calves almost knocking her down.

"Who are you?"

"I'm Ori. I'm just here to deliver a message. Your mom's name is Joelle?"

Drew took another step back, the waves splashing up her thighs. How did he know that? Her skin pricked with goosebumps. An icy air twirled in front of him, and she realized what he was. He was one of the wandering souls!

Drew folded her arms, her eyes narrowing on him. "How do you know my mother?"

"Look, I don't know a lot. But she's sent you—letters? Something like that?"

"Postcards. She sends postcards…and sometimes letters…I don't read them—"

"Well, I think you better start. She's in California." He gestured a hand over himself. "My home state. Well, it used to be."

"She can see you?"

"No," he said, "but for some reason, I can't seem to get away from her. She's driving me crazy. I'm stuck."

"What do you mean, you can't get away from her?" Drew was confused; it was too much information with no substance. "Wait, California? My mother is in *California*? I've got to read the postcards. What do you need from me?"

"Yes. That's right, read the postcards. I'm glad we understand each other," he said as his silhouette started to fade—just like Enid, like Ezra, like Iris. "Dammit. I've got to go. I'll see you again soon, Drew."

And just like they all did, he vanished.

Maybe she wasn't sticking around Atlas Cliffs this summer after all. Butterflies danced in her stomach as she looked up at the infinite night sky. She smiled to herself and braced for what unpredictable adventure awaited.

Acknowledgments

"Writing is a lonely job. Having someone who believes in you makes a lot of difference. They don't have to make speeches. Just believing is usually enough."

— *Stephen King, On Writing: A Memoir of the Craft*

This was one of the first books I read about writing a novel, and while Stephen King nails it with a ton of great advice, that quote stuck with me. I quickly discovered that having that person who believes in you really does make all the difference, especially when you're filled to the brim with self-doubt.

Back in January 2020, I took a Novel Writing workshop at the University of New Brunswick in Fredericton. I thought I'd learn some cool stuff about writing, meet new people, and bring creativity into my life. Little did I know that it would lead me down the path to writing my first novel, Wandering Souls.

Terry Armstrong taught that workshop, and it was the first of many that I attended. He pushed me out of my comfort zone and took on my novel as a developmental editor, seeing it through until the end. Terry, your well-delivered, constructive guidance, and encouragement, along with your belief in a storytelling ability that I wasn't so sure of, motivated me to keep going until the finish line.

I've been lucky to have met some incredible writers. I must give a shout-out to the most memorable writing group, The Eleven. Your support continues to overwhelm me in the best way. Em Whelly and Brandon LeBlanc—thank you both for always taking the time to be a sounding board to my many questions. I've taken your advice to heart and watching you both publish your own novels has allowed me to see what is possible.

The cover for Wandering Souls was a vision that Natasha MacKenzie brought to life. I'm beyond grateful for her patience and dedication to creating the perfect cover for this book—looking at it still makes me smile. I can't wait to work with this talented designer on the next one!

Many times, I've heard that writing is re-writing and re-writing again, and in my experience, those words are true. My editor and proofreader, the lovely Kayla Ramoutar, exceeded my expectations. Not only was she professional and skilled, but her personal touch and editor's notes were exactly what I needed to polish off this manuscript before releasing it into the world.

Formatting is a skill on its own, and my appreciation to Erika LeClair for swooping in and helping me with this critical step runs deep! Thank you!

My husband, Roman—you never waver in your

support when I set out to accomplish big dreams. You're the calm to my inner storm, and I wouldn't want to do this crazy adventure called life with anyone else.

I'm proud of my kids—more like teens on the cusp of adulthood. Lauren, you inspire me to tell the story as it's meant to be told, never holding back. Your matter-of-fact confidence in me to complete and publish Wandering Souls has been my superpower. Roman Jr., business and marketing comes so naturally to you, and I thank you for helping me navigate the crazy world of social media, websites, and beyond. You're both going to do amazing things and I love you so much!

Mom and dad, it's been a tough year, you've cheered me on through it all. Thank you for your continued love and support.

Cheers to my friends who've always been there for me. The kindness and positive energy you surround me with mean more than you know.

Thank you to everyone who discovered my first book, Wandering Souls. I hope that you've enjoyed reading it as much as I've loved bringing the story and characters to life. This newbie author has discovered a passion for writing, and I'm embracing the journey! Onto the next book… stay tuned!

Photo by Kelly Baker

Angela van Liempt is a music enthusiast, her playlist jumping from country to coffee house with 80s and 90s nostalgia sprinkled in between. When she's not writing, she's reading, listening to an audiobook, or binge-watching a series with her husband, Roman. Intrigued by the ocean, she loves the full moon and sunsets, doesn't miss Discovery channel's annual Shark Week, and can't get enough of big-wave surfing documentaries (seeing it from the sidelines in real life is even better!). Although most comfortable at home, she won't turn down an opportunity to travel, especially if it involves a beach and good food. Angela lives on the east coast of Canada in Fredericton, New Brunswick with Roman and their two teenagers… Three if you count her dog, Harley, aka 'Pippy.' Wandering Souls is her debut novel and the first in the Atlas Cliffs series.

Learn more at https://linktr.ee/angeladvl